BLACK LIGHT: EXPOSED

JENNIFER BENE

BLACK COLLAR PRESS

Black Light: Exposed

By Jennifer Bene

❀ Created with Vellum

This book is dedicated to all of my amazing readers who always lift me up with their comments, messages, and reviews. To my fantastic friend and co-crazy confidant Livia Grant, who came up with the idea for Black Light and let me be a part of this fun world, and a special shout-out to Nanette who helped me name this wonderful book.
Without all of you, lovelies, my life would be so, so boring.

Chapter One

Thursday Night

"Come on, let me hear you!" DJ Elixxir's voice poured like honey out of the speakers, and the crowd of college co-eds screamed on command while Maddie yawned and rolled her eyes. She just wanted a real drink, a fucking nap, and a goddamn story – but '*People Enjoy Dancing at Popular Dance Club*' was absolutely not a headline anyone would care to read.

"Everyone's already written about this fucking place anyway," she grumbled to herself. For the seventh time in two weeks Maddie was perched on a chair, watching a sea of writhing bodies as they had way more fun than her. Runway was the new *it* club in DC, and while she could understand the dense crowd of Georgetown students and tourists rocking it out to DJ Elixxir's latest set, she could absolutely *not* figure out where all of the random politicians, lobbyists, and other social elite were going after they arrived.

That was the story she needed, but for all her efforts she wasn't getting anywhere. Taking another sip of her diet coke she winced and rubbed at her temple as the pounding headache started to creep down her neck from the base of her skull.

"Fuck." Maddie tried to block out the flashing lights and moving laser show that seemed to bob and weave with the bass line, but that was a futile effort. No amount of caffeine, or head massage, or magical fairy dust was going to make up for the lack of sleep she'd been rocking for over three weeks. But giving up and sleeping wouldn't change the fact that Antoine was going to shut her out completely if she didn't give him *something* soon, and this was the only interesting lead she'd found after months of nothing.

Come on, Maddie, you can do this. Prove the assholes wrong.

With a deep breath she tried to shake off all the bullshit and lifted her head to glance back at the VIP area again. It was cordoned off from the main floor by a wall, as if the city's elite needed any further reminder that they were above the rest of the population, and while it held some barely dressed women who were also in the barely eighteen category, there was no one of interest. At least, no one she'd googled.

Tapping her phone she scanned her thumbprint and watched her iPhone come to life on the little counter in front of her. In another moment she had her list up, the one that held every single person of importance she'd seen pull up outside of Runway in the month it had been open. Black, shining town cars that dropped off some of the top A-list of Washington, DC for them to come party inside the club – and yet? She'd found nothing.

Nada.

Zilch.

Maddie was draining her meager savings coming to the club

almost every night it was open, and she knew she should stop, but the little puzzle kept pulling her back. If you watch someone enter a building, and then you go inside and they aren't there, then where are they?

It was the million-dollar question, or at least the seventy-two thousand dollar a year question if she could finally land a job at the Washington Post as a reporter. Antoine would have to give her a position if she could just figure out where everyone was going. Every part of her knew something was up. That tingle buzzing through her bloodstream with each new name she added to her list, and Maddie knew that *this* was it. This was the story that would let her finally work for a real newspaper, doing real reporting.

She just had to figure it the fuck out.

Finishing off her soda she tucked her phone back in the little black purse and abandoned her seat. She hadn't taken more than a step before some waif-thin blonde had snagged it, and Maddie could only sigh as she pushed past people to get to the coat check. The little ticket earned her the thick wool coat, and the bottle of Advil hiding in the pocket.

Tipping the last two dollars in cash she had on her she sought out the bathroom, praying there wasn't a line of chattering girls waiting to make her headache worse. As she navigated her way through the packed room she tried to remind herself that at twenty-four she was probably in the middle of the age range of the room, but she felt much older than the twenty-somethings grinding against each other on the dance floor. She'd never been interested in partying, never been the one to do keg-stands at Penn State, and being surrounded by drunk co-eds was not exactly one of her fantasies.

A Pulitzer? *That* was a fantasy she could sink her teeth into, and one that was currently way too far off working at her shit copy editor job.

With a push at the swinging door she found herself in the cool, insulated space of the women's room, and for the first time in hours she felt like she could breathe. Whoever had designed this place had clearly known how miserable it was to try and find a toilet at a club, because Runway was the first club she'd seen with eight stalls and a fucking sitting area with two full-length mirrors. It was paradise inside chaos, and the instant reduction in sound made her head a lot happier – even if her ears were still ringing.

There was only one girl at the sinks, applying eyeliner one-handed with the skill of a master, but Maddie didn't even have the energy to feel jealous. In the mirror she saw the silvery dress that clung to her hips, with a neckline that draped just low enough to reveal her moderate cleavage, boosted by Victoria Secret's best. It wasn't the nicest thing she owned, but she was running out of outfits for the club – which meant she really needed to do laundry. Just one more thing for her never-ending to-do list. *Great.* Stepping forward she turned the water on and rinsed her hands before pressing the coolness to her cheeks.

Wake up. Come on.

Meeting her blue-gray eyes in the mirror she took a deep, steadying breath as she stared at her reflection. There was not enough make-up in the world to hide the exhaustion she felt, it was drawn like an undeniable map in dark circles under her eyes.

"Perfect," she muttered, and the beautiful woman next to her glanced over. Maddie offered a slight smile as the girl started applying lipstick. The woman who was now pouting at the mirror had sleek, pin-straight dark hair, while Maddie's own fiery red waves were frizzy, and even though she'd spent twenty minutes carefully blow-drying it that morning around six am the effort was long dissolved.

As was her make-up, her ability to think, and her patience for the night.

Fuck it.

It was almost two am, and that meant if she could catch an uber back to her apartment quickly she *might* get two and a half hours of sleep. Another night wasted with absolutely nothing to show for it.

Popping open the Advil bottle she tossed three of the pills back and leaned down to the faucet, taking a few sips of water out of her hand to swallow them down. Ignoring the other girl's sideways glance, Maddie headed to the back of the bathroom. After so many nights inside the club she'd picked up on the second door off the sitting area that led to the rear exit of the club. Much less chaotic and easier to get to the street for the uber pick-up since the front of Runway would still be lined with people trying to get inside at this hour.

Tugging on her coat she dug her phone out of her little purse, and headed into the short hall behind the dance floor. Just as she pulled up the app to ask for a car, her eyes caught something out of place.

There was no security by the curtain for backstage, and the curtain itself wasn't pulled all the way across and latched to the wall like it usually was. *That* could be something interesting.

Locking her phone she moved quietly towards the curtain, suddenly grateful for the overwhelming music that felt like it was trying to vibrate her bones. It was a remix of Bad Romance, and Maddie sent up a silent prayer of thanks to Gaga as she leaned against the wall to peek into the backstage area. She couldn't see anyone, but light spilled from an open door just inside the curtain, and she slipped through to get a closer look. Three people were standing in what looked like a supply closet for the club, complete with shelves of cleaning products, and toilet paper, and other random stuff.

That would have been strange enough, but one of the big security guys was talking to a man in a suit, handsome with silvering hair at his temples, and in a flash she recognized him. He was one of the bigger lobbyists in D.C., David Alchert, and he was *definitely* on her google list. Next to him was a gorgeous woman, probably in her mid to late thirties, and wearing a black dress so short Maddie wondered how she wasn't flashing her underwear.

What the fuck are they doing in a closet?

They all started laughing, the woman wrapping herself around Alchert's arm, and then the security guy went to pick up a mop in the back corner – except it didn't move. He pulled it towards him, then pushed it forward, angled it to the side, and a door popped open.

Holy. Shit.

The couple waved at him as they stepped through into some room with pale purple light, and he waited there until the door snapped back into place. From where she stood there didn't even seem to be a seam to mark the door's existence, and there definitely wasn't a handle. Before he could turn, she darted back past the curtain as a smile spread across her lips, stretching them so wide her jaw ached, but she could feel that *tingle*. The same one that had appeared when she'd first caught sight of all those distinguished members of society hungrily lining up to gain entrance to Runway. A dance club started by a pair of male models embroiled in a messy sex scandal that had been front-page political news for an entire week. None of it had made sense, not one bit of it, but now there was a secret entrance frequented by some of the city's most affluent and influential people?

That had headline exposé written all over it, and Maddie O'Neill was going to be the one to break it wide open. Antoine would be positively *begging* her to work for the Post.

The sound of a door closing made her stumble back a few steps, unlocking her phone as she leaned against the wall a yard or two from the curtain. A gruff voice sounded a second later, "Hey, what are you doing back here?"

"Huh?" Maddie glanced over at him, playing the confused girl act as she navigated back to the Uber app with her thumb. "I'm calling a ride, why?"

"You shouldn't be back here."

Rolling her eyes with practiced annoyance, she showed him her phone screen. "Like I said, I'm about to leave," she pointed at the back exit, "out that door."

"Why don't you go ahead and leave then?"

"Oh, thanks for your permission!" Maddie pushed off the wall in a huff, stomping in her heels to the door to shove it open as she wrapped her coat around herself to fight the chill of early January – but the moment she was outside she couldn't stifle the grin any further.

She had a lead. A real, solid lead, and now she just needed to figure out how the fuck to get past Mr. Questions to that entrance so she could find out what secrets Runway was hiding.

Chapter Two

Friday

The next morning wasn't just brutal, it was post-nuclear blast destructive. Maddie felt like she'd been shoved into a meat grinder and then reformed into some shape that resembled a human being. Even as she slumped over her desk at the Daily Saver D.C. office, she couldn't make sense of the text on her screen.

It was like some evil eye test, and she was failing badly.

"Morning, Ginger!"

"Fuck off, Gilligan," she growled.

Jamar laughed as he took his seat at his desk, glancing back at her as he swiveled around to unlock his computer. "Bad night?"

"I'm going to shove a pen through your eye if you keep talking to me."

"Hungover?" he mused, looking over his shoulder. "Or did you just get laid and spend all night making an 'O' face?"

"Neither," she hissed and waited for him to turn back around, but she wasn't that lucky.

"Seriously, are you sick? If you're sick you should leave."

"Yes, I have the flu, and I licked all of your stuff before you got here."

"Always thinking of others, that's my Ginger." Flashing a wild grin at her he turned to his inbox, which was already full of ads and short articles to be edited before the eight o'clock print deadline.

"You're such an asshole."

"Hey, I'm not the one that looks half-dead. Has Brenda seen you yet?" Jamar's casual question made her flinch. Brenda had already commented once that she needed to pick up her pace, and on Monday she'd suggested that Maddie looked unwell – the last thing she needed was another chat with their taskmaster of a boss.

As if some shitty daily coupon paper was going to make or break the news cycle inside the Beltway.

"Why don't you pay attention to your own work, *Gilligan?*" As she snapped at him Jamar seemed to give up and tune into his screen with the kind of focus Maddie wished she could summon. She *also* needed to tone down the bitch-o-meter about ten notches. As snarky as she could be to him, she was grateful to have him and his playful jabs. Their nicknames for each other had formed her first week there, after she'd applied to every real newspaper in the D.C. area and finally settled for a job that would *just* pay the bills. Jamar had taken one look at her red hair, pale skin, and freckles, and immediately started calling her Ginger.

As in the soul-sucking-creepy-red haired kind.

By the end of the week she was fed up with the term, so she started calling him Gilligan. The dopey, accident-prone idiot from the show Gilligan's Island, the same show where Ginger was actually one of the hot girls on the island and not some rude Irish stereotype. But, instead of being bothered by it Jamar had loved the banter, and they'd quickly become friends – which would have actually made work pretty nice if they weren't both currently trapped in career purgatory.

A four-year journalism degree, top marks, and all she had earned was two years as a copy editor for a free daily ad paper. So. Fucking. Glamorous.

The Daily Saver wasn't doing much more than providing a shitty studio apartment, cheap food, and transport in and out of the city every day – but it was a job, and it meant she wasn't moving back home. That was all Maddie could hope for until she earned her a chance at a *real* job.

"Don't stab me in the eye, but do you want me to make you some coffee?" Jamar asked, hovering at the edge of her desk with his hand poised over her Penn State mug.

"For caffeine I will forgo the stabbing for now." She managed a small smile, but he just chuckled to himself as he wandered away with her coffee cup. Reaching into her giant sack of a purse she fished around until she found the hand mirror she wanted and opened it to look at herself. Somehow she actually looked worse than she had at the club the night before. Her skin was waxy pale, her eyes bloodshot, the bags under her eyes even darker, and when she tried to look back at her screen she knew she was fucked. A lead or not, she needed a night or two of sleep before she tried to unlock the mop-triggered secrets of Runway.

And if she planned on affording groceries this week, she'd need to make sure she got through the crap in her inbox before Brenda had more reasons to fire her and hire the next hungry, college grad looking for a job in the District.

Just as she opened the first email of the morning, an ad for one-hour phone screen repair, Jamar returned with her coffee and set it beside her. Cream and sugar filled ecstasy, the liquid inside looked closer to milk than coffee, and she practically groaned as she picked it up and took a sip. "You're too good to me."

"I know. I also added an ice cube so it wouldn't be too hot." He smiled and took a drink from his steaming cup of black tar.

"*This* is the benefit of knowing you, Gilligan. Sometimes I forget why I keep talking to you, and then you bring me caffeinated magic."

"First of all, I'm not even sure there's still caffeine in that concoction, and second, coffee isn't coffee unless it's hot, but –"

"There's a difference between boiling and drinkable."

"*But* you obviously need coffee, and since that lukewarm mess is all you'll drink that's what I brought you." Jamar leaned on the corner of her desk, his brown eyes catching hers. "No jokes, are you okay, Maddie?"

Plastering a smile across her face, she nodded. "Yeah, absolutely. I've just been working on some stuff at night, but I promise I'm going to take a break and get some sleep."

For a night or two anyway.

"You sure? If you need help with something, I can –"

"Nope! Nina would have my head if I bugged you after hours. I'm pretty sure she's already annoyed enough that I like your posts on Facebook."

Jamar didn't respond to that, which was all the confirmation she needed that his wife wasn't happy at how friendly they were. He took a long drink of his coffee and stood up. "Okay, well, the offer stands. I hope you know that."

"Right, I do." Keeping the forced smile, she met his eyes for a moment before glancing back at her screen as if she could really read it. "Time to work! Bye, Gilligan!"

"Drink your coffee, Ginger," he replied as he walked the few steps back to his desk, and Maddie blinked until the blurs on the screen turned into words.

Three hours, and four coffee refills later, and she was halfway through her inbox for the day. It still amazed her that the people who did the marketing at some of these small businesses couldn't do simple proofreading of their ads before paying money to have them printed. Without her checking the advertisement for *Caroline's Fabrics & More* they would have been offering 50% off 'patented' prints instead of 'patterned' prints.

With a grin, and a slightly less fuzzy head, she sent a screen shot of the error-filled ad to Jamar, but just as she clicked send Brenda appeared on the other side of her monitor. "Madeline, I need to talk to you, do you have a minute?"

"Sure." There was a sinking feeling in her stomach as Brenda sat down on the short cabinet beside Maddie's desk.

"Do you remember the Washington Cleaners ad from yesterday?" *Shit.* She was using her corrective tone, the one that already confirmed she'd made some terrible mistake. What was that ad?

Washington Cleaners, Washington Cleaners, Washington Cleaners...

"Of course!" Maddie lied through her teeth. "What's wrong?"

"Well, why don't you tell me?" Brenda pulled a Daily Saver D.C. from under her arm and laid it out beside her mouse, flipping to the second page where a red circle had been drawn around an ad for Washington… Clearers.

Fuck.

And below that it said they were the best in shirts, pants, and dreses. That's right, dresses with one 's'.

Double fuck.

"This was in your queue yesterday, right? And you approved it?" Brenda's tone was edging from corrective to outright irritated, and Maddie realized that five cups of coffee on an empty stomach was about to be a recipe for throwing up in her trash can in front of her boss.

"I don't know how I missed that, Brenda. I am —"

"Well, you did, and that's the fourth error in the last three weeks. I don't know what's going on with you, Madeline, but you need to leave whatever it is at the door. We don't have space for personal issues here at the Daily Saver, we have a reputation to uphold." With a steely gaze from behind her glasses, Brenda snatched up the copy of the paper as heat flushed into Maddie's cheeks. "Do you need to take a day off? Or two? You didn't take much for Christmas."

Swallowing in an effort to calm her churning stomach, and to cool the crimson blush that she knew was turning her pale skin into an embarrassing neon sign, Maddie spoke softly so that the audience in the cubicles around her wouldn't hear, "I'm fine, Brenda. It won't happen again."

"If it does it will be more than a talk, Madeline." The use of her full name for the third time made her teeth grind.

"I understand."

"Good. I really expect more of you than this." With that final jab, Brenda walked back towards her office at the end of the room, and Maddie bowed her head to avoid the bevy of eyes that suddenly focused on her from all over the floor.

So stupid. Stupid, stupid, stupid. You're going to lose the only job you have paying the bills trying to become some hotshot investigative journalist, won't that make mom and dad proud?

Opening the next item in her queue, Maddie could feel the burn in her cheeks slowly fading, but the embarrassment was like a branding iron over her chest. She had always been the A student, the smart girl, the over-achiever – and *this* was just not her.

As she threw herself into work, going over and over the ads and brief articles to ensure they were perfect, she ignored the dings of her email until a wad of paper hit the side of her desk and bounced off. Jamar was staring at her, pointing at his computer with a look of exasperation. With a sigh she flipped back to her email and saw a series of emails from him.

The first was a badly edited picture of a stack of fabric with ® and ™ symbols copy-and-pasted all over it. The second was a picture of one of the dragons from Game of Thrones breathing fire with the name 'Brenda' written on it in bright green text, and the last was a screen shot of an order for two subs from their favorite local sub shop, along with two large sides of fries. She couldn't help the smile that crept over her lips as she glanced up at him, and then Jamar pointed at Brenda's office and mimed shooting himself in the head.

Maddie grinned at him, and he shrugged and turned around, already brushing off the incident like it wasn't a problem. With a heavy sigh, she went back to work, committed to catching up and making no more mistakes – but then her phone lit up with a Google alert for Runway appearing in the news again, and she had to fight the urge to read it. Her hand hovered over the screen for a moment, her thumb itching to scan into the little device, but then she flipped her phone face down.

After work.

You can check it after work, and then you'll eat a sensible dinner, and go the fuck to bed. Runway and its secret door will be there Sunday night.

Chapter Three

Saturday Night

Thirteen hours of sleep, four trips up and down the elevator for laundry, and one grocery trip later – Maddie was finally nestled in front of her laptop again. She definitely felt more human than she had, and as she glanced at the clock it was tempting to head into the city. It wasn't even eleven o'clock yet, and that meant there would still be plenty to find at Runway if she could make it past the mop's security detail. Maybe just a few hours…

No.

You can go tomorrow night, when you get your dresses back from the dry cleaner.

Rolling her eyes at her own brain's responsible suggestion, she moved to the open Word document on her computer. It held her list of names, with notes next to each showing what they did in the city, and whether she had been able to find them inside. The badly lit pictures she had been able to take with her phone were below it. Some of those were marked because she'd yet to find out their names, but anyone arriving with a car service *had* to be of some interest.

"What are you hiding?" Maddie whispered under her breath as she opened a new internet window and searched Jaxson Davidson, the owner of the damn club, for the hundredth time. As usual, the first two pages of results were about the infamous display he'd put on at his father's campaign dinner.

Talk about a major political faux pas by a ménage-a-trois.

Searching Chase Cartwright brought up articles about his modeling in addition to the political shit, but she was still full of questions. What were they doing starting a nightclub anyway? And why would any of the D.C. elite get within a hundred feet of Jaxson Davidson after the stunt he'd pulled? He should have been toxic waste after destroying Senator Gregory Davidson's attempt at the presidency, and yet Runway wasn't just doing well, it was *still* the talk of the town over a month after opening.

Tapping a pen on a notepad beside her she started to write by hand in an effort to clear out the muddled mess inside her head. Question one… what would male models want to keep secret at a club?

Underground clothing line? A sweatshop?

With a groan she scratched through *sweatshop*. It would be stupid to invite a bunch of fancy dressed people into a sweatshop, but the secret clothing line wasn't beyond possibility – albeit relatively uninteresting.

Starting their own modeling agency? Possible, but weird to run it connected to Runway. Unless that was the reason they'd chosen the name and designed the stage that way… she starred that option and then tried to shift gears.

New angle.

Why were the people who went through that secret door dressed so nice? Maddie leaned back in her chair and took a long drink of her wine, a splurge purchase she'd made because she knew she needed to relax – even though all she was doing was obsessing while she drank. What was hiding behind the trick mop? Was it just a special VIP area? What would make it better than the separate VIP area already on the floor of Runway?

She scratched a series of question marks next to her terrible sketch of the mop, and began to tap her pen again. *Thump. Thump. Thump.* Could Jaxson be using his father's political connections somehow? Allowing a hidden place for people to broker deals out of sight of the police, reporters, and others?

It was another possibility, especially because while there were a lot of things you couldn't count on in the nation's capitol, there was always at least one of three things at play when it came to Washington, D.C.: power, money, or sex.

So, what was in play at Runway? *That* was the new question burning a hole in her mind as she tried to make herself sleep.

Sunday Night

Maddie had been at the club for over an hour, but every time she wandered towards the rear hallway the security guard at the backstage curtain was standing with his arms crossed like a formidable wall.

Damn him.

Curving her path as if she'd meant to, she headed into the bathroom and dropped onto the little love seat in the lounge area, staring at the door that separated her from her mop of destiny. Here she was well-rested, in her sexiest little black dress, her nicest heels, with her hair and make-up done… and it looked like tonight was going to be another bust.

No way she had enough money in all of her accounts combined to bribe the asshole into letting her past.

As she glared through the wall at her nemesis, a group of loud-mouthed Georgetown co-eds burst into the bathroom from the dance floor entrance, letting in the pounding beat of the DJ for a moment before it was muffled again as the door closed.

Then they all went into stalls, still talking to each other about nonsense.

"Can you believe Amanda showed up?"

"And with Riley? I mean, fuck *off*, right?"

"You know she only came with Riley because she was hoping to piss off Clarissa."

"Well, I already texted Clarissa and she said she doesn't give a shit. Riley cheated on her, and she's already going out with Mark on Tuesday."

"Why didn't she come out tonight? It would have been perfect for her to snag some hottie and dance with him right in front of fake-ass Amanda."

Maddie groaned and pulled out her phone to check the time. Barely eleven, which meant if she couldn't get back to the mop and into that secret door she'd be listening to idiots like this all night. Laughter echoed off the tile as toilets flushed and several of the girls gathered together at the mirror to wash their hands and check their make-up.

"Natalie! Are you coming or not?"

"One second!"

"Okay, we'll be on the dance floor. Meet us!" The larger group of girls left and then the last girl wandered out of her stall to wash her hands. Maddie was deep in thought as she heard the clicking of heels coming towards her, and that was when she saw the one called Natalie tugging at the hot pink crop-top as she stared at herself in one of the floor-length mirrors in the sitting area. She looked like every other college girl that was trying too hard and would probably end up puking in one of these stalls before the end of the night after one too many shots.

And *that* gave Maddie an idea.

"Hey, Natalie, right?"

Her voice made the girl jump, and she looked at Maddie a little nervously. "Uh, yeah... why?"

"I wanted to know if you could do me a favor?"

"Like what?" The girl looked even more freaked out as Maddie dug in her tiny purse for the twenty bucks she had tucked inside.

"It's not a big deal, I just need you to distract someone for me." She held up the twenty and the girl looked slightly less nervous.

"What exactly do you want me to do?"

A few minutes later she had her arm around Natalie's shoulders as they stepped into the back hallway. The girl suddenly lurched to the side and Maddie almost fell trying to hold onto her.

"I think I'm going to be sick," Natalie moaned in fake agony, bending at the waist to brace one hand on the wall.

"You'll be okay! We just need to get you some water!" Maddie raised her voice, glancing through her hair to see if the security guy had budged.

No such luck. Come on Natalie, play it up.

20

"No, I'm totally going to throw up." Some Oscar-worthy gagging noises came from the girl, and the security guy took a few steps forward.

Just a little more. "Oh shit! No, just stand up. You'll feel better if you stand up!" Pretending to try and lean the girl back up only brought an even more dramatic round of fake moaning and pre-vomit noises.

"HEY!" Security guy finally walked towards them. "Go back in the bathroom, do *not* throw up back here!"

"I can't *move*, I'll be sick if I move!" Natalie was playing her part beyond perfection, probably based on experience, while Maddie played the panicked friend.

"Shit, shit, I'll get you some water, and I'll grab Tiffany! Just wait!" Stepping away from Natalie, the girl started to slide to her knees, the fake retching increasing in volume. Security guy tried to grab her arm and lift her as Maddie took a few steps back, but Natalie just shouted that she was going to be sick.

"I've got a code four in the back hall by the women's room." He was speaking into something on his shirt, and he glanced over at her as she moved towards the doorway back to Runway's dance floor, but as soon as he turned to face Natalie's groaning form again she ran and darted under the curtain. With her heart pounding in her ears, Maddie steadied the fabric and then stepped away so he wouldn't see her heels under the edge.

She could still hear the soap opera style acting on the other side of the curtain, but the rush in her own veins was more powerful. It took a moment for her eyes to adjust to the dim lighting in the backstage space, but then she saw the door.

Thank you, Natalie.

Maddie couldn't stifle her smile as she eased it open, grateful it didn't make a sound, and she slipped inside. The bright, sterile light of the closet felt weird after the dimness of the club, but she saw the mop exactly where it had been before. Wrapping her hand around it she pulled the mop towards her, just like the security guy had, and there was a distinct click of some kind of mechanism underneath it. Pushing it forward she felt another click, and with a slight movement to the left she heard the snap of a lock as the edges of a door were revealed.

Bathed in pale purple light.

She stepped inside fast, pushing the door closed behind her just in case. It was a stairwell, brightly lit in that pale purple glow that emanated from recessed lighting in the ceiling, leading all the way down. Swallowing, Maddie walked down carefully, trying to get a peek of what awaited, but there was only another door.

"This is it," she whispered to herself, grabbing the door handle. Preparing herself for whatever lay beyond, she pushed it open and almost tripped as she stumbled into a large room. There were small lockers lining one wall from floor to ceiling, and another heavily muscled security guy sitting behind a tall desk.

Oh. Fuck.

Smiling with that *I'm-supposed-to-be-here* confidence, Maddie walked forward. The guy glanced up at her and arched an eyebrow. "Member or guest?"

"Guest," she answered smoothly, but inside new questions were firing to life.

"Of?"

"Hmm?" She asked as she fiddled with her purse to pull out her phone, trying to buy time.

"Whose guest are you?"

Shit, shit, shit. Her eyes roamed over the room, trying to memorize every inch of it, but there wasn't anything exciting to see. There was a glass window in the wall, just beyond some more lockers, that resembled a ticket window for a movie theater, and then a door. On the other wall there was yet another door tucked by some lockers, and the whole room seemed to glow with the same pale purple light of the stairwell. There was nothing helpful except for a sign that said all forms of electronics had to be left in assigned lockers, and while interesting, it did nothing to help her now. How the fuck was she supposed to get past this guy?

"Miss?"

The twin cameras aimed at her from the corners of the ceiling only made her heart pound harder as she struggled to think of an answer. There was so much security, whatever they were hiding underneath Runway *had* to be something huge.

This was it, the story she needed.

She just had to get inside, had to come up with something that would make the guy let her through whichever door led to the underbelly of the club. He was getting agitated, her brain was whirling with possibilities, and then the stupidest possible response fell out of her mouth, "Jaxson."

"Mr. Davidson invited you." The blatant doubt in the man's voice made a chill rush down her spine, but she flashed her brightest smile and nodded.

"Of course."

"What's your name?" Security guy lifted a tablet and started tapping away at it, and then she heard the door behind her open and shut.

Oh please don't be the other security —

"Evening, Daniel." The silken voice was most definitely not the security guy from upstairs, this was someone *much* higher on the income scale. As she turned to look at him Maddie had to swallow hard, because the newcomer was incredibly good looking. He had the aristocratic smile and tailored suit of someone that came from money, and his warm brown hair was trimmed to perfection.

"It's Danny, Mr. Hathaway, and good evening." Desk security guy, Danny, gave a brief smile, momentarily distracted from her trespass. "Get lost? You don't usually come in from Runway."

There's another entrance to this place? As she made a mental note of Mr. Sexy's last name, the man laughed warmly and gave her a once-over that sent a thrum of heat across her skin. "I had the urge to people watch for a bit tonight, my coat is at the front of the club. Now who's this?"

"Madeline." She answered before Danny Security could speak and stepped over to him, only to realize he towered over her by at least six inches. With a kind of old world elegance, he took her hand and leaned down to kiss her knuckles.

"I'm Thomas, and I'm very glad to meet you, Madeline." His voice did something funny to her insides, and she couldn't tell if it was the slight growl he seemed to add to her name, or if it was the intensity of his hazel eyes. Either way, for a brief moment the rest of the room seemed to fall away – that is, until security asshole interrupted them again.

"She says she's a guest, but I don't have a Madeline on the list."

There was a spark of something behind Thomas' gaze when he glanced back at her. "Why do you want to go inside?"

With a delicate shrug, she decided to play flirtatiously coy, which was not difficult as gorgeous as he was in his dark gray suit and pale blue button-down looking like he might be one of Jaxson Davidson's old modeling friends. "Curiosity."

"Just curious, or do you want to play?" His lips ticked up at the edge, a slight smile teasing his mouth, and she couldn't help but grin back.

Play? Holy shit, could it be illegal gambling? Jackpot!

"Oh, I definitely want to play, Thomas." Keeping the flirty confidence in her voice, she reveled in the brief flash of desire on his face.

He laughed, squeezing her hand before he released it to pull his wallet and phone out of his pocket. "Are you planning to play with someone else, or are you looking to have someone play with you?"

"Are you offering?" For a moment Maddie thought he was going to back down, or that she'd overstepped, and then she'd have no hope of getting inside, but then he shrugged.

"I don't have any other plans tonight, so I guess I am."

"She's not on the list, Mr. Hathaway," Daniel 'Danny' the security asshole chimed in and she wanted to throw something at him.

"That's fine, I'll have her as my guest for the night." Thomas walked the few steps over to the glass partition in the wall and pressed a button that resembled a doorbell beside it.

"Of course, Mr. Hathaway." The security guy gave her a long look, but she ignored him and stepped up beside her tall, gorgeous savior.

A young woman approached on the other side of the glass and slid the window aside. "Good evening, are you a member?"

"Yes," Thomas replied and opened his wallet.

Maddie couldn't stop smiling, because not only had she *actually* discovered a secret within Runway, she had *also* managed to get passage inside. The headline floated behind her eyes: *Illegal Gambling beneath Runway*. Which of the District's elite would she find caught in the act? The reporter inside her was positively salivating, but as a thank you to her white knight she'd leave him out of the article she'd write – as soon as she found out who exactly Thomas Hathaway was anyway. Trust fund aristo? Politician? Lobbyist?

He handed over a plain white card, and for a moment nothing was visible on it, and then the lighting in the room changed. All of the normal lights went out, and the purple glow was all that was left, revealing a logo and text on the card.

No way.

'BLACK LIGHT' was written in bold, all caps across the middle of the card, and underneath that was smaller text which simply showed 'Member ID' and then a series of numbers that she couldn't memorize before the lights came back to the normal pale purple. A combination of the black lights tucked around the room with the recessed lighting.

The girl tapped away at the tablet in front of her, and she smiled as she returned the card to him. "Mr. Hathaway, so nice to have you back. I see you have a guest this evening?"

"I do, this is Madeline…"

"O'Neill," she filled in, and blushed when she heard his quiet laugh.

"A beautiful name for a beautiful girl." He winked at her and then turned back to the woman inside the window. "A one-night guest pass, please."

"Of course." The girl gathered some pages together and attached them to a clipboard before offering them with a pen. "Madeline, please fill this out while I process the payment."

"Right." She took it and stared down at the dense legal speak, swallowing as she recognized what seemed to be a pretty serious non-disclosure agreement. The Post would surely defend her if they took the story. That's what they did when reporters exposed illegal activities, right?

"You'll just initial each page and sign the last one. Can I have your ID?" The woman was still looking at her, and now Thomas was too. Fumbling with the clasp on her little purse she tried to juggle the pen and clipboard, but he reached over and took them from her with a slight smirk.

"Sorry," she whispered as she pulled out her license.

"No need to apologize, beautiful."

The blush further heated her cheeks as she passed the woman her ID, but Thomas just smiled wider as he returned the clipboard to her waiting hands. She'd barely glanced down to start reading it when the woman spoke, "That's one-hundred and fifty for the pass, Mr. Hathaway."

"Sure." He didn't even bat an eye, but Maddie almost choked on her next breath of air.

Was that the buy-in for the gambling? Shit, that's a lot.

Quickly, she initialed the three pages and then signed the last one, clapping the pen on top to slide it back across the short counter. Thomas signed his receipt and then the woman handed everything back to them. "Alright, Madeline I'll just need to give you a stamp."

Maddie offered her left hand and the woman turned it over and pressed the stamp onto her wrist, where it was almost invisible to the eye. The barest shimmer of it showed, even more black light ink.

This place is bordering ridiculous with their security.

"Danny, can you open locker thirty-four?"

"Got it," the security guy replied to the girl and she heard the metallic clunk of it popping open behind them.

"Please remember, there is no technology allowed inside. This includes phones, wearable devices, recording devices, and anything mechanical that is not medical in nature."

Guess they were serious about stopping cheating, which meant there had to be some major money being exchanged behind that door.

Ka-ching, ka-ching!

"Thank you." Thomas nodded before turning that intense gaze on her again as he tucked his wallet away and pulled out his phone. "So, we're sharing a locker since you're my guest, but I want to make it clear that if you want to leave all you have to do is tell me. I'll bring you back out here to get your things immediately. Alright?"

"That works for me!" She followed him over to the locker that had its door ajar, and pulled her phone out of her purse. Thomas had already laid his phone inside and was removing an Apple watch while he looked her up and down.

"We'll talk more once we're inside and have a seat, but I just don't want you to feel like you owe me anything. I bought the guest pass because I want to get to know you better, and while I'd love to play with you, it's not an obligation."

Maddie rolled her eyes before she thought about it. "I promise, I'm fine."

Did this guy think she'd never played poker before? Did she really look that sheltered?

Thomas laughed low as his eyes roamed slowly over her curves. "Wonderful. No more technology under that nice dress?"

"No. Why, do you want to check?" Looking up at him she knew her cheeks were burning bright from the situation, the flirtation, and the fact that her offer wasn't an innocent one. He was hot, and it had been way too long since she'd even had a date. If he wanted to pat her down she'd let him in a heartbeat.

"Maybe in a bit." He answered softly and then offered her his hand and she took it, the next door popping open as they approached. There was low, wordless music coming from the room beyond, with soft, warm lighting – and then Thomas pulled the door wide and Maddie realized the error she'd made.

It was most definitely, unequivocally *not* gambling hiding underneath Runway.

What the fuck had she just gotten herself into?

Chapter Four

—————

Thomas squeezed her hand and pulled her forward with him into a scene out of the darkest recesses of her imagination. Leather, and chains, and the sounds of what could only be sex. The sudden snap of something striking skin, and the yelp of pain after, made her jump. Thomas turned to look at her and Maddie instantly summoned an easy, relaxed smile.

He leaned towards her with a hungry look, his voice meant just for her, "Let's go sit and talk."

"That sounds good." She nodded, trying to talk herself down into a calm state, while he walked forward confidently, obviously because he'd been here many times before. Hell, Daniel 'Danny' the security asshat had known him by name, and that meant Thomas Hathaway liked this stuff – and, more importantly, he wanted to play with her. Here.

Maddie, what have you done?

The sights and sounds were overwhelming, and her heart was pounding so hard she wondered if he could feel her pulse where their palms were pressed together. She wasn't ignorant, she knew she was in some kind of BDSM sex club, complete with everything she'd heard of and a lot more she had not. There were couches scattered across the dark carpet, most of them facing various raised platforms where women were strapped onto furniture.

This was beyond her imaginings, or at least out of some of the more secret fantasies she'd harbored growing up. A fucking sex club? Under the hottest new dance club in DC? How the hell had this happened?

It was started by Jaxson Davidson and Chase Cartwright – that's how.

Forcing a steadying breath, she tried to focus, but it was difficult. As they walked through the middle of the room she looked one way and saw a man draw back a thing with a lot of leather strips, landing them across a woman's ass and thighs. She jumped, and then squirmed, before he did it again. Looking another way she saw a woman ass up over a man's lap as he stroked her and then spanked her. From the cry she released, it did not seem to be the playful kind of spanking Maddie had tried experimentally in the past, but the guttural moan that followed spoke of anything but agony.

There were about a thousand warring thoughts inside her head, pinging between panic and interest, fear and arousal. A warm flutter in her lower belly was only amplified when Thomas stopped them for a moment and leaned close enough that she felt his breath against the shell of her ear, "See anything you like?"

She had to swallow past a dry mouth before she tried to speak, but all she managed was a crimson-cheeked nod. Fortunately, that seemed to be enough, and he continued to move towards the bar tucked in the far corner.

You've got an opportunity here, Maddie. A way to substantiate your reasons for being here, to give you an excuse to look for the people on your list, and most importantly… Thomas Hathaway is not bad to look at.

"Thomas!" A man called out and waved at him, and he raised his free hand in response, but she barely had the chance to see who it was before she was distracted by the mostly naked man wearing a ball gag, on his knees beside a high-top table. A leash was latched to a collar around his neck and tied off to a ring embedded on the stand. A woman in a beautiful dress was sitting in the tall chair next to him, chatting with a man in a long-sleeved shirt, casually running her fingers through the man's hair that knelt at her side.

Was she a dominatrix? Maddie knew that term, and it took a mental shake to make herself stop staring before they noticed.

Get it together. You need to be focused, memorizing everything, not gawking like a damn tourist.

Observe. Evaluate. Remember.

They stopped at a table, farthest from the action of the main floor, near what looked like a small shop that stocked everything from condoms to toys. A handsome man with long hair, wearing an elaborate leather harness, was sitting behind the counter reading a book, and Maddie had to steady herself to ease into the chair that Thomas pulled out for her.

He slid into the seat beside her, both of them facing out to the floor, and she noticed that now he carefully rested his hands on his lap, no longer touching her. "So, is it your first time at Black Light?"

Speak, Maddie.

"Is it that obvious?" She laughed, trying to summon back the flirtatious tone she'd held so well upstairs.

"You do have a charming blush on your cheeks and a bit of that wide-eyed wonder." Thomas smiled at her and gave a slight shrug. "I'm pretty sure I was a little wide-eyed when I first got here. There's really nowhere else like it."

"What do you mean?"

"Well, everything here is the best of the best, and they cater to pretty much any kink you could think of. Also, as I'm sure you noticed, you can't really beat the security here." Thomas leveled his gaze at her, a more serious tone taking over. "So, whose guest were you supposed to be tonight, Madeline? I'm very glad you agreed to come in with me, but I'm not looking to step on anyone's toes if you already have –"

"I'm not meeting anyone." Maddie shook her head and tucked a strand of hair behind her ear. "I mean, I was invited, but we didn't have plans or anything."

"Who invited you, Madeline?" There was a definite edge to his voice now, one that made her feel like *she* was the one being interviewed when it needed to be the other way around.

Summoning a wicked grin she leaned back, resting her arms on the sides of the chair, trying to display a casual comfort with her surroundings. "I'm not really sure I should name names, Thomas."

He leaned back as well. "Ah, I see. Well, that's probably a good idea considering that talking about this place is sort of against the rules unless you're bringing a play partner."

"Security is important," she answered, logging that bit of information away.

"It is. May I ask if it was a man or a woman that invited you?"

"You may, but I don't have to answer." The flirtation was finally back in her voice, and she bit her lip as he smiled slowly.

"What if I wanted to spank that bit of information out of you?"

33

Those dangerously attractive eyes were on hers, and she tried to stifle the sudden intake of breath his words brought on.

Be calm. Be confident. Act like you belong.

"You could try, Thomas."

"Feisty girl." Chuckling, he broke their gaze to let his eyes wander the room. The sounds of sex were coming from somewhere, the slap of skin accompanied by moans and groans, combined with a chorus of leather cracking, the clatter of chains, and the buzz of conversation – all overlaid atop that low thrumming music that seemed to call to all the basest needs of humanity. Hedonism at its finest. "So, before we get started we can have one drink to relax and get to know each other a bit. What would you like?"

Before we get started… right.

Maddie shifted in her seat, turning to look back at the incredibly well-stocked bar. "One drink?"

"Just one, you need to be clear headed and so do I."

"Of course." She smiled and blew out a breath, going for an old favorite. "I'd love a cape cod, it's vodka and cranberry and –"

"Lime. I know the drink." Thomas pushed up from his seat. "Just a moment, I'll be right back. Why don't you think of some of your favorite kinks so we can discuss them when I return?"

"Sure." Maddie answered confidently, but internally she was a ball of knots and anxiety. Kinks? What the fuck was she supposed to say to him? Looking around she wished she had her phone so she could quickly Google some BDSM terms, because relying on what she'd heard in movies, and read in a few naughty books, was probably not going to get her very far – and it may not even be accurate.

Shit.

Looking across the room, she left behind all her nerves and shifted into reporter mode. What could she see, and what did she already know?

To her right was a tiled area with a huge hot tub, but there were only two people soaking in it, and from the lack of straps it seemed the woman in it was topless. Beyond that was an open door to some showers, but getting completely nude in here was *not* on her to-do list. Swinging her eyes back to the middle of the room, she wasn't turned off by the idea of a spanking. Although she'd prefer being on one of the chairs or couches instead of the raised wooden platforms like some kind of showpiece.

There were various things in use among the thirty or so people inside, but since Black Light looked to be roughly the size of Runway above she knew it could hold a *lot* more. Maybe it had been wise to come on a Sunday after all?

"One cape cod for you, and a scotch for me." Setting the drinks down he took his seat and then lifted his glass. "To meeting new people."

"Thank you." Lifting hers she tapped it against his, and then took a larger sip than she probably should have. It was a cool, clean burn all the way down. Sitting up a little more she smiled at him. "So, do you meet new people here a lot?"

"Sometimes. Does that bother you?" Thomas rested his glass back on the table, his voice still light and casual.

"Not at all! I was just curious."

"Madeline." There was a chastising tone to the way he said her name, something about it making her want to apologize already even though she had no idea what she'd done wrong in his eyes. "It's fine if it bothers you, and I'm happy to discuss it. None of this works if we're not honest with each other. Honesty and communication are everything, and while I'm not asking you to blindly trust me right now, there does need to be some trust if you truly want to play."

The words settled like a weight in her chest, forming a lump in her throat that she had to take another sip of her drink to push down. Honesty was definitely *not* her forte. Licking a trace of vodka from her lower lip she glanced over at him, putting everything into maintaining the appearance of calm. "I know how important honesty is, and that was honest. I'm not a child, I know you've been with other people, as have I. We're both adults, right?"

He nodded and edged back to smile at her a little. "You're absolutely right. So, why don't you tell me what some of your favorite kinks are? I'm not saying we'll do them, but I'd like to get to know you better."

"Well, you brought up spanking." The grin that stretched her lips *was* honest, and he returned it.

"I did. Do you like to get spanked, Madeline?"

She felt her damnable blush returning, the curse of freckled people everywhere, but she spoke. "I do, and you can call me Maddie, by the way."

"Hmmm, Maddie…" There was a purr in his voice as he said her name and it made her press her thighs together. "Tell me, do you like to be tied down when you get spanked, Maddie?"

The sudden lack of air in the room made her head swim a little as she imagined what some of those leather straps would feel like across her limbs, and there was no denying the rush of wetness between her legs. "It's a definite turn-on." *Not a lie.* It was like he'd reached into her fantasies and plucked it free.

"What else do you like?" He leaned forward and rested his hand on her leg, inching up the hem of her dress just enough that the cool brush of his fingers teased the inside of her knee, and she realized she had parted them for him without thinking.

A crack of leather striking skin made her muscles twitch and she met his gaze. "That."

Thomas tilted his head with a smile. "I *think* that was a belt, or a strap. Do you like to be spanked with a belt like a naughty girl?"

If anyone had asked her that on any other day of the week she might have thrown her drink in their face, or flipped them off and said something about misogyny, but the low growl in his tone made her pussy clench with unexpected anticipation. "Maybe," she admitted, and his fingers traced a little higher on her thigh, sending a rush over her skin.

"You're blushing, Maddie."

"I'm sorry." Pressing her drink-cooled hand to her cheek she felt the burning heat. Her cheeks had to be flushed bright red from her own nerves and the beginning surges of the vodka. "I can't help it, it just happens."

"I don't want you to help it. It makes you look so beautiful, just... a little touch of innocence." Thomas slid his touch higher, brushing the place where her thighs still touched and she was tempted to spread her legs wider for him. To offer herself up like some sacrifice. "But you're not that innocent, are you, Maddie?" His hazel eyes bored into her with an eerie kind of power, and she felt her breath grow shorter as arousal stormed through her veins.

"No, I'm not," she whispered. *Truth.*

"Do you want to play with me tonight?"

"Yes." *Definitely not a lie.* She wanted him. Probably more than she'd ever wanted any stranger. There was some dark mystery in him, some forbidden thing that called to the good girl in her and beckoned her closer. Some thing she wanted to taste, to feel, and this could be her only chance.

"Say 'yes, sir' for me." Not a request, a command... and, strangely, it only made her heart race.

"Yes, sir," she repeated.

He gave her a look that promised corruption, and she realized she actually wanted it. Wanted all of it. The spanking, the leather, the bondage, and other things she couldn't even name but she knew he could give them if she'd just give in. And she was *definitely* going to give in.

For the sake of the story, of course.

Lie.

She knew it was a lie as soon as the idea passed into her head, because while she was sure this would make for one hell of a headline, the fact that she was easing her knees apart in hopes that this absolute stranger would inch his fingers just a little higher was all about her own wicked little desires and the epic sexual drought she'd been in for almost a year.

Dragging his trimmed, manicured nails across the delicate skin of her thigh, he captured her eyes for a moment – and then sat back and removed his hand completely. She leaned forward as if she could somehow follow his touch, but then caught herself and snapped her knees back together.

He chuckled softly at her obvious self-correction. "You're a lovely submissive, Maddie, that's for sure."

"Thanks," she replied lamely, her mind wrapping around the term and aligning it with everything she'd ever heard, or read, and everything she could see now. Time for a gamble. "And you're dominant."

"I figured that was pretty clear." He watched her carefully over the rim of his glass as he took a sip of the golden liquid.

Right. Alcohol. That was a good idea.

She took another hearty drink, appreciating the warmth blossoming in her stomach that matched the heat in her cheeks and the growing fire between her thighs. "So, question. Do *you* want to play with me tonight?"

"I do." He inclined his head towards her as he tilted his glass back and forth on the tabletop. "But I want to remind you again that although you're my guest, you don't have to do anything you don't want to do. I paid for your admission here, not for *you*."

Ah.

While she hadn't been thinking of it that way, hearing him say it aloud did bring some level of comfort to her. He was like some white knight, *no*, a dark knight. The kind of knight that would rescue a princess and do a hell of a lot more than kiss her when he found her – and for the first time in her life she definitely wanted to be the princess in the story. "Thank you for saying so, but I'm fine."

Just hopelessly turned on and soaking wet, but fine.

"Good. Back to your question, I would absolutely enjoy playing with you. The idea of tying you down over the end of one of those couches and turning your ass as beautifully red as your cheeks has me, admittedly, very turned on."

Talk about honesty. Her throat was dry, and she tilted her drink up only to be disappointed as she swallowed the last bit of the only alcohol she'd have before whatever came next.

"Does that interest you, Maddie?"

She nodded slowly as she lowered her empty glass, forcing herself to speak. "It does."

"Look at me when you answer me, please." That edge was back in his tone and she lifted her gaze to his, unaware that she'd been staring down into the ice and lime.

"It interests me."

"Sir," he corrected.

"*Sir*," she repeated.

"Wonderful." Thomas smiled like a wolf and finished the last sip of his scotch before standing. He offered her his hand again, and she took it, abandoning her glass to the tabletop. Only Maddie stood more carefully than he had, because her legs seemed to be as unsteady as a newborn foal. "What is your limit for our play tonight? I won't go beyond a belt or a strap, since that's what we've discussed, but may I touch you?"

"Oh God, yes, please." She answered too quickly, borderline pathetic and desperate due to the pulse pounding in agreement between her thighs.

Smooth.

His laugh was full of dark promise as he lifted his free hand to brush a thumb across her cheek, tucking a strand of unruly hair behind her ear. "I would love to watch you come under my touch."

Maddie's knees almost buckled as she stared up into his maddening eyes, sometimes a hint of green, or gray, amidst the forest-tinged brown. "That would be fantastic."

"Sir," he added for her, again.

"Sir," she repeated, again, and the smile he gave her was full of approval that she devoured like she was starving.

Gripping her hand a little tighter he started to lead them back into the maelstrom in the center of Black Light. Everything was more intense now, people were half-dressed, a woman was crying as she held onto a bar embedded in the back of a chair, the man behind her using a riding crop across her thighs. Instead of the fear she expected, Maddie felt a heady rush that made her breathing grow short.

Then she almost tripped over her own feet when she realized she was looking at Senator Robert Paulson getting a blowjob from a woman on her knees in front of him, his hand clenched in her dark curls. More shocking was the fact that his wife, the woman she'd seen pictured at a charity event in the Post just a few months before, was sitting next to him, nibbling her way down his neck before he pulled her into an open-mouthed kiss.

I have fallen through the fucking looking glass.

Thomas led them towards a wall that had a series of doors, one of them propped open to reveal what looked almost exactly like the exam room at her doctor's office, including a set of stirrups tucked into the table. She swallowed, relieved when he paused at an oversized, plush leather chair away from it, but from somewhere deep inside there was a flicker of regret that he hadn't led her into that room. Hadn't shown her what possibilities existed there to lead her even deeper down the rabbit hole.

'Next time,' a tiny voice inside her whispered, but she balked.

What next time? You didn't even get invited tonight!

Stepping behind her Thomas pulled her back to reality as he brushed his hands across her shoulders, down her arms, before transferring them to her waist. He settled his grip at the swell of her hips, pulling her firmly back against him, and there was no mistaking the erection pressing against her ass. "We're going to use the club's safe words, Maddie. Yellow if you want me to slow down, and red if you want me to stop. I will always respect them and listen for them, and I want you to repeat them for me so I know you remember them."

There was a buzzing in her ears, an intense rush in her blood-stream that made it hard to focus, but she managed it as she shifted her hips against him to the rhythm of the low music. "Yellow if I need you to slow down, red if I want you to stop."

He stilled her movements with a groan, digging his fingers more firmly into her hips. "You will not hesitate to use them. Promise me."

"I promise." She gasped as he slid one of his hands up her stomach to tease the underside of her breast through the infuriating barriers of the dress and bra. "*Sir*," she added and he pressed his hips more firmly against her.

At least she wasn't the only one drawn tight by their tempting discussion and the orchestra of sex around them.

"I want this dress off, are you okay removing it?" He barely finished speaking before she dropped her little purse to the floor and started reaching back for the zipper. With a soft chuckle he brushed her hands away and began to slide it south.

It was agonizingly slow, his knuckles brushing each newly bared inch of skin, and there was static electricity rushing through her in his wake. Finally, he nudged the shoulders of the dress forward and she pulled them down, letting the fabric fall to pool at her heels.

"Step out," he commanded, and she did, his touch grazing her ankles as if he were ready to steady her in case she lost her balance. Such a tiny gesture, but it caught her attention in the oddest way. Nothing had ever been like this, *no one* had ever been like this. Making her somehow feel important moments after she'd met them. Feeling special, protected, even though she was in a room full of people who were now seeing her in her favorite bra and panty set.

Thank God I did laundry, she thought to herself as his fingers trailed up the outsides of her calves, her thighs, her hips, her waist, and then he cupped her breasts and pulled her back to his chest. She felt the buttons on his shirt, the strained fabric of his pants in front of his hard cock, and her body responded instantly. A surge of wetness between her thighs, her pussy slick with need, urging her forward with the pounding beat of her heart. Urging her to dive in to whatever he had planned.

"You are so gorgeous," he whispered directly into her ear. One hand roaming lower over her soft belly, the curve of her waist, and then squeezing in at the hips she always complained were too wide – and yet, against him she believed his words. Not too pale, too curvy, too speckled by freckles, but *gorgeous*. "Are you blushing for me, Maddie?"

He nudged her hair away from her neck, leaving chaste kisses across the flesh leading down to her shoulder. With a quieted moan she arched against him and nodded. "Yes, sir."

A low groan thrummed against her back, the rumble of it felt by her ribs. "Bend forward, arms outstretched to the other side of the chair."

She followed his direction, pressing her hips against the arm of the chair and reaching to the other side. Thomas ran his warm hand over the swell of her ass, toying with the edge of her underwear. Then he spanked her, a sharp sting that made her jump, but she returned her hands to the other arm of the chair quickly.

"What did you forget, beautiful?"

"I don't know," she breathed, so beyond aroused that she was struggling to think straight. Fuck the story for the moment – this was intense, kinesthetic, experiential research.

"Whenever I give you a command, let me know you've heard it by saying 'yes, sir', alright?" There was infinite patience in his voice, and she nodded as she looked down at the dark brown leather of the chair's seat.

"Yes, sir."

"Mmmm, I do love the way that sounds when you say it." Thomas Hathaway, her tall, gorgeous, incredibly hot savior ran his hand over the place he'd just swatted, squeezing the flesh in a firm grip. "Stay right here, do not move. I'm getting something to tie you up with. Would you prefer rope or leather cuffs?"

His touch hadn't left her yet, and she chewed on her lower lip, imagining the texture of both and unable to decide. "Surprise me, sir?"

The devious laugh that came from him was followed by a gentle kiss pressed to her spine. "Alright, Maddie. Don't move." Then he stepped away, and she could feel the air cooling the dampness of her underwear.

How on earth was she so turned on before he'd actually *done* anything to her?

It felt insane, *she* was insane for being half-naked and bent over a chair in public, in front of at least one senator and God only knew who else. Doubt and panic started to edge their way in, competing with the mind-numbing arousal that had owned her so completely a moment before, but then he was back. He trailed his fingers over her lower back, then up the line of her spine before he gathered a fistful of her hair and gently lifted her head.

Thomas crouched on the far side of the chair, his eyes level with hers. "Still okay, beautiful?"

"Yeah," she nodded, and it made her hair pull slightly against his grip. The tingle of each little pin-prick like sting made her squirm against the armrest. He tightened his fist in her hair and the short moan that escaped her lips was unconscious. "I mean, yes, sir."

"Good girl." Those words flooded her with warmth, and there was no hiding the self-satisfied smile across her lips. "So beautiful," he mused as he released her hair and lifted the rope. It was shiny and black, not the coarse rope she'd imagined in her head, but she quickly realized *that* was probably a good thing. He fiddled with it out of sight for a moment, his chestnut brown hair falling over his forehead as he worked. Then he lifted what looked like cuffs, except in the center was a coil of rope instead of chain.

"Wow," she whispered, mostly to herself, but he smiled.

"They're called Texas Handcuffs. Now, put your hands through."

She obeyed, and with the tug of the two ends of rope the silky cuffs tightened. The effect was immediate, her heart rate increasing further, and the knotting tension in her lower belly grew stronger. He pulled her arms straight, straining her over the middle of the chair, and she lifted her head to see him working.

Oh, shit. He's tying the rope to the chair.

For a moment she felt a flicker of panic, but then the arousal was back as he met her gaze and pressed two fingers to the centers of both of her palms. "Squeeze for me."

"Yes, sir," she replied as she obeyed.

"If for some reason they get too tight, you tell me. Say yellow, and I'll check in and fix it. You shouldn't lose circulation to your fingers, alright?" His concern for her safety edged back the hint of panic even further. When she stayed silent he tilted his head at her, his brown hair shifting across his forehead.

"Oh! Yes, sir." Maddie swallowed as he grinned at her, reaching a hand forward to trace her still flushed cheek.

"I've got some questions for you, Maddie." He stood, withdrawing his touch as he walked around the chair to where she couldn't see him.

"Questions?" she asked. *Wasn't she supposed to be asking the questions?*

"Yes." Thomas' voice was a low rumble behind her, and then the sharp sting of a spank landed on her ass. It shocked her more than it hurt, but she still gasped loudly and pulled against the rope. "Keep your heels on the floor, beautiful, and listen to me."

"Okay." She nodded and then another swat landed, a little harder. "I mean, yes, sir!"

"That's a good girl." He had a smile in his voice. "Let's get you warmed up." He began to spank her, sharp stings followed by warm heat that bloomed over her skin. Never truly painful, but always a shock that made her push up onto her toes before she forced her heels to press back into the carpet.

The three-inch lift from her shoes seemed to have her ass at the perfect height for him to pepper every inch of her skin, and he did. Starting out slow, with a breath or two between each smack, but then they grew faster. More intense, until the stings started to overlay one another and she knew she was squirming, tugging against the rope that slid like silk across her wrists without giving an inch. Murmuring incoherent pleas that she bit down on, because she knew he was being gentle, that the teasing burn he was building was nothing more than that – a tease.

Because she'd had spanks like this before, and she wanted to know what came next.

"There." He stopped, running his hand over the warm skin of her ass, and she could feel the low heat in it as he squeezed. "So beautiful… all pink and ready to play. Are you ready, Maddie?"

The bravery came from some dark, hungry place inside her, but she nodded and pushed her voice to give more than a whisper. "Yes, sir."

"Alright, now tell me the truth. Were you invited here tonight?"

"Yes, sir." A hard spank landed on her right cheek, and she cried out as the shock made her gasp. "What the –"

"Want to try that again? Remember, honesty is important." His hand brushed over the place he'd just struck, and she shivered. "Were you invited here tonight, Maddie?"

"Yes, sir." She lied again, and this time the swat to her other cheek was even sharper. It was a burst of fiery sting that made her bounce her hips trying to settle it, and if her hands hadn't been bound she would have reached back to soothe the skin.

Thomas leaned over her back, the brush of his shirt across her ribs making her shiver. "See, I don't think that's true, beautiful. It's in the rules that any member bringing a guest has to be present. So, either your *friend* broke the rules and didn't meet you, or you heard about this place from someone who should not have been talking about it and you tried to come in on your own." He pressed an all-too-gentle kiss to her ribs, and she drew in a shuddering breath as her nerves ramped up. "And I sincerely doubt that anyone would invite you and then not be here to play with someone so impeccably beautiful. So… which is it?"

Shit. Shit. Shit.

"Maddie?" His voice had that edge in it again, that chastising tone that made her want to apologize for things she couldn't possibly admit.

"You're right, I, um, I heard about it, but I can't tell you their name. It's my fault, not theirs… sir." *Another lie,* but this was one she hoped he'd believe.

"So, you planned to just come in here and… what? Offer yourself to the first Dom that wanted to play?" He delivered a hard spank to the place where her ass met her thighs and it hurt even more, forcing her up onto her toes before she dropped her heels again.

She nodded, agreeing to the lie. "Yes! Yes, sir. I just wanted to see it."

Thomas laughed low, standing up behind her. Another hard swat, but she gritted her teeth to stifle the whine. "You've been a very naughty girl, Maddie… and while I'm very glad I was the one to find you, I don't like it when subs lie to me, and I like it even less when they put themselves at risk. *Anyone* could have offered to let you in."

"I'm sorry, sir." *Not a lie.* Guilt surged inside her, and she felt bad for continuing to lie, but there was no way out now. She was in, she'd already seen one senator embroiled in this devious little underground sex club, and where there was one – there had to be more. A whole new, exciting layer to the Jaxson Davidson scandal.

It had front page written all over it.

Suddenly, Thomas slipped his hand between her thighs, cupping the evidence of her arousal as he applied the barest hint of pressure to her clit. The shock of it pulled the brake on her thoughts, shifting gears to the thrumming heat inside her, the pulse of desire that beckoned her ever closer to the darkness all around her. Maddie pushed her hips forward, seeking a little more, and she knew that the story wasn't the only reason she was bent over this chair. No, she'd let him tie her down because some piece of her wanted this, wanted *more* than what she knew, and he seemed more than willing to give it to her. "Please, sir…"

"Please what?" he asked, his hand staying still against the damp fabric of her underwear as she rocked more urgently against his touch.

"Please touch me!" It was begging, something she wouldn't have imagined herself capable of, but her mind was spinning out of her control, and her nerves were a network of need that she knew instinctively Thomas Hathaway could satisfy.

"Oh, no. Not yet." He pulled his hand away and she actually whined, twisting against the rope and shifting her weight from heel to heel in a miniature fit. The dark tone in his voice instantly quieted her, "You know the deal, Maddie. Naughty girls don't get rewards, they get punished. Then, *if they're very, very good,* they get a reward."

The next swat from his hand was so loud it seemed to bounce back off the ceiling, and she tried her best to swallow the shout as the full outline of his hand burned to life atop the still aching skin.

"Are you going to be good and take your punishment for lying to me? For trying to get into Black Light without any kind of real invitation?" She could hear the slightly playful tone in his voice, but deep inside her guilt twisted like a knife. Thomas thought he was punishing her for just sneaking in because she wanted to play at the club, when the reality was so much worse.

Maddie nodded her head, the fiery red of her hair probably

competing with the shame-filled crimson of her cheeks. *At least he can't see that.* "Yes, sir."

"Good girl. Remember your safe words."

There was no warning except the barest whisper of leather cutting air, and then a line of molten fire landed across both cheeks of her ass. She screamed, digging her nails into her palms as the pain peaked and then faded into the burning heat. *'Red'*, danced on the tip of her tongue, some part of her brain desperately enacting a fight or flight instinct urging her to shout it, but instead she clenched her jaw tight. Another lash from the leather, either a belt or a strap like he'd said, and the pain was unlike anything she'd ever felt. Sharp, unforgiving for a moment, and then it would fade and she would suddenly gasp in air.

Again.

And again.

And again, and again, and again.

Somehow always on a new place, a little higher, or a little lower, and she would cry out, but she knew she deserved it. She quietly begged him to stop, but there was no sincerity to the words. She knew she deserved the pain that had her so tense she was scratching furrows into her palms with her nails. There was no way she'd speak the words he'd given her to *really* stop this.

She didn't deserve them, didn't need them.

It was an unvocalized apology for using him like she was. Using him to gain entrance to this place, using him to lie her way past all of their elaborate security, and using him to explore this new, dark place inside herself that was steadily tipping her from the agonizing pain into some kind of humming energy.

There were tears on her cheeks, capturing strands of her hair against her cheeks. Her breathing had been ragged at first, but it was calming, and as the next strike landed she felt the burning heat of it, the flash of pain, but it faded so quickly into the blur of sensation that she almost couldn't track it.

Another crack of the leather, another distant sting, and Maddie was floating somewhere outside herself. Somewhere the guilt was but a tiny blip in the sea of her mind. It was glorious, and quiet, and so much simpler than the chaotic torrent her brain was on a daily basis.

This is incredible.

The first lash across the backs of her thighs, just below her ass, made her lift her head, a quiet yelp of pain, but then she was limp again. A soft, low sound escaping her lips, and she couldn't imagine using a safe word any more. Why had she ever wanted to escape this? It was catharsis embodied. It was perfect.

She just needed it to continue, to keep going. To wait in this place where her body was a lightning storm of tingling energy, where her mind was hushed and guiltless and free.

Another snap that she heard rather than felt, and she was warm and glowing through and through.

"Such a good girl, you're such a good girl, Maddie..." Thomas' voice filtered its way back into her awareness, and then she felt his hand between her thighs again. Rubbing, pressing the soaked fabric of her lacy underwear between her folds as he found her clit and focused his attention in delirious circles that had her hands twisting in the ropes again.

"Oh, *God*," she whispered on a moan, arching her back to lift her head and push back more firmly against his touch. Her head was swimming, so close to some kind of glorious, sparkling horizon, as the tense pleasure built and built. Every touch was expert, and when his other hand landed in the small of her back, pressing her down, she reveled in it. In his strength, the wicked rhythm his fingers maintained on the focal point of her body, and the constant assurances he voiced from behind her.

"That's it. You did so well, come for me, beautiful. Go on, let go and come for me. You did so well, you're such a good girl…" His sweet lies pushed her to the very edge, the pleasure building until it was an almost agonizing boundary that she teetered over, her body tense to the point of pain – and then she fell.

White light burst behind her eyes, and she called out something incomprehensible as she came against his hand, every thought obliterated once more for a blissful moment of nothingness where she drifted in warm, golden perfection.

Bliss.

This was what that word meant. Languid, pure, unfettered by the bounds of reality.

Thomas' touch left her a moment later and she felt lost for a second, confused, until she felt his deft, talented fingers at the rope near her hands. He released her and then his arms were under her, lifting her like she weighed nothing before he spun them and settled her in his lap in the chair. His strong arms wrapped around her, holding her firmly until she melted against his firm chest. Cool cloth brushed over her skin and she opened her eyes to see that he'd covered her with his suit jacket, the silk lining set against her. "Shhh, Maddie. Relax. That was… incredible."

She mumbled something in agreement as he adjusted her in his lap and pulled her closer, letting her heels drape over the side of the chair.

"You are so beautiful," his voice purred against her hair and she let herself just *be*. All of the pieces of herself, the parts that were usually in such a frenzy reminding her of her never ending to-do list, her failures, her mistakes — they were all hushed and calm. Sated beasts sleeping in the corners of her mind.

For a few minutes she wasn't the disappointment she always saw herself as, she was just Maddie. Just a languid set of muscles, and bone, and still tingling nerves wrapped in his warmth.

If only the world would really fall away.

Awareness returned slowly, first with the steady brush of his thumb up and down her arm, the gentle touch of his hand near her knee where he held her in his lap. Then the strong, pounding beat of his heart under her cheek. Even and powerful. When she went to shift she felt the *other* strong thing nudging her... Thomas Hathaway was still hard as a rock under her ass.

Twisting in his arms, he relaxed his grip a little so she could move, but as soon as she reached between them to brush the steel of his cock through his pants he moved his arm from under her legs and caught her hand. "Just rest, Maddie."

"But you're —"

"Fine. I'm just fine, I want you to relax. That was intense, and I'm not sure I've ever had a sub drop into subspace so quickly from a belt." He laughed and it was a warm, shaking feeling since she was propped against his chest. "You kind of surprised me."

"Subspace?" she asked, still a little dazed.

He leaned forward to look at her, his hazel eyes shadowed with concern. "Has no one ever put you in subspace before?"

The blush that fired to life in her cheeks seemed to answer for her. "Thomas, I —"

"Oh, Maddie... that's..." He sighed. "It's terrible that no one's taken care of you. You deserve so much more." His interruption cut off her confession, and she bit down on her lip. He was too good. Too good to have stumbled into her twisted plans. "Masochists don't always get treated well, but you deserve that. You know that, right? You deserve to be treated well?"

Her brows pulled together, because *that* was a word she definitely knew. Masochists were people who liked pain, but that wasn't her. She wasn't messed up like that... right?

"Madeline." His use of her full name made her look up into his gaze, shifting in his lap until they were almost eye-to-eye. "Just because you enjoy this, doesn't mean you don't matter. People can't just take advantage of you, and you can't let them. Okay?"

"Okay." She nodded, still unsteadied by everything that had happened, and then she cursed herself silently. "I mean, yes sir."

Thomas chuckled. "Play is over, beautiful. You can just call me Thomas."

"Alright, Thomas." Maddie went to get off his lap, but he tugged her back.

"You don't have to get up, I'm enjoying holding you. Aftercare is one of my favorite parts of play." He leaned his cheek against her hair, hugging her against him once more. "Has no one done this for you either?"

"No," she confessed, but when he sighed and held her a little closer she flinched. Aftercare? She didn't even know what the fuck that was. No one had ever done any of this, *any* of it, because she was pretending to be someone she wasn't − or she was discovering something she was for the first time − or she'd lied so thoroughly the whole damn night she couldn't tell anymore − but regardless, she didn't deserve this kindness. This warmth, this generosity. Not from someone like him.

"I was only going to give you ten with the belt, but I thought I felt you teetering on subspace, so I went for it. You sure you're okay?"

"It was wonderful, I can't think of the last time my head was that quiet."

He hugged her tight again. "Oh, Maddie... women like you are so unique. I have to admit I'm glad you showed up tonight trying to sneak in, even though that was *very* wrong." There was a playful tone in his voice, but her guilt woke up like an angry bear inside her chest.

"I'm really sorry, Thomas, I never should have –"

"Oh, no, beautiful... shhh..." He adjusted her on his lap, tucking his coat tighter around her to trap his body heat against her skin, warming her when she hadn't even realized how cold she'd been. "That's the beauty of punishment. You make a mistake, you take a punishment, and all is forgiven. I think it's one of the many things BDSM gets right when it comes to relationships. Vanilla people will sit on things for years, bring it up later just to toss it in their partner's face, because it's never really been resolved. *This?* All resolved. Over and done with, and I won't speak another word about it."

"Thanks," she whispered, but his words had only poked the bear of guilt. The punishment had felt good because she'd known she needed to be punished, but *he* didn't know what she was really doing here.

What she was *still* doing here, if she were honest with herself.

As she'd slowly woken up out of her daze, her eyes had been roaming the room. Catching sight of different people, memorizing faces just in case she recognized them later. Building up her little list inside her mind so she could update her notes when she got home.

Good for you, Maddie, you're just like every other selfish, self-righteous reporter out there now.

It's what you've always wanted.

Despite the undeniable guilt for how she was using him, she knew that it was secondary to the whole mission of the night in the first place. Before she'd been sidetracked by his handsome face, his tempting flirtation, and his wicked words – she'd come for a story, and now she had the beginnings of one hell of an article. A chance to expose a fresh layer of scandal to the Davidson story – Antoine was going to lose his mind.

"How about one more drink before I tuck you into a car home?" Thomas' low whisper tugged at the guilt again, and she sat up in his lap to look him in the eye, the insistent nudge of his erection still present.

"But I haven't taken care of you."

"I got what I wanted, beautiful. Trust me." He lifted her in his arms and then settled her on her feet, his suit jacket still held against her front. "Let's get you dressed."

He was as good at getting women back into their clothes as he was at getting them out of them, and when he finished zipping her up, he turned her around to take his jacket, smiling as he pulled it on. Then he checked both of her wrists, rubbing them with his thumbs in an effort to ease the redness with a kind of gentleness that belied the actions that had put them there, before he ran his hands over her hair and cupped her cheeks.

"You are wonderful, you know that?"

"Sure," she whispered, but it was half-hearted. Thomas pulled her into a hug anyway, and pressed a kiss to the top of her head, then he caught her hand and walked them back to the bar. The chorus of moans, cries of pain, and the whisper and crack of leather in the room now seemed to be nothing more than background noise to her.

He settled her on a bar stool, and she hissed as the pressure of the stool woke up the welts across her ass and thighs. "Oh, hell. Are you okay? Would you rather sit on one of the chairs?"

The sudden concern for her pain made her genuinely smile, because, after all, he'd been the one to cause it. Maddie shook her head, and squeezed his arm. "I'm fine, I promise. It just surprised me."

"Well, I'm sure those marks will look even more beautiful tomorrow." He winked at her and then waved down one of the bartenders. "Order whatever you want, I just need to run to the bathroom. I'll be right back, I promise."

"Okay." She maintained the smile as he walked away from her, and she waved when he glanced back at her. Then she turned around to find a pretty bartender in front of her with pin-straight blonde hair, tan skin, and a curious expression on her face.

"Hey, what can I —" The woman slowed her speech and then paused, leaning forward on the counter. "You okay?"

"Yeah, I'm fine." Maddie tried to smile, but it felt brittle. She could feel the sting of tears at the edges of her eyes, and she shook her head and looked down trying to hide behind the curtain of her once-again frizzy hair.

"One minute," the bartender spoke, but by the time Maddie felt comfortable lifting her eyes, the woman was down the bar pouring a drink.

Forcing a deep breath, she tried to settle her emotions, but they felt like they'd been shaken up so hard that none of the pieces were falling back into place. *What the fuck had she just done?*

"Here you go. It's an *actual* cape cod, the other girl shorted you on the vodka, and it looks like you need it." There was a hint of frustration in the woman's voice, but it was directed at the other bartender and not her.

"Thanks," she whispered as she pulled the glass towards her. Taking a small sip, she had to admit it tasted better than the one earlier, and the immediate burn in her stomach confirmed the presence of more alcohol.

The bartender smiled brightly and leaned her head down to catch Maddie's eyes. "Your hair is unbelievable, you know that? I'm sure people tell you that all the time. Is it natural?"

She was a little surprised by the question, but she nodded. "Yeah. Just as red as my mom's. Irish families, you know?"

"I love hair colors, so much cool stuff you can do with it. I went red for a while, but it's a bitch to maintain when it isn't natural." The woman smiled. "Just know lots of girls are jealous of that hair, and probably your dress. It looks nice."

Maddie felt a blush creep into her cheeks, but it pushed back the urge to cry a little further. "Thanks, it's my favorite."

"Well, your date certainly seemed to like it, and damn if he's not cute." The almost wistful tone in the bartender's voice made her lips lift at the edge in a weak smile.

"Yeah, but it was just kind of a spontaneous thing. Not a real date."

"Working the bar I've seen a million dates. Trust me, the way he looked at you? That looked like a *date*, with a guy that's pretty into you. Lucky girl..."

"Right." Maddie's stomach turned, the guilt roaring in her chest, but she took a hearty drink of the vodka in an attempt to silence it.

"Anyway, where do you work?"

"It's this daily ad paper, it's called the Daily Saver D.C., I do copy editing, nothing fancy." She shrugged, still embarrassed to admit she had such a shit job in one of the most incredible cities in the country.

The bartender tapped the counter in front of her. "I know that thing! It's in a bin outside my apartment in Adam's Morgan! Found this great local Chinese place..." The blonde rested her hand against her stomach like she was already hungry. "Happy Family meal with an egg roll and rice for just eleven dollars, it's my favorite pre-shift dinner."

Maddie shrugged and smiled despite the sour feeling in her own stomach. "I'm glad it helped you out."

"Sure did. Girl's gotta eat on the cheap before D.C. prices suck you dry. Coupons make my world go round. I'm Klara by the way. I keep the sailors salty every night we're open." She leaned forward conspiratorially, all smirks and trouble. "Until I can whip my cohorts into shape, make sure you order from me. Otherwise you'll get *that* kind of shit." Klara angled her head towards the other bartender, and then laughed.

"I'm Maddie."

"Nice to meet you, Maddie, and oooh it looks like your *date* is on his way back over." She winked at her and then put on a professional face for Thomas as he approached. "What can I get you, sir?"

"I'll take a scotch. Bowmore, twelve year?" Thomas met Klara's gaze and smiled as she nodded.

"Neat or on the rocks?"

"Rocks, please. Thank you."

As Klara walked away, Maddie took another hefty drink before she met Thomas' beautiful hazel eyes. "So..."

"So, this is where I'm supposed to be a gentleman and get your phone number, and then wait a few days to call you, but I'd

really just like to ask you to dinner on Wednesday night."
Thomas stunned her again with his casual confidence, but at
this point she shouldn't have expected any less. It was just the
layers of lies she'd constructed that held her back. He was
perfect, or he *would be* perfect if she hadn't already fucked it all
up so bad. "Come on, Maddie. Say yes."

"Thomas…" She flinched and was grateful when Klara
returned with his scotch.

"Anything else you two need?"

"We're good," Thomas answered, offering his stellar smile
before they were once again alone. "Come on, Maddie. Did you
enjoy tonight?"

She sighed. "Of *course* I enjoyed tonight, it was fantastic, but I
don't think —"

"Then don't think, just say yes. Let me at least give you a chance
to get to know me outside of Black Light. I'm not going to lie to
you and say that I don't have a dominant personality, hell, it's
what got me elected, but I can be a normal every-day man too."

Elected?

Maddie felt like the ground was moving under her feet, quicksand waiting to swallow her whole, but as she shifted on the seat
and felt the sparks of pain reminding her of the delirium he'd
given her — she wanted to say yes. Wanted to let the quicksand
swallow her just so she could taste what it was like to be with
him one more time.

Just once more.

Once more wouldn't hurt, right?

"Okay, Thomas."

The pride that lit up his face was infectious, and as he let out a quiet cheer and raised his glass of scotch she couldn't help but smile back. "That deserves a toast. To second dates being even better than first dates!"

"You're counting this as a first date?" Maddie laughed as their glasses clinked together.

"Oh, absolutely. Makes for one hell of a story, doesn't it?" He laughed and took a sip, but her heart sank as she drank too.

"Right, one *hell* of a story." Her eyes roamed the room, and she saw David Alchert, the lobbyist from Thursday night that had helped her discover the mop marked entrance to Black Light. He was leading the same beautiful woman he'd had with him then, but now she had a collar and a leash as they walked towards one of the raised platforms. Tearing her eyes away she upended her glass to finish it, almost choking as she tried to swallow too much at once.

"Whoa, Maddie, are you okay?"

Plastering a smile on her face, she nodded. "Absolutely. Just tired, you know? And I've got work in the morning, and –"

"Say no more, I'll get you home quickly. Where do you live?"

"Arlington. Near the Ballston metro stop," she spoke as he dug out his wallet and laid a black AMEX down on the counter.

Shit. He's really *got money.*

"That's not far at all, we'll have you in bed in no time." He chuckled to himself, pushing a hand through his hair as Klara swung by to snag the card. "I mean, *you* will be in bed in no time."

His correction made her smile, because they both knew he could have her if he just asked. Fuck, she'd offered to take care of his hard-on earlier in the middle of the club, but he'd refused her – and what guy did that anyway?

Thomas Hathaway was unlike any man she'd ever met, more interesting, more confident, more tempting, more *everything* – and she was going on a second date with him. On Wednesday. The reality settled on her as he scribbled a tip and his signature on the tiny receipt, and then put his wallet away. "Ready?"

"Yeah." She let him help her off the stool, and she glanced back just in time to see Klara wave at her before walking over to another couple.

They were back outside in a matter of moments, but everything seemed to be moving in fits and spurts. They were walking through the still active play area, then they were in the pale purple locker room, and Thomas was pressing her phone into her hand.

He had his phone already, and he touched her shoulder and the world seemed to come back into focus. "Maddie, are you okay? I asked what's your number?"

"Yeah, I'm great. Sorry." She smiled and rattled it off, and then opened her phone to add his, typing in *Thomas Hathaway* with a bitter taste on her tongue.

"Alright, you definitely need some sleep." As soon as he'd given his cell number, he was on the phone with his car service. In another flash they were upstairs moving through Runway, in another they were gathering their coats from coat check, and then they were outside. It was almost two am, and she was shivering on the sidewalk as he wrapped his arms around her. "I don't know about you, but I'm going to be counting down to Wednesday when I'm stuck in meetings all day tomorrow."

"Me too," she agreed, and tried to focus on him instead of the guilt gnawing away inside her. A few minutes later a sleek, black sedan pulled up and a man jumped out of the driver's side to open the back passenger door for her.

Just like the people she'd watched before. The same people she had listed in her phone, and in a growing document at home that was now going to include a *lot* of research on BDSM clubs for the article.

You're such a bitch, Maddie.

She swallowed, hesitating when the driver gestured to the interior. "I really don't need to take your car, Thomas. I can grab an Uber, it's okay."

He kissed her on the forehead when she stopped speaking and nudged her towards the car. "I'd rather know you made it home safely. Please drink some water when you get there, and if you think of it, send me a text so I know you made it?"

"Sure." Maddie dropped onto the seat.

"I'd like to check on you tomorrow, if you're okay with that?" There was a charming softness to his tone now, a concern, but she flinched back from it internally.

I don't deserve this.

"Okay." Nodding, she looked down at the phone in her hand to break eye contact, and he waved at her as he shut the door. The driver was inside an instant later and they were pulling away, leaving Thomas on the curb. Nothing felt right as they drove towards her apartment, but it *was* nice not having to worry she'd need to stab someone with her keys in case the driver turned out to be crazy.

It didn't take long at all in the night traffic before she was inside her tiny apartment and turning the locks. She stripped out of the dress and tossed it onto her bed, grabbing a glass of water from her kitchen, which was only about fifteen feet from her bed, and ten feet from her desk. Living in one big room had some benefits. Opening her laptop she drank some of the water before she brought up Google and searched the one thing she knew she wouldn't be able to sleep without knowing: *Thomas Hathaway election.*

A second later the results returned, and she clicked on the first link which showed a smiling headshot of him, looking even more gorgeous. Underneath the picture were the words she hadn't even known she'd been dreading: Congressman Thomas Hathaway (D), New York.

He was a politician, a fucking member of the House of Representatives, *and* a member of Black Light. The club she was going to expose to get a position at the Post.

And she had a date with him on Wednesday night.

Fuck.

Chapter Five

Monday

𝒯he decision to sleep on the couch in his office had been a good one, because at six o'clock in the morning his desk phone was already ringing. With a groan, Thomas shoved himself into an upright position, rolling his neck before he took the few steps towards the phone. "Hathaway," he answered, and then sighed and walked the rest of the way around his desk to drop into his chair as one of his fellow representatives started talking fast.

Off to a stellar Monday already. As he let his peer rant about their need to get more support behind a proposed bill, Thomas unlocked his phone and frowned when he was still missing a text from Maddie.

"Right, I'm listening," he half-lied as he tapped out a text to her. *Just checking to make sure you got home alright. Looking forward to Wednesday night.'*

Locking the phone he tried to block out the images of her draped over the chair at Black Light. The curve of her ass, outlined by those lace edged black panties, the delicate curve of her waist and the swell of her hips. His cock twitched behind his slacks and he clenched his teeth, forcing his attention back to the call. "Do you want me to talk to Donna for you? If you're so concerned about her vote, I'll just ask."

He waited for the frenzy on the other end of the phone to calm down while he opened his laptop. Fifty-three unread emails. *Great.* This was why he'd headed to Black Light the night before, he'd needed to take the edge off before this shit started up again.

"Eric. *Eric,*" Thomas interrupted him, channeling the authoritative tone that calmed both upset members of Congress and submissives alike. "I will speak to Donna today, now go have some breakfast and we'll talk later in the meeting. Alright?"

Nodding, even though Eric couldn't see him, he listened to the man's blood pressure drop, and then he smiled as the volume of his voice finally reached normal levels again.

"Wonderful, see you then." Hanging up the phone, he blew out a breath and scratched a note on a pad of paper on his desk asking his assistant to set up the lunch with Donna and explaining he was heading off for a workout. Grabbing his gym bag, and a change of clothes, he stuck his cell phone in his pocket, and dropped the note on Alan's desk as he headed downstairs.

Wireless headphones blaring Nine Inch Nails he was in mile two of his treadmill run when 'Closer' was interrupted by an incoming call. Glancing down at the screen he was disappointed to see Jaxson Davidson's name plastered across the screen instead of Maddie's. He tapped the decline call button and upped the incline on the treadmill with a sigh. Whatever Jaxson wanted could wait until he'd showered, and that wasn't going to happen until at least mile four. Just as his mind had started to drift back to Maddie's delicate blush, the impossibly arousing way she'd squirmed under his hand, the fucking phone rang again.

Declined.

Dammit, Jaxson, lay off. It's barely seven am.

As 'The Downward Spiral' album picked back up in his head-phones he shook his head and focused on keeping his breathing steady for the run. It's not like he wasn't already distracted enough, but a hard-on was only going to make finishing impos-sible. Shifting gears from thinking of the beautiful submissive to reviewing the particulars of the bill he'd be discussing with Donna, and then Eric, he mentally zoned out on work.

Just as he started to really *think* his phone dinged with a voice-mail alert. He didn't even have to glance at his screen to know it was from Jaxson. The guy had gone from jet-setting model party boy to obsessive businessman almost overnight. He barely recog-nized him anymore, but no matter how much they'd changed one thing was still true about both of them – they were domi-nant. It was actually Jaxson's decision to open Black Light that had brought the two of them back together after so many years on vastly different paths.

Still, long-time friend or not, he could wait thirty fucking minutes for him to finish his morning workout.

Turning his phone face down in the little tray, he cranked up the volume on his music and pushed himself until the haze from his few hours of sleep was obscured by a wave of endorphins. Four point six miles later and he hit the cool down button, pouring sweat in the uncomfortably stagnant air of the cardio room.

He was walking with the treadmill when he turned his phone

over, hoping to see a reply from Maddie – but there was nothing more than the reminder of the two missed calls, the voicemail, and a few news alerts. Swiping it open he was about to text her again when he stopped himself.

Do you want to look like a creep? Calm down and go take a shower.

Locking his phone, he took his own advice and went to make himself presentable for a day on Capitol Hill.

"So, you've got that meeting with Congresswoman Taylor at 9:30, then the waterworks brunch at 10:00, which you *will* be late for," Alan glanced up at him from his notepad, and Thomas just shrugged. "I was able to get Donna Mueller for noon, but I know that's two –"

"I won't eat at both, Alan, don't worry."

With a slight smirk, his assistant returned to his list, scratching something off with a pen. "Then you're in committee meetings from 1:30 to 4:30, and there's the cocktail reception for the Carrindi Foundation at 6:00."

"Did I agree to go to that?"

"You told me to RSVP last month."

"Are you sure?" Thomas groaned and took a long drink of his coffee. "I'm pretty sure I wouldn't have –"

"You said RSVP, and I did, and I got your tux cleaned on Friday for it, so you're going." Alan gave him a serious look, and then waved his hand to the side. "Honestly, if you didn't want to go, why did you agree to it?"

"I probably *did* want to go then, but now I'm tired."

"Too bad, you're going. You already paid for a plate." His assistant ticked off another thing on his list.

"Wait, I'm paying to go to this thing I don't want to go to?"

"Yes."

"You should go instead of me. Rub elbows, enjoy the drinks and the food. I already paid after all." Flipping over his cell phone he checked again for a text, but the only person he'd received one from was his brother back in New York asking about their father's birthday.

"If only I were three inches taller and had your shoulders." Alan gave him a smart-ass smile, and Thomas raised his eyebrows at him. With a sigh, Alan dropped his hands to his sides. "You're going, Congressman Hathaway."

"First of all, you know to call me Thomas, and second of all, I seem to remember being your boss, and not the other way around?"

"Whatever makes you feel better. I snagged you some fruit and a bagel, whole wheat, low-fat cream cheese, it's on your filing cabinet because there wasn't a single *inch* of desk space visible." Alan headed towards the door.

"Wait, I need dinner reservations for two on Wednesday night. Around eight. Somewhere nice, alright?"

His executive assistant froze in place and turned to face him. "Do I get to ask questions about this?"

"Not at all, Alan."

There was blatant curiosity on the young man's face, but after two and a half years of working together, Alan knew when he could push his luck, and when he couldn't. "Alright, I'll get you reservations, but your scary glare doesn't work on me, remember? It's why you keep me around."

"Right. Thank you, Alan." He couldn't help but smile as his assistant shrugged and pulled his door closed behind him. Spinning around in his chair he found the little plate of food next to a stack of files that he really needed to sort through so he could find them again. If he asked Alan to do it, they'd be put in some kind of alphabetical order that he'd never be able to remember.

Stabbing a piece of pineapple with a fork he took a bite and continued through his email, making notes on where different people stood on various discussions happening on the hill. It was a few minutes after nine when he felt his iPhone vibrating on his desk.

Jaxson Davidson.

Again.

Thomas answered and tucked the phone against his cheek so he could continue working before his first meeting showed up at 9:30. "Good morning, Jaxson."

"Avoiding my calls, or just pretending to be a busy, important politician, Thomas?"

"Being an asshole on purpose, or just for the usual reasons?" He smiled as he heard Jaxson's heavy exhale on the other end of the line.

"You were at the club last night." There was an odd note in the other man's voice, and he could feel a headache coming on before their discussion even started.

"Yes, I was."

"With a girl."

"Why, *yes*, with a girl. I don't bat for both teams, remember?" His chuckle died on his lips when the frustrated growl that Jaxson returned rumbled over the line.

"I remember, and I still don't care, asshole. How exactly do you know this Madeline O'Neill girl?"

"Why do you ask?"

"Because she gave *my* name to Daniel at the security desk in the locker room and said that *I* was the one to invite her."

"Ah." Thomas couldn't help but smile. Maddie *was* a naughty girl, and she probably had no idea just how poor of a choice that was. If there was one thing Jaxson hated, it was someone dropping his name without permission.

Perhaps that could be their next corrective discussion.

"Ah? That's all you have to say? This girl of yours shouldn't be using my —"

"Stop." He used the commanding tone automatically. "First of all, she's not mine, I met her last night."

"What the fu—"

"And second of all," Thomas interrupted before Jaxson could go on a rant, "Maddie was just curious about the club. She'd heard about it from a friend and she showed up. Her choice of listing your name was bold, but I dealt with it."

"You *dealt* with it? What the fuck, Thomas? We can't just have a bunch of people wandering into Black Light! It's supposed to be private, secure. That's the entire fucking point." The growl in his friend's tone spoke of his frustration, but he just shrugged and replied to an email as he talked.

"Look, it's not my fault someone talked to her about it, but I'm just glad I was the one to meet her, and the club needs more single subs anyway. You told me the lack of pick-up play would change, but it's been over a month and Maddie is only the second one I've seen."

There was a grumble on the other end of the line, and then the silence stretched. Not in a rush to continue the argument, Thomas used the time to finish his reply on the email and click send. He took a bite of his bagel as he waited for Jaxson to decide if he wanted to argue or crawl back into bed with his lovers. "Fine. So you *dealt* with it."

"I punished her appropriately for trying to get into the club without an invitation, and potentially putting herself at risk by waltzing in with the first Dom to offer to pay for her guest pass."

"Yeah, she could have done better."

"Kindly go fuck yourself, Jaxson."

"I don't have to, remember? I'm well taken care of, and I'm more concerned about all of *your* pent up frustrations." There was humor back in his friend's voice, and Thomas knew the potential fight had been diffused, which was good for him – and good for Maddie. Jaxson was not an enemy she needed to make. "So, you said we needed more single subs. Is this Madeline O'Neill single?"

"I have a date with her on Wednesday night."

"Is that a no?"

"It's an *I don't know*. Nothing is set in stone." Thomas rolled his eyes at the question. She hadn't even texted him back yet after all.

Maybe she's backing out of the whole thing.

"Then if she shows back up at the club, I should tell Daniel to let her in? Let her test drive someone else? You *did* say we needed more single –"

"I'd prefer if she didn't play with anyone else before Wednesday, but she's an adult. She can do what she likes." Hitting the enter key a little too hard on the email he was writing, he felt the tension in his shoulders as he imagined someone else with their hands on Maddie.

It had only been one play session, but she was spinning circles through his mind. Every moan, every whimper, every shift of her body playing on repeat. He wanted his hands on her again, wanted to make her come again, he wanted to do so many things with her. *Dammit.* His cock was getting hard just remembering her and that was the *last* thing he needed before a meeting.

You don't have any right to feel possessive right now, rein it in.

Think of puppies, Christmas carols, the awkward relationship chat you had with mom – and that did it. Erection avoided.

"Hmm…" Jaxson murmured. "Did you enjoy yourself getting to actually play and not just be a voyeur?"

"I did." *Don't think about her, don't think about her.*

"You know, there have been plenty of couples that would be glad to have you participate if –"

"I don't share well, Jaxson. You know this." Thomas wanted to hang up, but Jaxson would just call back until he said his peace. It was easier to just let him get it out.

"I'm aware. Does Madeline know how possessive you are?" He was taunting him, and it was tempting to rise to the bait, but he didn't have the time for it.

"I've played with her once, we'll talk more when we meet again."

"Alright. Are you coming to Black Light on Wednesday?"

"We're going to dinner."

"After dinner, then?" There was an odd tone to his friend's voice that made the hair on the back of his neck stand up.

"Why are you asking, Jaxson?"

"I'm just curious as to what's so special about this Madeline that has your voice sounding like *that*."

"Like what?" Thomas wasn't sure what he was referring to, but he was definitely starting to feel irritated.

"Edgy. Usually you only break out the asshole voice around subs and people who piss you off."

"*You* are pissing me off right now." Thomas went to click on a new email before he realized he hadn't even read the one that was open, he'd just stared at it while trying his damnedest not to remember pale pink skin covered in stripes from a belt. A belt he'd had in his hand, with a beautiful, willing, wonderful masochist of a submissive giving him the chance to play.

"No, I'm not, you're just worried that I'll scare the girl off if I meet her."

"Are you planning to try and scare her off?" *Like hell I'll let you meet her anytime soon.*

"She might thank me." Jaxson had a hint of a laugh in his voice, but the twist in Thomas' stomach gave the comment too much validity. He didn't want to act like a possessive jerk, and that meant *not* texting her every hour, even if he wanted to.

"Remind me why I ever started talking to you?"

"Because we were both bored out of our minds at bullshit dinners for our fathers, and I was at least interesting conversation."

"You were eight when I met you, and I talked to you because you wouldn't stop following me around." Thomas rolled his eyes at the memory of the first dinner when they'd been sat near each other, both restless. He'd been thirteen, but because his older brother wouldn't even speak to him at the time, the young dark haired kid with an attitude had been his only entertainment. "Also, you kind of worshipped me for a few years. That was nice for my ego."

"I *never* worshipped you, Tommy."

Thomas' teeth creaked with how hard he gritted them. "You know how I feel about that nickname, Jaxson, and *this* is a perfect example of you trying to piss me off."

"Look, I won't try and scare her off, I'm just curious what this redhead could possibly have that interests you so much. You literally just met her, and when the fuck was the last time you took someone out on a date?" *Redhead.* He must have looked up the security footage, which meant that by tomorrow morning he'd probably have researched Maddie into oblivion.

"I go on dates sometimes, Jaxson, but not all of us live the life of a playboy in front of the cameras. I have an actual job, remember?"

"Right, I forgot you're the good kid that followed in his father's footsteps. I'm the disappointment." There was bitterness in his tone, but Thomas had met Gregory Davidson too many times to not understand why.

"You *did* make out with your girlfriend, *and your boyfriend*, in front of an entire press corps at a campaign event."

"True," Jaxson preened, "and it was worth it to show all those assholes –"

"May I remind you that *I* am one of those assholes?" Thomas sighed as he glanced at the clock in the corner of his laptop, just over five minutes before his meeting.

"I'd never forget what an asshole you are, but I also know your voting record. You and your father never exactly agreed with my father's politics, it's why we're still friends."

"Wonderful. Listen, I've got a meeting in a few minutes, if you're done berating me I need to prepare." Thomas gathered together the papers he needed to refresh his mind before Taylor arrived.

"If you say you have Madeline O'Neill under control, I'll back off. Just make sure she doesn't drop my name again."

"Consider it taken care of."

"Great."

"Hey," Thomas spoke again before Jaxson could hang up, "one more thing, if you want to stay friends, don't do your insane research thing on this girl."

"We look into all members, Thomas."

"She's not a member, is she? She's my guest, and I don't want you rooting around in her life."

"You really like this girl, don't you." It was a statement, not a question, and Thomas blew out a breath as he shut his laptop and evaluated how he wanted to respond. The sudden tap on his door cut his time short.

"Look, I just want the chance to see what might happen. Pay attention to your own love life, you have more than enough to handle. My meeting is here, I have to go."

"Fine, go be the politician, asshole."

"Go back to bed."

Jaxson laughed low, and Thomas heard the soft voice of Emma over the line, sleepy and feminine. A pang of jealousy struck him just as his friend replied, "I already am."

"Right." He ended the call and flipped his phone face down on the desk, taking a cleansing breath to push away all the personal stuff so he could get to work. Shaking off the memories of the night before, and the strange conversation, he raised his voice, "I'm ready, Alan."

Chapter Six

*S*itting in the break room, Maddie picked up her phone again and started a new text: *I'm not sure dinner on Wednesday is a good ide-*

Backspacing she erased the twelfth attempt at a text to Thomas and slammed her phone down on the table, spearing her salad with an angry fork jab. If she were a decent human being she would cancel the date with him. He was kind, a veritable *nice guy*, who also happened to be incredibly hot and kinky and everything her darkest fantasies had ever dreamed up. Maddie groaned to herself. Representative Thomas Hathaway, democrat from New York, did not deserve to be used like some cheap ticket.

How are you supposed to get back inside Black Light without him?

Right. That was the issue, because there was no way she could get past Danny Security again, and the likelihood of getting another savior was slim to none.

Do you even want someone else?

She growled under her breath, stabbing another bite of salad to shove in her mouth so she wouldn't start cussing, because she didn't want anyone else. If it were a perfect world she would have met Thomas in a normal way, and there'd be no complications in trying out everything hidden in that club buried underneath Runway. No issues with having dinner on Wednesday. No problems except for the normal ones, but life seemed to take great joy in screwing her over.

As if the gods were listening, her phone buzzed with a text message, but it wasn't Thomas this time – it was Antoine from the Post. *Fuckity fuck.* All it said was 'call me'.

Swallowing her last bite of food she took a sip of her diet coke and pressed the call button. It rang twice before Antoine answered, "Hey, Maddie."

"Hey! How is everything?" she tried to sound peppy, but he didn't return the favor.

"Listen, I want to help you out, but you've got to give me something. They've filled the other open position, and I can't stall on the last one forever. You either have a story, or you don't."

"I'm working on one, right now, and it's going to be big, I swear." Maddie put her forehead in her hand, feeling the guilt twist a little further.

"You've been telling me that for weeks. I'm not just being an asshole, you wouldn't be able to pull this if you worked here either. Can you at least give me an outline?" Antoine was trying to help her out, and she knew it, but she also didn't want to hand the story over to him. They were only friends, acquaintances really, and she couldn't trust him with something this big.

It had to be hers.

"I'm still researching, but I have a way into the place now. I'm gathering names and details, and I swear it will be a big story."

"Maddie…" He sighed. "You know I believe in you. The first time we met I told you that I saw the spark in you, that hunger for a good story. You could be a great reporter if you just get after it. Pound the pavement, do the grunt work, get –"

"I *am*, Antoine! And it's kind of hard to do this without any support, you know? I'm the one that caught onto this thing, I'm the one that's spent weeks pounding the fucking pavement, as you say, to get the details on this story. I just got a break in it last night, and I'll get you the story, I just need time!" She'd raised her voice, and she felt bad about it, but her heart was racing. It felt like her dream of working at the Washington Post was dangling by a slowly unraveling thread, and Antoine was holding a pair of scissors ready to just cut it completely.

Silence reigned for a moment, and she thought about apologizing for her outburst, but he spoke first. "Alright. Shit, Maddie, I want you to work here, but you've got no experience and I'm putting my neck out anyway. This better be a fucking amazing story, got me?"

"It is, I swear. I swear to you, it's got front page written all over it." Relief washed through her, and she found herself nodding at the coke machine as if Antoine could see her.

"Okay, just give me a hint. What's the subject matter?"

"Sex," she said it softly, a blush creeping into her cheeks as she remembered the feeling of Thomas' hand between her legs, the delirious orgasm he'd pulled from her with expert skill.

"Sex always sells. I'm assuming there's a politician involved?"

"More than one." Her blush went full crimson, the heat in her cheeks almost uncomfortable.

"Well, well, well, that *does* sound like a good story, Maddie." Antoine blew out a breath and she could hear him shuffling papers. "How long do you need?"

"Another week or two."

"You've got it, but you owe me. Bring me something hot and the job is yours."

Hope filled her up from the inside, crushing the guilt to a pinpoint. "Thank you, Antoine. Seriously, thank you. I won't disappoint you, I promise."

"I look forward to hearing more about it. Email me an outline as soon as you can."

"Definitely."

"Bye, Maddie." He hung up before she could say goodbye in return, but it didn't matter. She had his attention again, and assurance that the job was hers. By next month she'd be a reporter at the Washington Post, and she'd be out of Daily Saver D.C.'s dimly lit offices forever.

Cradling the phone in her hand she pulled up Thomas' text message again: *Just checking to make sure you got home alright. Looking forward to Wednesday night.*

Taking a deep breath she replied: *Thanks! I did, sorry I didn't text last night. Wednesday works great, where did you want to meet?*

She cleaned up her lunch and tossed the remnants in the trash, refilling her water bottle before she headed back to her desk. It hadn't been more than a couple of minutes when her phone buzzed with a text from Thomas: *Fiola at 8:00. I'm glad you messaged, I was starting to worry you'd changed your mind.*

"If only you were that lucky," Maddie mumbled under her breath, but it only took another thought of standing in the Washington Post offices to get her fingers moving again. *Why would I change my mind? I still haven't returned the favor.*

The blush in her cheeks was back as she set the phone down

and tried to focus on work, but Jamar walked by and stopped in his tracks. He laughed, bright white teeth amidst his mocha complexion. "Okay, now I know what that face is. Who's the lucky guy?"

"None of your business, Gilligan."

He sat down on her filing cabinet, leaning on her desk. "Come on, tell me. I've been married almost ten years, let me live vicariously through your exciting night life!"

"No."

"Ginger."

"No." She yanked a folder from under his elbow and he grinned.

"Ginger, Ginger, Ginger, Ginger, Ginger, Gin–"

"Stop it! I'm not telling you anything." Her phone buzzed and Jamar went to grab it but she caught it first and his hand landed on hers. "Let go."

"Then tell me who it is!"

Ripping her phone away, she tucked it under her leg on the chair. "Not a snowball's chance in hell."

"Is he important? Is that why you're being secretive?" His grin grew even wider as she felt the redness in her cheeks reach for her ears. "It *is*, isn't it? You've got a boytoy from inside the beltway, don't you?"

"Drop it, Jamar."

"You got some from some politico. Didn't you?"

"Actually, no." She'd come harder than she'd thought possible, and spent time in what Thomas called subspace after he'd taken a belt to her ass, and spanked her, and tied her up – but they had *not* had sex.

"Just blink twice if he's a politician."

Maddie turned and stared at him, trying her best to keep her expression flat. "Who says it's a guy?"

Jamar laughed too loud and the graphic designer on the other side of her, Brad, who never spoke to anyone, looked over the cube wall at them with an irritated glare. "Alright, I get it, Ginger. You don't want to tell me. Just invite me to the wedding, okay?"

"Ha. Ha." She flipped him off and he stood, raising his hands up in defeat.

"Look, whoever he is, I'm happy for you." Shrugging, Jamar moved back to his desk and she gave him a smile. Sometimes it was good to have friends like Jamar, and sometimes it was a liability. The last thing she needed was someone snooping around her evening activities.

Pulling her phone free she checked the last text message: *'Naughty girl. Now I'm distracted from my lunch meeting. Looking to get punished again on Wednesday?'*

A tingle rushed down her spine, blooming into warmth between her legs that made her squeeze her thighs together. *Punishment.* The word felt like it purred through her mind. Pure temptation. She never thought the idea of getting spanked with a belt would actually excite her, but as she wiggled in her seat she felt the dull ache of the bruises at her sit spot and it made her wet. *'Maybe I am'*, she replied, and then plugged her phone in to charge under her desk.

Their date, and whatever came after, would be there soon enough. Until then, she had to focus on work, and on her research for the article in the evenings. Antoine wanted an outline, and she needed to start writing that story. One of the top dance clubs in the city, owned by the trio who'd already had one sex scandal on the front page last year, and now they were running a BDSM club out of the basement where the well-connected were coming to play. The Post wanted something hot? Well, she'd see how hot they could handle.

Wednesday Night

The Uber driver stopped in traffic several cars back from the entrance to Fiola, but it was already 8:03 and that meant she was late. "Hey, I'm just going to get out here. Thank you!"

Before the guy could respond she was out of the car, slamming the door behind her as she hurried over to the sidewalk. Her legs were freezing, but the dress didn't exactly work with leggings, and the tights she wore were not enough to keep out the cold. It was a very nice Italian place on the corner of a building, but she didn't care much about the exterior – she just wanted out of the frigid air. When she stepped inside, wind-blown and shivering, Thomas was standing there with his coat over his arm, even more gorgeous than she remembered.

Wow.

Talk about an award-winning smile. He was in a sharp suit, again, only this time the little US flag pin on his lapel made her breath catch. *Right,* make that election-winning smile. Maddie had to swallow before she could speak, summoning a bright smile to her face as the door closed behind her to block the wind. "I'm so sorry I'm late, traffic was worse than I imagined."

Thomas smirked, a wicked little tilt to his lips as he glanced down at his Apple watch. "Four minutes, but I've already been here fifteen."

Her eyes widened as she tried to tame the mess the weather had made of her hair. "Right. Sorry, I really didn't –"

Laughing, he took a step forward and leaned down to press a kiss to her cheek, his lips pausing by her ear for just a moment. "Don't worry," he whispered, too low to be heard in the din of the restaurant, "You said you wanted a punishment, didn't you?"

She felt her lips part in shock, but he stepped around her without the slightest change in expression. His warm fingers lifted her coat from her shoulders as she quickly undid the two buttons holding it on so he could take it. "I, um…" Maddie's mind had short-circuited somewhere now that she was back in his presence. Something about him had her heart racing before he'd even spoke, but after those words? She was lost. *Speak, Madeline.* "This place looks nice."

Smooth.

"My assistant said it's great. Apparently I've been here before, but I honestly don't remember." Thomas winked at her and then one of the staff arrived to take the coats from his arms. "Ready for dinner?"

"Absolutely!" She nodded, praying that she wasn't as much of a disaster on the outside as she was on the inside.

They were seated in moments, and he offered her the booth side of their little table, while he took the chair opposite. It was a long bench accompanied by a row of tables, and she wondered what kind of conversation he expected to have when the couple beside them was three feet away. "Do you like wine, Maddie?"

"Huh?" She glanced at him, drawing her attention back to his hazel eyes and away from the beautiful décor. "Wine? Oh, yes, I love wine. Doesn't everyone?"

He smirked again, and she cursed herself internally for acting like such an idiot. "I think wine might be a good idea. You look like you're tempted to run out of here, and I'd hate to have to chase you down." The purr was back in his voice as he lowered it. "Actually, that's a lie. I'd love to chase you down, and do all kinds of things when I caught you, but that's probably not appropriate for a Michelin Star restaurant, is it?"

The shock on her face must have been entertaining, because he leaned back and laughed. It took several seconds before she reminded herself to shut her mouth and nod, but the growing wetness between her thighs was enough of an answer on how she felt about Thomas Hathaway chasing her down. Swallowing, Maddie did her best to make her voice steady, "Wine does sound like a good idea."

"Agreed." Thomas glanced back at one of the waiters and they were beside him in a moment. As he asked for a wine list, she tried to center herself. She'd had plans to arrive in control. She'd planned to actually *stick to* her plan, but then she'd changed outfits five times, and there had been traffic, and then there was Thomas Hathaway. The man looked like he'd fallen out of some high-end men's magazine, all charm and sophisticated grace, but he also had this aura that spoke of sin. An edge to his words, to the looks he gave her, that promised dark, unspeakable things. Well, unspeakable for her at least, he seemed to have no trouble saying whatever was on his mind. No matter how it made her blush, or maybe *because* it did. "Maddie?"

"Yes?" She lifted her eyes back to him and he looked like he may have already said her name once. "Sorry, just a long day." *And night.* Short on sleep again since she was up until two working on the damn article, and she'd read so many websites about BDSM that she had actually dreamed about a St. Andrew's Cross.

"You sure you're okay tonight? We can resched—"

"No!" Her voice had been a little too loud, but she smiled and tucked her wild hair behind her ears. "I promise, I've been looking forward to tonight all week."

Get your shit together, Maddie.

"Me too." The menus interrupted him as they arrived, along with two glasses of ice water. She stole a drink of hers before he reached across the table and slid his hand under hers, those hazel eyes capturing her gaze. "In fact, you've been pretty much all I could think about. Very, very distracting."

"All those texts you've been sending have made it difficult to focus for me too." Finally, the flirtation was back in her voice, and she felt like she'd found her footing in this verbal dance. "Specifically… the ones mentioning a belt."

"How *are* those marks of yours?" he asked quietly.

"Quite pretty, actually. Why, do you want to see?" The slow smile that stretched her lips felt like a victory, because for the first time it was actually Thomas who had to gather his thoughts.

Clearing his throat, he smiled at her. "You're a naughty girl, Madeline O'Neill."

"I think you like it."

"Oh, I do. Very much." Squeezing her hand before he released her, and lifted up the menu. "What do you think you'd like to try tonight?"

"Other than you?" She grinned when only his eyes lifted back to hers, his warm brown hair almost brushing his eyebrows.

"It feels like you'd like to skip dinner, which would *not* be a good idea because you're going to need your energy." The chastising, playful tone was in his voice, and she squeezed her legs together to fight against the urge to squirm in her chair.

Licking her bottom lip she pulled it between her teeth to bite down for a moment and his gaze tracked each tiny movement. "Then I think we should probably eat."

"I'll be eating later too, but dinner does sound like a smart choice." The wicked grin that flashed across his mouth brought her pulse to life between her thighs.

How did he always manage to push things a step farther than she thought he would?

A bottle of wine arrived, and it tasted delicious, and expensive. Just like the rest of the meal. Maddie had just let him order after she'd scanned the menu and seen about ten words she didn't even recognize, but Thomas had done well. Everything they tried was perfect, and the conversation stayed light. She talked about working at the Daily Saver, and had to literally bite her tongue to keep from saying she wanted to work at the Washington Post. He talked about his father working in Congress, and then the Senate, and how he'd followed in his footsteps. One term under his belt, starting his second. Thomas had an older brother, she was an only child, and they both laughed at their penchant for over-achieving. She'd beat his college GPA by 0.2 points, but he'd only smiled and told her that he found intelligence and drive very attractive.

The way he'd looked at her, combined with the glass of wine she'd already finished, made the blush unavoidable.

With a barely touched chocolate dessert concoction between them, *that she'd also been unable to pronounce*, he leaned back in his chair to sip the wine. The restaurant was much quieter now, even though there were still plenty of patrons buzzing with conversation, but those hazel eyes were focused on her like she was the only one there. "So, Maddie, I have a question for you."

"Ask away." She smiled, toying with the stem of her wine glass, turning it one way and then the other.

"I'd love to know why you told Daniel that Jaxson Davidson invited you to the club." The slight curve to his lips didn't change at all as he spoke, and she tried desperately to read him as her lungs clenched tight – but it was to no avail. Was he amused? Angry? How had he even known?

Maddie cleared her throat, sat up in the chair, and told the truth. "I'd looked up some stuff about Runway and read that he owned it. When he put me on the spot for a name it just sort of came out."

"Hmm." All he made was the single humming reply as he studied her face. "Well, that wasn't very smart, and we both know how smart you are."

"Did Daniel tell you what I said?"

"No, Jaxson did."

She almost choked on the sip of wine she'd taken, but managed to swallow it down instead of spitting the cabernet sauvignon all over the white linen. "*Jaxson* told you?"

"Yes, he was... irritated that you used his name." Thomas' smirk grew a little. "It's one of his pet peeves."

"I – um..." Her words trailed off as her mind went into overdrive, and panic made her heart race a little faster. Thomas Hathaway apparently knew Jaxson Davidson well enough to be told about her little indiscretion. He knew him well enough to know about his pet peeves, and she was planning to blow the lid off of Jaxson's secret little club. *Fuck.*

"Don't worry though, I handled it. Jaxson's temper has been appeased." *Temper?*

"How?" Maddie asked the word on a breath, so quiet she was worried he hadn't heard her.

"By telling him that I would handle *you*."

"Handle me," she repeated.

"Yes, and you've been a very bad girl, haven't you, Madeline O'Neill?" Thomas leaned forward on the table, nudging the dessert to the side so he could reach for her hand. Holding it palm up he traced his touch across the center, leading up her pointer finger. "You lied more than once trying to get into the club, and didn't admit all of it to me on Sunday. That's one."

"One what?" Her heart was pounding from the borderline panic attack, but the tingle rushing over her skin from the point of his touch was from something entirely different, and much farther south.

"You sent me so many teasing messages in the last few days, just begging to be punished." He traced over her palm again, up her middle finger. "That's two."

"I thought you liked them?" she whispered, incapable of making her voice any louder.

"Oh, I did, but I was always planning to oblige your requests." Again he traced over her palm, leading up her ring finger this time, the smooth edge of his nail sending a shiver over her skin. "And then you were four minutes late, so that's three."

"Three what, sir?" The title seemed to insert itself onto the end of her question without a conscious decision, but the dark flash in his eyes made it clear it had been a good choice.

"Three sets of whatever punishment I deem appropriate, unless you've decided you don't want to play anymore?" There was a wicked edge to his words again, more promises of corruption hidden in the breaths between them. He paused, waiting until she lifted her eyes to meet his again. A storm cloud of desire swept through her, and his next words were as powerful as a clap of thunder. "Well, Madeline O'Neill, do you want to be forgiven?"

He removed his hand from under hers, leaving it on the linen tablecloth that suddenly felt much cooler without the heat of his skin. *Forgiven?* She found herself nodding, chewing on her bottom lip again to keep the words she wanted to say inside.

Yes, she wanted to be forgiven, for all of it.

Not just the things he'd listed, but the whole situation.

Unfortunately, that wasn't possible.

"I need to hear you say it, beautiful. We don't do anything without your express permission." For a moment his voice had lost the cool, chastising tone, replaced with warmth. He was too good. She should say no. She should get up and walk away. She should apologize.

"I want to be forgiven. I'll accept your punishment, sir." The last sane part of her damned her mouth for speaking the opposite of what her mind had commanded, but the fire in her blood and the humming wetness between her thighs was running the show. All of her reading on BDSM 101 websites had paid off, because judging by the hungry look on Thomas' face, she'd said the right things – even if they were so very, very wrong.

"I'd like to take you back to the club."

"When?" Maddie raised her voice so she could hear herself over the pounding of her heart.

"Now, actually." He touched her hand when she reached for the still half-full wine glass, shaking his head a little. "No more alcohol. Finish your water."

"Yes, sir." She obeyed without question, and she wanted to evaluate that. Wanted to figure out what it was that let Thomas twist her up so easily, tangle her mind into a spiral of desire and an urge to please him.

"Good girl," he purred, and from that moment she lost the ability to even care about why it was all happening.

Chapter Seven

---

at some point he had paid, and she had finished her water, and now they were pressed close in the backseat of his car as it wound its way through the District towards Black Light. Thomas had one hand on her knee, inching up the hem of her little maroon dress, while the other was wound in her hair. His fist tightened at the base of her skull and her lips parted on the softest of moans before she bit down on her lip to silence it.

He chuckled beside her, easing his fingers a little higher, and her knees parted to give him room. Brushing his lips against her ear, he spoke, "I love seeing you like this, Maddie. Flushed and panting and wanting."

Was she panting?

The quick rise and fall of her chest answered her, but before she could think twice about it he had turned her face towards his and she looked up into his confusing eyes. Now some dark shade of forest brown and gray, and they were tracing her mouth.

"I want to kiss you."

"Okay," she answered, distracted by just the idea of it, but then he did. Warm and soft, his tongue brushing her lip like a question before she opened to give him access. The first taste of him was heavenly, chocolate and wine, and just as he pulled at her hair to angle her back so he could control the kiss, his hand found the juncture of her thighs. A gasp escaped her between their lips, but he didn't relent. He nipped at her as he delicately stroked the soaked fabric of her tights, the barest of touches sending her head reeling.

She was helpless as her hips tried to lift, to seek more, but he held back. Never stopping the delirious caresses, but never increasing the pressure, or relenting on the demanding way he took her mouth. Maddie was lost. Lost inside the energy thrumming under her skin that whispered to her that there was more, so much more, if only she would give in. Completely.

Someone cleared their throat, and Thomas broke off their kiss, his eyes holding hers for just a moment before he turned toward their driver.

Their driver. Fuck.

Maddie snapped her knees together, and she was grateful Thomas had shifted his hand to her thigh, skillfully drawing the hem of her dress down to a more reasonable level.

"We're here, Mr. Hathaway." The driver's expression didn't change at all, even when Thomas tightened his grip in her hair once more, causing her body to arch away from the seat against her own wishes. As embarrassing as that was, she managed to silence the moan that tried to slip from her throat.

"Wonderful, thank you Paul." He turned towards her, that wicked grin back along with the unmistakable hunger in his gaze. "Are you ready?"

"Mmhmm." She nodded, not confident enough in her ability to form actual words to even try.

When he stepped out of his side of the car and walked around, she looked out the window and realized they were *not* in front of Runway. Instead, it was a dimly lit store with a neon sign in the window in the shape of a hand with the word 'PSYCHIC' in purple letters beneath it. Thomas opened her door and helped her out onto the curb. Pulling her coat tighter around her, Maddie looked up at the store and somewhere under the haze of arousal two of her brain cells bumped together to elicit speech, "This isn't Runway."

"We're not going to Runway, are we?" He smiled and took her hand, leading her to the door of the shop. It jingled as he held it open for her, and she stepped inside to the smell of incense and candles. Colorful decorations and scarves were everywhere, but he walked them straight to the back. Just past a half-drawn curtain, they found a Hispanic man sitting on a chair, the light of his phone highlighting the scar on his cheek.

For a moment he looked foreboding, and then he smiled and stood, holding his hand out to Thomas. "Hathaway, nice to see you again. Who's the girl?"

"This is Maddie." They shook hands before Thomas went to pull out his wallet.

The man waved his hand. "No need for that, I know you. Danny will want it for check-in though, you guys can go ahead."

"Thanks, Luís." Thomas reached for her again as Luís opened a door behind him, revealing another set of well-lit stairs.

As they walked by, the man winked at her, and she summoned a smile. "Yes, thank you."

He nodded at her as they descended, Thomas keeping a hold on her hand over his shoulder. Then she heard the door shut behind them a moment before they reached a tunnel. It was brightly lit, but cold, and as she moved to walk beside him she tried to memorize everything that had just happened.

A second entrance. Another security guard. A fucking tunnel.

Black Light was beyond her imagination, and it would make for one hell of a story when she could think straight again, but the lingering buzz of Thomas' touch on her skin was keeping her higher brain function to a minimum. She touched her lips and found them as swollen from their kisses as she thought. Making out in the back of a car like she'd never even dared to when she was in high school – but if she were honest with herself, a tiny part of her had always wanted a guy to take control like that. To grab her hair and...

Just before they reached the next door Thomas spun her in front of him and then pressed her back to the wall. His body was firm against hers, hard into soft. It was like he'd read her fucking mind, like he could *always* read her mind.

Would she ever be able to catch her breath around him?

When his lips found hers again she decided the answer was *no*. He cupped her face with his hands, one of his thighs pressing between her legs to rock against the core of her. Desperate sounds slipped from her mouth as one of his hands slid down to hold firmly to her hip.

Dominant.

In all of her research *that* was the word that appeared a million times, and it was the perfect word for him, the perfect summary of everything that he was. The aura of power that caught her whenever she was near, like the dangerous gravity of some dark star.

Breaking their lips he trailed kisses down her jaw, ending in a nip to the place where her neck met her shoulder. A sinful shift of his leg between hers, and then he was kissing her again. She moaned against his mouth, wanton in their solitude, clutching at his coat and wishing she could feel the heat of his skin on hers. He pressed more firmly against her, the friction of the layers of fabric on her clit causing her to rock her hips forward. "Please," the whisper escaped before his lips collided with hers again, his teeth tracing a path before his tongue rejoined hers.

"Beg me again," he growled, one hand across her neck, lifting her chin to make her look up at him.

"Please, sir…" She sounded as pathetic as she'd imagined, the cold of the wall behind her slowly leaching through her coat, but she couldn't bring herself to care with those eyes locked on hers.

"Oh, Maddie. You are so perfect." His thumb brushed across her lips, and she flicked her tongue out to taste his skin. The groan that left him was just as full of need as her soft pleas, but he grinned slowly, wickedly, and shook his head. "It's too bad you were such a naughty girl, or we could skip straight to the pleasure."

"What?"

"You've earned three sets. Remember?" He tapped her lower lip. Once, twice, three times. "And I wouldn't be a very good Dom if I forgot them, now would I?"

"Sir —"

"You told me you wanted to be forgiven, didn't you, Maddie?" *Fuck.* If only she could bottle his voice. The rough sound of it when he dropped his tone that low. It had her squirming against him in a moment, but he stilled her with a sharp push of her hip back towards the wall. "Madeline O'Neill, answer me."

"Yes, sir." Nodding against the hand he had holding her, she felt a flood of relief when he smiled at her. That bright, aristocratic, election-winning smile.

"Good girl. Now…" He slid his thigh between her legs once more, a slow teasing friction that had her whining. "I think you're just about ready to come, aren't you?"

"Yes, *please*. Please, I want to come, sir."

"You sound so incredible when you beg me like that." Thomas crushed her to the wall with his body, the hardness at his hips finally pressed to her stomach, and she suddenly had a very clear image of what it would be like to have those eyes staring down at her on her knees. "But I need you to listen very carefully." He had leaned down just enough to speak against her ear, pulling her back from her fantasy. "If you come during your punishment, I will add a whole new set. Do you understand, beautiful?"

Maddie whined, *actually whined*, in her desperation.

"You have to say it."

She forced the words through her lips, even though what she wanted to do was beg until he relented. "I understand, sir."

"Wonderful, then let's go inside." He stepped back, and she sagged against the wall in his absence, her heart drumming a tattoo behind her ribs.

"Where?" Maddie asked quietly. Brain completely fuzzy again, drowning in the singular urge to have him touch her with his skilled hands, to find oblivion with his lips on hers.

Thomas Hathaway smiled like the devil, "Black Light, of course."

Chapter Eight

"*O*f course," she whispered.

Thomas took her hand and pulled her forward, and she managed to walk after him without tripping over her own feet – which was its own kind of miracle. When he opened the door, she was stunned to see the pale purple locker room. Complete with Daniel 'Danny' the security guy. The smirk on the man's face made her brows pull together, because it looked like he knew a joke she wasn't a part of.

"Thomas," he nodded, the smirk only growing wider. "I see you brought Jaxson's friend back."

If she hadn't already been completely flushed from all of Thomas' calamitous touches, that comment completed the process. She was speechless, and while that was definitely *not* normal for her any other time in her life, it was quickly becoming normal in Thomas Hathaway's presence.

"Danny, it's not nice to torture the subs outside of the club." The chiding laughter in Thomas' voice made her look up at him in shock, but he winked at her and brushed his hand down the line of her spine, renewing the rush of tingles across her skin.

"Looks like you got a head start already."

"I had an invitation." There was that warm flirtation again, and he squeezed her hand as they walked over to the window. Waiting for someone to respond to the bell, he leaned close and whispered, "Don't let him torture you, beautiful, that's my job."

Her lips parted to respond, but then she closed her mouth tight. Every inch of her was still a mess of hormones, the buzz of need between her thighs louder than her thoughts. A man arrived at the window this time, and she barely tracked the discussion they had, only providing her ID when she was prompted.

No contract this time, because she'd *already* signed the NDA she planned on breaking.

He took their coats through the window, handing Thomas a slip of paper that he tucked into his wallet. A fresh stamp for her, then another receipt for him, and she swallowed as the guilt flickered to life somewhere amidst the fog of arousal.

You're lying to him, the little voice whispered, and she flinched before trying to push it away.

It only took a minute to lock their things up before they were walking through the door into Black Light. He rested his hand on the back of her neck as soon as they were inside, the pressure of his grip making her shiver as he stepped close. "Take off your dress, Maddie."

The club was laid out before her, so many others in various states of undress. Tied to different things, kneeling, crawling. It was a world with different rules, a place where she could do exactly as he said and there would be no consequences.

Only rewards, a different voice inside her spoke up. Urging her to let go, to ignore the guilt, to stop trying to control every single moment.

There was only one person in control right now, and she knew it.

"Maddie." A hint of that chastising tone, but she loved it. Loved the heat blooming low in her belly, the return of that breathless feeling that sent her pesky thoughts spinning somewhere else.

Before he spoke again, she reached back for her zipper and started to lower it. Thomas' hand touched hers and he took over, gliding it smoothly down. His thumb was rubbing in circles on her neck, and it felt soothing, and enticing – amazing. It seemed like everything he did with his hands was custom meant for her. Nudging the fabric at her shoulders, he slid it down, and she pulled her arms free of the three-quarter length sleeves.

When the dress was a pool at her feet, he spoke again, "What did you forget, Maddie?"

Yes, sir, the inner voice prompted, and she turned to look at him over her shoulder. "I forgot to say yes, sir."

"That's right." He smiled and then ran his palms over her waist, before catching at her hips. Slowly drawing her tights down, he paused in a crouch to free her feet of the heels and tights. Always ensuring she was balanced, one hand on her calf. With a gentle push, he nudged her forward so she was out of the nest of fabric. There was humor in his gaze when he stood, so close to her bare skin she could feel the heat of him. "What happens when you forget to respond when we play?"

"Spanking, sir." Even saying the word made her body wake up in a whole new way, the drugged languor his kisses had brought on fading into the shimmer of expectation, her skin waiting for the sting of his palm. Instead of a swat, he slowly ran his palm over the round of her ass.

"Right again." Leaning down he scooped her things from the floor, and placed the bundle of cloth and shoes into her arms. "I'll just add that to the list, won't I?"

"Yes, sir," she answered, wondering exactly what was on that list. *Three sets of what?* Thomas returned his touch to the back of her neck, walking her through part of the play area. Her eyes flickered over the people there, a few faces bringing sparks of recognition, but just as she tried to focus, to memorize, his fingers would squeeze and she'd find herself facing forward again.

They stopped at an older looking wooden door, which seemed both completely out of place, and somehow appropriate in the hodge-podge of items scattered across Black Light. It had a small window with iron bars about head height, and he peeked through before he opened the dark, metal handle. "Inside, beautiful."

Her breath caught in her lungs as soon as she stepped through. It was dimly lit, a much more yellow tone than in the main club, and everything about it looked like it had been taken from a dungeon. An old world kind of dungeon. "Sir," she whispered, her voice wavering, but he was right beside her as soon as the door was closed.

"Do you remember your safe words, Maddie? Repeat them for me." There was a rough edge to his voice again, the one that had her melting from the inside out.

"Yellow if I want you to slow down, red if I want you to stop. Sir." Goosebumps rushed over her skin as he traced his fingers down the line of her spine, even more intense now that her dress was gone. Just his skin on hers.

She needed more of it.

"We're going to warm up just like we did before." He started talking as he led her to a corner of the room, lit by what looked like actual medieval sconces, except the flickering light was artificial instead of a flame. "But with each set of punishment you've earned, I'm going to choose something a little more intense. If it's too much, you'll use your safe word. Understand?"

"Yes, sir," she spoke quietly, unable to be any louder because he had stopped them in front of the St. Andrew's Cross. It looked even more foreboding than the one in her dream. Braced to the dull gray wall with dark iron rivets that were flush with the surface of the wood to leave it smooth, gleaming, a warm reddish tone in the fictional firelight.

"Tell me the implements on your limits list."

"What?" Her eyes found him just behind her left shoulder, and his eyebrows pulled together like he was concerned, or maybe upset. "Sir?" she added, but it didn't change his expression.

"Your limits. We didn't really need them last time, but I need to know what your limits are before I choose implements tonight."

Maddie shook her head and looked back at the cross, her wrists tingling as she stared at the beautiful leather straps. Two for each arm, and two for each leg. *What will that feel like?* "I don't have any, sir."

"Madeline." Thomas grabbed her arm and turned her to face him, her shoes almost tumbling from her arms before she adjusted. "You have to have limits. It doesn't matter what anyone else has told you, you are *always* allowed limits."

"But I trust you." Turning to look back at the cross, she remembered the way the belt had felt at first, and then how the pain had changed. Morphed. Become something better with him.

Suddenly, she was looking into his eyes. Intense, forest brown. His hands were on either side of her head, and Maddie didn't look away this time. He was searching for something, and she was curious if he'd find it in her. After a slow breath, in and out, he nodded. "Okay, Maddie. Alright. Promise me you will safe word if you need it."

"Yes, sir," she answered automatically, but she wasn't sure if she would. If tonight would be more intense, how much better would she feel after it? What could he see in her that she couldn't identify in herself? What would she learn if she just gave in?

The shift in him was felt before she saw it, the intensity was back, and she bit her lip to try and stifle her smile. "Put your clothes down, out of the way. Then get against the cross. Arms up."

The authoritarian tone made her instantly wet. Well, *more* wet.

She obeyed, tucking her little pile of clothes to the left of the cross, and then she stepped up to it, raising her arms to brush against the smooth wood. "Yes, sir," she remembered to answer once she was in position. *In position*, another phrase she'd learned in all her research.

Watching him work this time was fascinating. Instead of him building rope cuffs out of sight, he was touching her. Holding her in the right place as he threaded the leather strap through, and then locked it in place. Left arm, then wrist. Right arm, then wrist. He ran his hands down her sides, pausing at her hips to squeeze. "I want your underwear off this time. Are you okay with that?"

"Yes, sir." Nodding, she wiggled her hips, and he tugged them down in a single movement, touching her ankles so she could step out. Without her underwear in the way her mind spun off in a hundred directions dreaming up what it might feel like to have him touch her again. To have him slide his fingers inside her and push her over the edge, or fuck her against the hard wood of the cross. A soft sound left her lips, and she knew she was one brush of his fingers away from coming apart.

He'd wound her up on purpose. Made her delirious with need – but it wasn't necessary. She would have walked back into Black Light without the teasing touches, the fevered kisses. Would have returned to this place even if it wasn't him… but because it *was* him she found herself pressing her ribs against the hard wood of the cross, fantasizing about the first licks of pain he'd promised her.

Thomas spread her legs wide, and when she tried to lift onto her tiptoes he pressed her heel back to the floor. "No need to strain your legs, you'll be uncomfortable enough in just a few minutes."

Right. Three punishments.

He draped his jacket over a hook on one wall that she assumed was not actually *meant* to be a coat rack. Her breaths were getting shorter as he undid each cuff on the sleeves of his button down, rolling them up his forearms. When he caught her staring he smiled, a wicked gleam in his eyes. "So many messages this week, Maddie. You liked the belt a lot, didn't you?"

"Yes, sir." Crimson heat flushed her cheeks.

"I have to admit that having a sub like you is a rare gift." His cool hands touched her ribs as he moved behind her, out of her line of sight. "A real masochist… tell me, Maddie, are you excited, or nervous, about what you've earned?"

"I –" Whatever answer might have left her disappeared as one of his hands slid over her hip, trailing down her soft stomach to swipe at the damning wetness between her thighs.

"Naughty girl," he growled against her hair, lingering his touch at her core without the slightest brush of her clit. "I think the answer is excited. Just remember, beautiful, this is punishment for your transgressions. There will be no coming, no subspace, no matter what. Understand?"

"Yes, sir." Maddie agreed, even though his words still felt strange to her ears. When he pulled away she almost asked how she could possibly come during anything he called *punishment*, but then the sharp crack of his palm against her ass made her hips jolt forward into the cross. It stung, but it had been so sudden she'd not even thought to cry out.

"That was for forgetting to respond properly inside the club." Without more than a heartbeat of a pause, he started to land spank after spank across the round globes of her ass, a warming burn building slowly after each spike when his hand met her skin. "*These* are because I like how your ass looks when it's pink and glowing."

Maddie was chewing on her bottom lip, soft whines slipping out, but even though he was spanking her harder than he had the first time – she knew *this* was not the punishment. Each snap of his palm was a fresh surprise, and she found herself shifting from foot to foot, already reaching for that confusing place where the sting would become something else.

"Beautiful." Thomas stopped as quickly as he'd begun, and then his footsteps moved away to her left.

Peeking through her hair she saw him in front of some kind of black cabinet, gathering things into his hands. *What will he use? The belt again?* Maddie twisted her wrists in the restraints, anticipation making her even more antsy now that she couldn't move.

"What was the first reason I gave you for punishment tonight?" The question floated over to her and she looked away from him, turning her eyes up to the sight of her hands loosely fisted on the other side of the leather cuffs. *What had he said at the restaurant?*

"I told them Jaxson invited me," she answered, and Thomas returned to his place behind her.

"Do you know Jaxson, Maddie?"

She shook her head, feeling her wind-torn hair catch on her shoulder. "No, sir."

"Have you ever met Jaxson Davidson?" There was an odd tone to his voice, but she couldn't think straight enough through the fire in her blood to evaluate it further. Her heartbeat was picking up speed as she waited.

"No, sir."

"Then you understand why that was a mistake? To name him as your invite into Black Light?" Leather stroked over her skin, and she dug her nails into her palms in preparation.

"I do. Yes, sir." Nodding, she tried to focus on him, on the cross pressed into her skin, on what was about to happen – but at the mention of Jaxson her mind was pulled back to the teensy, tiny, itty-bitty detail that the man behind her knew *the* Jaxson David-son, the owner of Black Light, the man who had built ridiculous levels of security to keep out people just like her.

Fuck.

A line of fire across the right side of her ass lifted her onto her toes as she hissed air between her teeth. Its twin landed on her left, and she jerked her wrists against the cuffs on instinct, biting down on the cries she wanted to release as the pain segued into heat.

"I promised him that I would deal with your little indiscre-tion..." In the pause between his next words he delivered a hard swat of the leather a little lower than the first set. "Ten sounds like a good number, doesn't it?"

Two more blistering stings, and he paused when she shouted something unintelligible. Maddie was tense, up on her toes, pressing forward against the cross as if she could escape – but she was bound, exposed, and had no intention of avoiding whatever punishment he'd deemed appropriate. No matter what fell from her lips, it wouldn't be *red*.

If only naming Jaxson was my worst sin here.

"What number are we on?" Thomas' voice was lower, a rolling thunder that made her shiver as she tried to think through the stinging skin and the throbbing need between her thighs.

"F- five?" The word turned into a question as she doubted herself, and his chuckle behind her didn't help to validate it. Another snap of the leather and she arched, biting down on the cry, but he tapped her foot with his shoe and she pressed her heels back to the floor.

"Right, so now there's just four more with the strap."

Strap.

Her mind wrapped around the word, focusing on the differences between this and the belt. The belt was slightly more forgiving, longer, and it stung more, while this felt more powerful, heavier.

Sting versus thud.

All of her research snuck that phrase into her brain, and she knew exactly what they meant now. There was more weight to the strap, more – "Fuck!" she yelled as he landed the next one just below the curve of her ass.

"Oh no, we're not even done with the first set yet, beautiful. Any possibility of *fucking* is still far off." Another hard swat.

"Please," she begged, but his only answer was the last two snaps of the strap on the backs of each thigh. The whine that left her lips had more to do with the sudden assault on the delicate skin of her legs, than with the plea for him to have her, even though the visual had her hips shifting.

"Strap is done, Madeline, but that set wasn't for me, was it?"

"Sir?"

The sound of him moving behind her was distracting enough that she was able to let the heat of the strap settle. There would be new bruises, she was sure of that, but she was *also* sure he wasn't done. He was close again when he spoke, "That set was to appease Jaxson. So, tell me, are you sorry?"

"Yes, sir." She tried to swallow down the pique of troublesome guilt that attempted to emerge from the waves of confusing arousal, discomfort, and newfound submission.

"Say it."

"I'm sorry."

"Say what you're sorry for." Thomas' voice was colder, stronger, and she felt a little breathless as something swished through the air behind her.

"I'm sorry that I said Jaxson Davidson invited me to Black Light. Sir."

"Forgiven." There was a snap just behind her, and she jumped, but nothing touched her. The purr to his tone became more seductive than threatening as he asked, "What is your second punishment for tonight?"

"It's for, um…" Maddie wracked her brain. "You're upset about the texting? Sir?"

His shirt brushed against the bare skin of her back, his lips grazing her shoulder. "I'm not upset at all, Madeline. *This* set you asked for yourself. Each time you referenced the belt." Teeth caught her skin for a moment, sending a vibrant rush through her nerves. "Every time you told me how much you wanted to feel it again. Did you lie about that?"

"No," she whispered. *Truth.*

A spank landed atop the marks from the strap and she gasped.

"Sir!"

"Such a good girl. I'm just giving you what you asked for now. Another ten −" A swish through the air again made her tense. "With the crop this time."

The crop.

A riding crop.

"Shit!" she shouted as the hard, thin, leather bound object landed almost perfectly across both globes of her ass, the barest hint of a sting wrapping to her right hip.

He had said ten, but then two, three, and four landed in such quick succession that Maddie found herself squirming against the cross, her arms pulling at the leather cuffs as she tried to stifle the sting of the tears in her eyes while the already blistered skin of her ass screamed.

"Please!"

"Please what, Maddie?" There was humor in Thomas' tone, a hidden challenge there, and she bit down on the request for him to stop. Swallowed it. Each line was still vibrant, somehow different than the lingering burn from the strap, but the initial panic had ebbed as he paced behind her, as the throbbing faded into a dull ache surrounded by heat.

"Nothing, sir," she whispered.

"Are you sure?"

"I have six more, right?"

A sharp snap of the crop at her sit spot, that painful place where the curve of her ass met her thighs, had her bouncing on her toes, and the tears she'd been struggling to hold back spilled onto her cheeks. "Five now," he answered.

Despite the pain, there was something else inside her. The beginnings of a blur to the peak of each painful swat, the hum of her arousal filling the gaps, and *there* was the promise she'd sought. The dark promise of more, of oblivion, if only she could hold on. Steeling herself, she settled her body on the cross, reveling in the hard press of it against her ribs, the way she could brace her knees into the wood so she could take it. *Five more.* "Yes, sir…"

Two more, back to back, but she held in the cry. *Three more.*

Another across her thighs, and she jerked, crying out as her mind walked some indelible line between pleasure and pain, teasing her with the possibility of some warm and sparkling quiet place just beyond the bite of the damn crop.

"Your screams are lovely."

Lovely?

The impact of the crop on his next swing criss-crossed with a blur of other marks, waking them all up, and sending another cry out to echo in the room. As she tried to breathe, tried to sniffle and hold back the tears that were blurring her vision, a single thought floated to the surface – could all of those D.C. elite hear her through the door? Did they think her screams were lovely too? Were they listening to each powerful crack of leather against her skin?

"Are you wet for me, Maddie?"

"Sir…" her voice wobbled, her breath catching on the next inhale.

"Answer me." A command. Cold, and dark, and hard.

She nodded. As insane as it was, she could feel all of the heat in her skin focusing between her thighs. Her clit was pounding in time with the still throbbing ache of her ass, and while there was no way she could have explained it to anyone, the answer was, "Yes, sir."

"Fuck, Maddie…" Thomas' words were almost a groan, and then the crop landed for the tenth time, forcing her up onto her toes as she shouted, whining as more tears fell.

This hurts. It hurts.

There was a buzzing in her head, a delirium that was mercifully dulling the edges of the lingering pain.

"How's my girl doing?" he asked, stepping around to lift her head up and push back her hair. It took a minute for him to brush it off her damp cheeks, his thumbs running over her skin. Beneath the hazy green-brown of his eyes was a veritable forest fire, an intensity that stole the last of her breath. "You are so beautiful like this, you know that?"

Slowly, she shook her head. Her nose was trying to run from the crying, and it had to be as red as her cheeks at this point. With her luck, her mascara and eyeliner had probably smeared into raccoon eyes – and Thomas Hathaway was calling her beautiful? *Impossible.*

A smile crept over his face, and then he kissed her fiercely, one hand shifting to tangle in her hair and pull, holding her lips in place as tiny sparks raced across her scalp. His tongue clashed with hers, fierce and hot, and he was breathing as hard as she was when he broke away. "Beautiful. Absolutely beautiful. Can you take more?"

There was no doubt inside her that he would stop if she said no, that he would take her off the cross and do all kinds of wonderful things if she just refused. Her body was a conflicting swarm of messages, urging her to end it, and begging her to continue. Questioning her sanity at staying tethered to the wood, and rewarding her for holding on with a tingling rush that flooded over her skin in a shiver. As she stared into his hazel eyes again, she knew one thing for sure — *she hadn't lied* — she trusted him. "Yes, sir. I can take the last set."

He groaned and kissed her again, nipping at her lip and tightening his fist in her hair until pinpoints of electricity burst into life and rushed across her body to nestle between her thighs. His voice purred against her lips when he spoke, "I'm going to make you scream."

Maddie was dizzy with arousal, and that buzzing hum in her veins was getting stronger, but it was his words that left her breathless.

Stepping back, Thomas kept his eyes on her as he unbuttoned his shirt. The fabric slid from his shoulders, and he dropped it on the floor. His undershirt came off next and she had to swallow to keep herself from staring. Lean, muscular lines, with a hint of the abs under his skin. Strong arms, a hint of dark hair scattered across his chest and another line leading down from his belly button to where his belt stopped her eyes. None of that hopped-up-on-steroids, vein-bulging insanity — just real, and incredibly sexy. "How late were you to dinner tonight, beautiful?"

It took a mental shake to get her to focus enough to answer. "Four minutes, sir."

"Then, I think you deserve one for each minute you were late." His fingers wrapped around a thin, long wooden thing that had been lying on the floor. "And one more to help you remember how important it is to be on time."

"What —" *is that?* The question evaporated as she stared at him. Asking would reveal just how uneducated she was, but whatever it was... it looked like it was going to hurt. A lot.

"You'll take five as your punishment, and then you'll be forgiven. Think you can handle it?"

No. "Yes, sir."

"You're incredible." A smile tugged at the edge of his lips as he walked behind her, holding the wooden implement down at his side.

She tried to breathe, tried to prepare, but the first swish of the wood cutting the air made her tense. It landed evenly across both cheeks, and for a heartbeat there was nothing, and then she screamed. Pain, worse than anything she could remember, rushed out from the thin line of fire. *Red* surged to the tip of her tongue, pleading with her lips to shape the word. Instead, she bit down and whined as the torment slowly receded into a pulsing ache.

Thomas waited longer than he had between any of the other things he'd used, but then the soft whisper of it moving again filled her ears. Strike. *One, two...*

Maddie sobbed as her body caught up to the impact, failing to hold in the sounds as the burn enveloped her and she twisted in the restraints. This mark was just below the first, and every synapse in her brain was focused on it, her mind pulling the proverbial fire alarm. Urging her to run, fight, flee. Words were leaving her lips, pleas and desperate requests for him to stop, but he stayed silent somewhere behind her. The flickering light of the false torch made the wall in front of her eyes dance through the haze of tears as she tried to calm herself.

It would just take one word.

The little voice in her mind sounded like him. It had the same purr, the same low rumble that caught her attention, and she knew it was what he was waiting for. It was why he was quiet and still behind her – he expected her to use the safe word.

With a strength she hadn't been aware of, Maddie pressed her heels into the floor and clenched her fists tight until the distant sting of her nails digging into her palms competed against the echo of the last strike. Thomas was closer when he spoke again, "Are you ready to continue?"

Unable to make her vocal chords form the *yes*, she simply nodded and braced. Another quiet swish, another bolt of agony, but she clenched her teeth tight against the scream. The pain crested, and ebbed, as she whined behind closed lips. A brief lull of peace followed, her body shivering, and then the fourth landed at her sit spot. Maddie's legs buckled for an instant as the torturous thing struck, pulling her wrists hard against the cuffs, but she was restrained too well to the cross to actually fall.

Had she screamed?

The raw feeling in her throat suggested she had, but there was a humming edge inside her, the glistening horizon of that thing he called subspace – the same thing he'd forbidden her from at the onset – and she wanted it. It was quite possible she was crazy, more than a little realistic to imagine some deep place in her was damaged in some way, but the thrum in her veins was a call she couldn't ignore. All of the darkness his wicked words promised, the strange pull she felt whenever she was around him, it all beckoned her to hold on. To wait just a little more.

Just one more.

Soft steps across the hard floor buzzed in her ears, as if she could sense his presence even though she couldn't see him. In her mind she tracked him, pacing to a place on her right where she could see him if she just looked – and then moving back to her left. The sensation of his eyes over her skin felt like a heated touch.

He stilled and she froze, air held in her lungs, sealed behind her lips as the object cut towards her again. Her breath exploded on a wail, but as she cried out she was already falling through something indescribable. Pain on the surface, pure and impossible, and then just beneath it – a warm rush. A promise fulfilled. The ache fled her consciousness even faster this time, leaving behind just the memory of it. The dulled surprise that she had done it.

Five.

Forgiven.

Swimming. That was what her head felt like, swooshy and fuzzy, but not quite gone. Not back to that place from before, from the first time.

"Maddie." Thomas' voice was a light at the surface, calling her back to a place she didn't want to rise to. Not yet.

There was so much more to see in the dark. She was almost there.

"One more." It was barely a whisper, but it hung between them like a tangible thing. A wicked and dangerous request, gleaming in the darkness she was sinking into.

He was pacing again, quiet footfalls, the shuffle of his shoes across the floor. The debate as much in him as it was in her own head, but then she heard the low hiss of it, felt the blinding burst of pain – but the wash of delirium that flooded in to wash it away was worth it. Static tingles, a sweet buzzing inside her head that pushed away everything else and left her limp against the cross. A clatter of something falling met her ears just before his bare skin pressed against her back, one arm slipping around her waist to support her, but she was beyond caring about the cuffs biting into her skin. His fingers brushed over the welts, raised and tender, and then he squeezed, waking up the pain to make her whimper and arch against him.

"Sir..." she murmured, and he responded with a groan as his hand trailed over her hip to find its way between her thighs. One stroke at her lips and she became aware of the silky, liquid heat that had her open and waiting.

"You're so wet." There was awe in his voice, the edge of a growl in his tone as his hips pressed against her bruised skin, the hardness behind his zipper a reward she intended to receive.

"Please –" Her words were cut short as he delicately toyed with her, brushing her clit to send her back into the blurry place in her head where language wasn't possible.

"Please what, beautiful?" The arm around her waist squeezed, and she dropped her head back against his shoulder, pulling languidly at the binding leather as he slowly teased her. She was a dreamy grouping of muscles and tingling nerve endings, floating in the hushed emptiness of her mind. "Tell me what you need," he urged her, his lips grazing her neck.

"Please touch me. Fuck me. I need –"

Thomas groaned as he pushed his fingers inside her effortlessly. A shiver pulsed out from the place where he stroked her, so close to the edge, an unspoken summons to fall over the edge and be done with it. "Maddie..."

Her hips shifted, grinding into his hand, her pussy squeezing at his fingers. *So close.*

"Fuck." His voice was a whip crack as he slid his touch from her, immediately working at the buckle binding her wrist to the wood. He moved quickly, the leather falling away so that her left arm dropped until she made the effort to lift it again. Then her right was free and she grabbed onto the mid-point of the cross as her head swam. Blood rushing through her limbs as Thomas crouched beside her, legs free, but uselessly trembling like a new fawn.

He must have seen it, because without a word he scooped her up, tucking her against his warm, bare chest to spin her away from the cross. Gently, he sat her in a strange chair like thing, also bolted to the wall, and covered in straps. The welts stung, but the pain was a distant flutter amidst the desperate buzzing between her thighs. Lifting her eyes to peek through her hair she watched as he hurried back to the cabinet – *did he really expect her to take more?*

You deserve it, a nasty, small voice piped up inside her, and inside the blurry swirl of her head she flinched at the truth of it. *Liar, liar, liar…*

Maddie opened her mouth to speak, tears burning at the edges of her eyes as she tried to imagine how she could explain, but then he pulled open the door to reveal a red, velvety interior. Grabbing a blanket from a lower shelf he turned and laid it out on the floor, the flickering lights highlighting the strength in his arms. The gleam in his eyes when he looked up at her again was hungry, and the truth died on her lips.

Thomas was with her again in an instant, his kiss so powerful he forced her back against the rigid wood of the chair, tongues tangling in a war that dissolved any thought of ruining this perfect moment. She pushed her hands into his hair, silken strands running through the spaces between her fingers, his quiet moan buzzing against her lips. It was wrong, she wasn't worthy of his caresses, but she didn't even attempt to stop him as he unclasped her bra. "Say it again," his harried whisper forced her to look at him to understand what he was asking.

"Sir?"

"Tell me what you want, Maddie."

"You." That was all it took for him to tug her last shred of fabric free of her arms to toss it to the floor before lifting her. All that strength, wrapped around her as she tightened her legs around his waist, it was more than she deserved. His unbearable gentleness as he eased her to the floor with him almost brought the tears back, but his lips found hers as soon as she lay down. A nipping bite, a teasing tug at her nipple, and she was arching up. Knees spread wide and inviting.

"Are you sure?" His question was barely audible, the tension between his brows as he stared down at her making it clear the restraint it took for him to wait, to hold back for her consent.

"Please fuck me," she begged without a shred of modesty, and Thomas answered her with another fierce kiss. Their lips collided almost painfully as she poured every humming wave of desire into it, telegraphing her need so he would believe her – and it worked.

He pulled away to kneel between her legs, working at his belt before he stood completely to push his pants down. Shoes toed off, fabric kicked away, but her eyes were drawn to the boxer briefs sealed to his skin, outlining his erection so perfectly that her mouth watered. Sitting up she reached for him, intent on fulfilling the offer she'd made on Sunday, but Thomas caught her hand and she froze. "Maddie…" his voice was a low rumble, his eyes alight with forest-tinted fire as he looked at her. "After the show you just put on, you can either taste me *or* I can fuck you, but not both."

Biting her lip, weighing the options for a fraction of a moment, she leaned back onto her elbows, naked before him.

"Good choice." He smiled, but instead of climbing on top of

her, he moved between her legs, shifting backwards until the dark tousle of his hair brushed her inner thighs.

"Sir?" She sat up, but he was already tracing a finger between her wet folds, brushing her clit just enough to have her lifting her hips. The heat that had dimmed to a simmer flared to life as he dipped his head and licked her in one long stroke, the hum of his low moan vibrating through her.

Thomas looked up at her from between her thighs, a wicked smirk on his lips. "I still want to taste you, beautiful."

"But —" There was no arguing as he started to lap at her in earnest, torturing her with indolent licks, only to draw her clit into his mouth for the briefest of moments, a completely different kind of agony as he dragged her to the edge of bliss — and then he would pull back. Warm breath brushing across the center of her, wordless whimpers escaping as she fisted her own hair, her hips lifting into empty air as he chuckled, waiting. "Please!" she shouted when he started up again, delirious tension twining like a line of silver light down her spine, the pinnacle of it bound just under his tongue.

"Breathe through it, beautiful. Push it back and wait, I promise it will be worth it."

Impossible. He was asking the impossible in that damnable calm voice, that wicked low tone that was just as much of a tease as his licking, stroking, sucking. She was soaked, finally aware of the wetness spilling from her to slide down her ass and dampen the blanket underneath her.

Wait? He had to be more insane than she was.

When he drew on her clit again she let out a scream of frustration, digging her heels into the floor to try and push away, but he caught her hips, yanking her back to his mouth to scald her nerves with his devious tasting. "I can't! I can't hold it, I can't, I can't, I can't…"

Her babbles were bordering incomprehensible when he finally sat up, chin wet with her, and he grabbed for his pants, ripping a condom free from his wallet. His gaze was stunning, dark, pupils dilated as he stared down at her and tore the wrapper between his teeth. In another instant he'd pushed his boxers out of the way, gripping the hard steel at his hips before rolling the condom down in a smooth motion.

"Please," she begged, and he finally leaned over her, nudging her thighs further apart as he brushed against her. With a tilt of his head he kissed her, and she could taste herself on his lips, his tongue. Her moan met his as he pushed her legs wider with his knees, opening her up, and she dug her nails into his shoulders, trying to pull his skin to hers.

"Tsk, tsk." He captured her wrists and pinned them above her head, holding them with one hand, the weight of him crushing the fine bones against the floor – but she didn't care. She loved the ache, the power of him as he lined up between her thighs. His eyes met hers just before he thrust inside her in one sharp movement, completely to the hilt, and their soft moans blended as he stretched her.

"Oh, fuck…" The whisper left her lips as she arched off the floor, but he didn't wait. Bracing his elbow into the blanket beside her he kissed her, drawing back and thrusting hard again so that her next cry was trapped against his mouth.

"You're perfect," he breathed against her lips before he dropped his head beside hers and spoke again, "You can come as much as you want, beautiful, but I'm not going to be gentle."

Tugging at the merciless grip he had on her wrists, she lifted her hips sharply. "I don't want you to be."

Thomas growled as his hips swung back and drove home, each brutal thrust making her ache, but the swimming feeling of pleasure was building and she knew she was going to drown in it. *Happily.* It was close, so close that she could feel the tension in every muscle, every inch of her reaching for what he'd denied her for too long.

Releasing her wrists he reached down and lifted one of her knees, pushing it towards her chest so the next thrust was even deeper. A sharper twinge as he bottomed out, and Maddie released a cry as she finally came, that line between pleasure and pain fracturing into a million golden splinters that filled her with light.

Perfection.

She was breathless, gasping under his weight as he continued to move inside her, spiraling her higher and higher, the orgasm drawn out until she thought she might shatter as well. Dissolve into the blur. They were slowly inching across the blanket, each hard drive forcing her forward, but he shifted and grabbed onto her shoulder to hold her still for his next thrust.

The full power of each swing of his hips met her, and she slid her arms under his, her nails digging furrows into his back as his fingers left bruises on her skin. It was all too much. Too much waiting, too much pain, too much pleasure, and suddenly she was back at the edge of some unknown void.

"Come for me," he commanded, and she obeyed instinctively, taking her bliss.

Guiltless and warm as it washed through her.

Arching against him, holding on to the firm strength of him, she felt the shuddering pleasure as she came again, squeezing him inside her. "Fuck, Maddie," he groaned, before thrusting deep, his cock jerking as he joined her.

Their breaths competed in her ears, unsure whose was quicker as his weight settled over her, keeping them linked. He was warm, *hot*, and they were both slick with sweat as he kissed his way from her neck back to her lips.

Sinfully sweet. That's what the gentle press of his mouth to hers felt like, because she was damned by how much she reveled in the taste of him as their tongues brushed. "You're incredible."

"You are," she replied lamely as he chuckled and slid from her, instantly shifting to her side so he could pull her against his front.

"How in the hell was I lucky enough to be the one to stumble upon you?" With his face buried in the nest of her hair, she let herself flinch.

Lucky?

"I don't know."

His quiet laugh was warm as he hugged her to him, more kisses pressed to her neck, her shoulder, her hair. "You did so well. Rest, beautiful. I'm right here."

It wasn't until he said the words that she realized how close she was to sleep, the yawn cracking her jaw as she tucked her arm under her head, his strong body curved around her.

"I can't believe you asked for another stroke of the cane..." Thomas was smiling, she could hear it in his voice, but she was barely able to focus as the exhaustion finally sucked her under.

"A cane?" she asked.

"Yes," he answered.

"I didn't know..." she trailed off as sleep urged her into quiet. Relaxing into the silence inside her head. No guilt, no to-do list, no constant checks – just a hushed peace, wrapped in his arms.

Thomas watched her profile as Maddie's breathing evened out, her body softening against his. All lush curves and sweet skin, skin that she'd let him mark. Over, and over, and over.

A cane.

Had she really not recognized it? The furrow between his brows was going to give him a headache if he didn't stop it, but he was confused. His heart was still racing in his chest, his body still coming back from one of the most incredible orgasms of his life, but Thomas couldn't shake the idea that something was very wrong with how Maddie had been treated.

Running his fingers lightly over her waist he leaned back to trace a few of the marks on her skin. Raised, wide, pink ones from the strap. Narrower lines, already leaning towards bruises, made by the crop. The strange little double lines the cane always left, thin cuts in the skin from each stroke. She'd taken each set like an experienced sub, even her momentary panic with the cane hadn't been accompanied by anything more than begging and pulling at the cuffs. Totally normal, expected... but sometimes the things she said triggered little warnings inside him.

No hard limits.

No recognition of the risk associated with playing with the first Dom to find her.

She hadn't even expected aftercare on Sunday.

Had some bastard just been abusing her?

Anger flooded through him, plucking at the temper that he usually kept in check, but when he imagined some asshole taking advantage of her – of her submission, her masochism, her incredible tolerance for pain – he felt like he wanted to hit something. Instead, Thomas pulled her closer, reaching over to wrap the blanket across her front in case someone peeked in through the opening in the door.

A surge of protectiveness pulsed through him as he stared down at her soft lips, the delicate arch of her eyebrows. Noticing a strand of her fiery red hair angled over her still blushing cheek, he tucked it behind her ear before running his knuckle along her jaw. It had only been a few days since he'd met her, not even an entire week. Just two evenings together, but he already wanted more time with her. He wanted to show her what it was like to be cared for, taken care of, treated like the wonderful person he knew she was.

"Don't worry, Maddie, I've got you." The words were barely a whisper, but he meant them. Which meant he needed her off the fucking floor of the dungeon space inside Black Light, and then into a real bed.

Carefully easing away from her, he draped the blanket the rest of the way across her and then started to clean up. Disposing of the condom in a basket tucked in the corner, he got dressed, shook out her clothes to drape them over the spanking bench near the door, and then stacked the implements he'd used at the base of the cross so they could be cleaned.

A soft rap on the door made him lift his eyes, and he saw one of the dungeon monitors through the small window. Glancing back to ensure Maddie was safely hidden from view, he walked over and cracked the door. "Hey, Garreth."

"Mr. Hathaway." The tall man nodded at him, angling his head to look past him. Thomas sighed and pushed the door open wider so that the monitor could see Maddie curled up beneath the blanket.

"Is there a problem?" he asked.

"No, just checking in. I believe a few other members were hoping to use the dungeon tonight –"

"Right." Thomas cut him off and cursed under his breath, pushing his hair back from his forehead. *How long had they even been in here? What time was it?* "We're about to leave."

"Is she alright? I got a nice earful, it sounded –"

"Of *course* she's alright."

Garreth smiled a bit and raised his hands at the defensive tone. "I wasn't trying to offend. It's kind of my job to make sure she's okay, especially when play happens in these more private spaces."

"It's my job too," Thomas added, and then realized how aggressive he sounded when it definitely wasn't necessary. Giving himself a mental shake he forced himself to offer the other man a smile and a handshake. "Listen, I appreciate you watching out for the subs, I do. I'm going to wake her up and take her home."

"I understand." Shaking hands, Garreth stepped back from the door, making it clear he had no intention of pushing any further when it came to Maddie. "Want any help?"

"I've got it."

You're being a possessive dick, Thomas. Somehow that internal voice sounded like Jaxson, and he had to admit it was true.

"Alright, if you do just flag me down. I'm hanging out over by the wet area, there's some needle play that I need to keep an eye on." Garreth turned to walk away, waving a hand over his shoulder.

"Thank you," Thomas finally answered with something resembling a civil tone, and closed the door.

As he turned to see Maddie curled into a smaller ball under the covers he knew he felt something for her, or at least that this *could* be something. That is, if he didn't scare her off by acting like a possessive jackass.

Jaxson's choice of words, not his.

Moving closer he sat down beside her and ran his fingers through her hair, plucking at the tangles he'd given her throughout their fun. "Maddie... hey, beautiful, I need you to wake up."

Her face scrunched slightly and she curled up even tighter, grumbling softly.

Thomas couldn't help but smile, she was cute, but they really needed to leave. Reaching to fist the hair at the back of her head, he tightened his grip just a little so that a gasp slipped through her pretty lips. "I said wake up, Madeline."

"Huh?" Her blue eyes finally opened, and when her tongue flicked over her bottom lip he momentarily regretted not taking the chance to feel her mouth on him.

Focus.

"I'm not sure how late it is, beautiful, but I know I need to get you to bed."

"Late?" she asked, her voice still groggy. Maddie was likely exhausted, maybe even experiencing a little drop after their intense play.

"Yes, I want to take you to my place so you can sleep, and I can keep an eye on you. Okay?" Thomas immediately let her go when she pushed herself into a sitting position, the blanket falling away to bare her breasts. It took an act of willpower not to move his eyes from her face.

"No, no, you don't need to do that. I just need to get home." As soon as she shifted onto her ass, she hissed air between her teeth, leaning forward again to ease the pressure on her welts.

He lifted his eyebrows. "You're going to be sore, just —" *let me take care of you.* Swallowing the rest of the words, he made an effort to pull back, to respect her answer. "I'm happy to let you sleep at my place, in your own room. I can make sure you get to work on time, I have morning meetings so I promise we won't sleep in."

"Thomas…" The way she said his name was a soft whine, and it made his very sated cock twitch in his pants.

"I promise I'm not a serial killer?" he joked, and she paused the efforts of combing her hair with her fingers to stare at him. He shrugged. "That was supposed to be funny."

"I know you're not a serial killer." Maddie sighed and pushed herself to a standing position, and he rose with her, reaching out in case the sudden change of elevation made her dizzy. She wavered for just an instant before she stepped away from him towards the cross, and he clenched his fist at his side to keep from touching her.

"Your clothes are over here. I picked them up, moved them to the bench."

"Thanks," she muttered and walked towards it, sifting through the cloth to find her bra. He felt suddenly awkward standing next to her as she began to cover all of her curves, hiding the marks he'd given her beneath underwear, tights, and then her dress. Memories of the way she'd arched against him, of the tight, warm feel of her squeezing him, the sounds she'd made against the cross and underneath him – they all ran through his head – but his questions were still there too, and it felt like she was avoiding his touch when all he wanted was to wrap her up and make sure she was okay. Doubts flickered to life in his head, coloring their fun in ways he didn't like, in ways that made his stomach turn.

"Maddie, I need you to be honest with me, are you okay?"

She paused for a second as she slid her feet back into her heels, holding onto the wall to steady herself. "I'm fine, just tired."

The weak smile she tossed him as she brushed her hair back from her face wasn't enough, and he was standing in front of her before he could stop himself. Gently holding her shoulders, he waited until she looked up at him. "Did someone hurt you, Maddie?"

Rolling her eyes, she gave a short laugh. "Um, you? Earlier?"

Thomas took a slow breath to keep his voice calm, and the little smile on her lips faded when his eyes returned to hers. "I mean before tonight, before I met you. If this is going to work I need to know things like that, I need you to be honest with me so I can keep you safe."

"No, nothing like that." She tried to shrug out from under his hands, avoiding his eyes, but he held on.

"You can talk to me."

"Thomas –"

"Honesty is the foundation here, you know that, nothing works right without it. Look me in the eyes and tell me the truth. Did you have a Dom that took advantage of you? Some asshole who just liked to hurt you? It was absolutely *not* your fault if it happened."

Maddie stared up at him, and he could have sworn there were tears at the edge of her eyes. "No. None of that. There was no one, Thomas." When she twisted away from him this time, he let her go and stepped back.

"Okay. That's good." He nodded and rubbed the back of his neck, trying to ease some of the tension forming tight little knots beside each of his vertebrae. "Okay, Maddie. I just – I don't want to ever cross a line with you. Was this too much? Are you sure you're alright?"

"I'm fine." When she turned back to look at him, her smile looked real. "I promise. I mean, I'm sore, but I think that's pretty normal."

His eyes flicked her over face, taking in all the little non-verbal hints he could, trying to see if what she was saying was true. *Had he crossed a line, and she wasn't telling him? Was there something in her past she didn't want to discuss?* She looked like herself. Beautiful, all put together in that maroon dress with the fire of her hair brushing her shoulders, and she sounded normal too. Still, there was something bugging him, ticking away inside his head like a problem he hadn't solved yet.

Are you going to give her the third degree, or are you going to let her sleep?

"Let's get you home." Reaching out for her, he offered his hand, and there was a moment he was nervous she wouldn't take it – but then her palm touched his and her fingers interlaced to squeeze.

"I really did have fun tonight," she spoke quietly as they left the dungeon room.

"Tonight was phenomenal." He smiled, some of the tension easing in his chest as he tucked her to his side and leaned down to kiss the top of her head. "You amaze me, Maddie."

She didn't answer him, but her arm went around his waist and they paused just before the exit door, embracing tightly for a solid minute. As he stood there, with her held close, smelling the lingering shampoo in her hair and the scent of her skin that was some heady mix of warmth and flowers, he knew he had to watch himself. Madeline O'Neill was the kind of girl he'd fall hard for, the kind that would fill his thoughts, and that made it even more important not to push too fast, not to be too intense – not to scare her off.

And at least she's letting me touch her again.

"Come on, beautiful. I think someone might complain if you fall asleep and I carry you out of here over my shoulder like a caveman." He managed to finally crack a joke that made her laugh, breaking the tension between them as she reached for the door.

"That might be something fun to try, having you carry me off to your cave." That wicked, enticing tone was back in her voice and it was working miracles on his cock, his body getting too interested in the idea of another round with her.

She needs sleep.

"You can text me about that fantasy tomorrow." Thomas swatted her ass and she groaned, but ended up smiling as they left Black Light. She was beautiful, and beyond anything he'd imagined, and the way she lifted her blue eyes to him as Danny opened their locker almost took his breath away.

Oh, yes, he was in very deep trouble with Madeline O'Neill.

Chapter Nine

*W*alking into her apartment, Maddie leaned back against the door, clutching the small box in her arms that she'd found in her mailbox. It was almost three, and Thomas had spent the entire car ride to her apartment apologizing for the late hour – but she didn't even care. The moment she'd seen the time on her phone she'd immediately decided to call in sick.

Kicking off her heels she padded over to her desk and dropped the package and her purse. With a sigh, she cracked open her laptop and tapped the space bar to wake it up, the glowing light of her screen filling the space. The browser window was still open with twelve different BDSM websites in different tabs – all of her pre-date studying – and now she could add her crash course in impact play to the things she'd only skimmed before.

Switching to the Word document she tried to memory dump as much as she could: *cane, crop, strap, chair with straps, bench. How does Jaxson know Thomas? 2nd entrance to BL. Psychic shop – what street? Luís.*

"Shit, the stamp…" Hurrying into the kitchen area she ripped open a drawer and found her scissors. She tucked them under her arm and pulled open a cabinet to fill a glass with water before she moved back to the desk. Setting the water down, she cut into the box and tossed the air packs onto the floor beside her until she found the packaging. "Bingo."

The easiest thing to find in her research had been a flashlight equipped with a black light, and it had arrived just in time, but she growled when she tried to turn it on and nothing happened.

"No batteries? Really assholes?" Dropping it back into the box she flipped on the lights in her kitchen area, digging through drawers to scrounge together three AAA batteries. She found one in the bottom of a drawer, and then gave up and tore the last two from her blu-ray remote. As soon as it was on she grabbed her phone and went into the bathroom to shut the door where it would be the darkest. Then she aimed the purple light at her wrist. The stamp was a little blurred from sweat, and all of their efforts, but the words were still mostly legible as 'BLACK LIGHT' with 'guest' underneath it in a swirling script. Holding the black light in her teeth she started snapping pictures with her phone, adjusting the settings until she had the best photo she could manage.

Real. Evidence.

As exhausted as she was she still gave a little cheer as she stared down at the image, and then moved back to her desk. Maddie dropped into her chair without thinking twice and the sudden pressure made her let out another flurry of curse words. Welts and bruises instantly reminded her of what she'd done, and for a flash she was back against the cross, filled with that thrilling anticipation. Waiting for Thomas' voice, waiting for what he'd do next, and she knew she was growing wet again. He was dangerous. Dangerous, because every minute she spent around him made her want to stay longer. When he'd offered to take her home, to watch over her, it had been too tempting. Everything about him was temptation. His voice, his words, his smile, his fucking body with his ability to know *just the right way* to touch her, to fuck her, to make her come apart. "Stop it, Maddie."

Growling under her breath she emailed the photos to herself, and focused on the article. The opener was done, a revisit of the drama between Jaxson Davidson, Chase Cartwright, and Emma Fischer. Juicy in and of itself, especially with the added bit about Senator Davidson's withdrawal from the presidential race, but then she segued into the reveal that their ménage-a-trois was *also* connected to a kinky secret hidden under their new enterprise, the popular dance club called Runway.

The paragraphs on Black Light were probably too long, too descriptive, but she didn't want to miss anything. Sex did sell, after all, and Antoine could trim out whatever he wanted. Taking a sip of her water, she started to edit, and add to it. Words flowing out about the second entrance, the levels of security, weaving it all into a narrative – and then she got caught down a rabbit hole of research trying to find the name of a man she'd seen there. Scrolling through backlogs of articles on the Post's website to try and remember at what event he'd been photographed.

Maddie had always been good with faces, and she knew she'd seen his. Specifically, in a photograph, in a tuxedo, and she had to know if this guy was a politician, or some other D.C. elite. Was he more important than David Alchert? Less important? The article needed more names. It had been pure luck to see him, and recognize him, the night she'd discovered the entrance, and then *again* the night Thomas had let her into Black Light.

Like a wolf among sheep.

Guilt nagged at her, but she kept typing, researching, outlining

Black Light's secrets in detail before she lost them. The only thing she left out was Thomas.

Eventually, her alarm went off and she jerked back in her seat, surprised to realize it was already 5:45am. Wandering to the clock she turned it off, and then went back to her desk. A text to Brenda about being sick, an email to Jamar's work inbox so he knew, and then she was back in the article.

A couple of hours later, as the winter sunlight started to peek through her windows, she realized she was just staring dumbly at the screen, her fingers frozen on the keyboard. She'd been up for too long, and the pounding headache behind her eyes was bad enough to dull the lingering ache of her ass. Pulling up her email, she wrote to Antoine explaining that she was confident in the article and gave a few very vague bullet points that wouldn't allow someone to scoop her if he decided to share it. Concluding it with a snarky comment that he wasn't going to get a full outline until they talked about a job offer, she sent it and shut the laptop.

In a matter of minutes she had stripped out of the dress and tights, and dropped into bed. Hiding her face under the covers to block out the sounds of the city waking up outside her building, she tried to sleep.

Buzz. Buzz. Buzz.

The clatter of her phone against her desk pulled Maddie from a groggy sleep. Every inch of her was sore as she woke up, flinching as she went to stretch. Not only did the welts hurt, but so did her shoulders, her back, and her head wasn't too happy either.

"Shit." Throwing the covers back she squinted against the

daylight as she stumbled to her desk to snag her phone. Two texts from Thomas, another from Jamar, and then a missed called from Antoine. Blinking and shaking her head to wake up further, Maddie opened her laptop to check her email.

Yes!

Antoine had replied that morning, saying he wanted to meet for lunch. Around one. Glancing at the time in the bottom corner of her screen, she almost screamed. It was 11:43am. Pushing back from her desk she ran into the bathroom to start warming up the shower, using her other hand to call him back.

"Maddie?"

"Hey! Antoine," she spoke up as she stepped out the bathroom so the water couldn't be heard. "I just saw your email, where do you want to meet?"

"You tell me, can you do one o'clock?"

"Sure, how about some place near the GWU metro stop?" Her heart was racing, but she was trying to make it sound more like excitement in her voice.

"Let's meet at CIRCA. After the morning I've had I need a drink and some good news. You *are* bringing me good news, right? Your email was a little short." Antoine sounded stressed and distracted, but she found herself nodding.

"I do, I do have good news." *Rein it in, Maddie.* "I mean, I have good news, if *you* have good news."

"The job is still open, if that's what you're hinting at."

"Obviously." She smiled, and Antoine chuckled.

"I'll see you at one, Maddie."

"See you then." Tossing her phone onto the bed, she stripped the rest of her clothes off and hopped in the shower. It was probably the fastest she'd ever got ready, but she caught the silver line and made it to the Foggy Bottom/GWU station in plenty of time.

Maddie ordered two glasses of white wine, the last thing she'd seen Antoine drink, and waited nervously at the table, refreshing her email on her phone obsessively as the time got closer and closer to one. At three minutes past, she would have been bouncing in her seat if she wasn't still very aware of all of the marks she'd caught sight of in the mirror after the shower. A rainbow of colors, with several dark red lines she knew were from the cane.

Thomas.

Thinking of the cane brought him to the forefront of her mind, and as she gripped the phone in her hands, watching the time tick by, she couldn't forget that those marks had been earned because *she* had been late to meet him. At a restaurant.

As if the universe was trying to mock her, the phone clicked to 1:04PM just as Antoine walked through the front door. *Four minutes late.* She raised her hand to wave him over, flipping her phone face down to ignore the time as he slipped past other diners and took his seat. "You're wonderful," he said as he snagged the glass of wine and took a sip, groaning. "That is *exactly* what I need right now. Promise me that when you start working at the Post you won't be one of these prima donna journalists talking about how I'm destroying your *vision.*"

The quotes he put in the air, accompanied by the huff and rolling eyes, had her smiling – but she smiled further when she processed what he'd actually said. "*When* I start working at the Post?"

Antoine laughed, glancing at the menu before he took another drink. "You did say you have a great story. I think your bullet points were: the people involved have already been front page stories before, lots of kinky sex, and that you had the names of people inside the Beltway involved. Did I miss anything?"

"Just the stuff I haven't told you yet."

"Well, I'm all ears." He smiled at her, and Maddie took a sip of her wine, that turned into several drinks as she tried to figure out what she was willing to share.

Fortunately, the waiter arrived a moment later. They ordered, chatted about a few updates with mutual friends, and then she was prodding the salad in front of her with her fork as Antoine waited.

"So, your story. You can tell me the details, Maddie." He leaned forward, lowering his voice to a conspiratorial whisper, "How high profile is it? Well-known politician? Does it touch the White House?"

"Now, Antoine… if you think I'm just going to hand this over to you without a job offer so you can hand it off to someone already on your staff you've got to be —"

He had started digging in his messenger bag as she'd been talking, but she stopped when he slapped a stapled packet of paper on the table between them. "You were saying?"

Hands unsteady, Maddie picked up the pages. The Washington Post emblem blazed across the top like the light from a lighthouse. It looked official, and it even had the details on the job title and salary level — with her name in bold in the first full paragraph. Lifting her eyes back to Antoine, she swallowed. "Is this real?"

"As real as the story you've been teasing me with." Antoine took a bite of his sandwich, taking a drink of his water before he picked up his wine. "It's all there. You turn in the story that touches on those key points you sent me this morning, and the job is yours."

"Wow…" It was all she could say as she stared at it, and then Antoine's phone rang and he lifted his hips in the seat to dig it from his pocket.

"Dammit – what? No, *no*, that is not what I fucking said!" He growled and pulled his wallet out to slap two twenties on the table, giving her a look that told her just how much of a mess was back at work for him. "Look, I'm ten minutes away, just don't do anything until I get there."

"Problem?" she asked as he ended the call.

"Just more obnoxious journalists pulling shit they're not supposed to." Antoine pointed at her, and then dropped his finger onto the paper she'd settled beside her salad. "Read through it, finish your damn story, and send it to me so I can hire you. At least then I'll be able to commiserate with you about these fucks."

"Oh, so now you're all confident in my story?" She smirked at him as he stood up from his chair, tugging his coat back on.

"Maddie, I was always confident in *you*, I just need you to show it. So, get on it. I've gotta run." Antoine waved as he dodged a waitress carrying a tray of drinks and then ducked out into the winter sunshine.

She sunk down in her chair, flipping through the pages of the document as she finished her wine, and then Antoine's. It was everything she wanted, everything she'd dreamed about since she'd moved to the District, so why wasn't she already signing?

Friday

Work had gone by too slowly, and Jamar had been grumpy

because he'd had to pick up her slack when she'd called in, but all of Thomas' teasing text messages had made it better.

He'd spent Thursday checking in on her, making sure she was okay, and then he had started flirting. That night he'd asked about her marks, a teasing comment about if she'd found it diffi-cult to sit, and she'd responded by sending him a picture of the bruises on her ass. The dirty conversation that had followed had left her soaking wet, and convinced her that phone sex was a lost art that Thomas Hathaway could probably bring back with a 1-900-HOT-REPS number on some late night channel.

She'd be his first customer.

As soon as she'd woken up today, it had been more of the same. More teasing, more flirting, more hints of dark promises she wanted him to fulfill. He'd even sent her a selfie of him in some room at the Capitol, full of other representatives, and he had looked completely miserable. It had been accompanied with a simple reminder that during their phone sex she'd agreed to go out with him again. Tonight.

He had promised it would just be dinner, that they wouldn't be heading back to the club, but now that she was back at home, in front of her desk, Black Light was all she could think about. The job offer was tucked under her mouse pad, and she stared at the screen reading and re-reading what she'd written for the article, because she wasn't satisfied with it. It was missing something, and she was pretty sure she knew what it was.

More names.

More high-profile attendees.

More politicians, more movers and shakers inside the Beltway. Just *more*, and there was only one way to get that. Another trip to Black Light – with Thomas.

Growling under her breath she opened her phone and checked

the address of the restaurant he had picked this time. It was maybe fifteen to twenty minutes away, so she still had an hour or so to burn before she needed to call a car. Trailing her finger over the track pad, she pulled up the separate document she'd been using for information on Thomas that she wasn't including in the article.

It had bits and pieces of his life that she'd pulled from the internet, mostly articles about his campaign and election, but she'd barely scratched the surface on his history with Jaxson Davidson. Both of them were the sons of politicians, but Michael Hathaway had spent years of his political life as a representative in Congress, before he'd eventually become a senator. Gregory Davidson, on the other hand, had become a senator earlier in his career. More importantly – Hathaway was a New York Democrat, and Davidson was a Republican from Virginia.

When would they have ever been together outside of Capitol Hill?

Maddie sighed and scrolled back through her documents, her bookmarks of old stories about the two politicians whose sons had taken such different paths, searching for anything that hinted where those paths crossed. Jaxson Davidson, international model, poster problem child, lived a life of excess until he seemed to suddenly settle down with Emma and Chase. In what seemed like the complete opposite path, Thomas had gone to Princeton, received a degree in Political Science, with a minor in History, and then started working with his father on campaigns and around the Hill. Then Jaxson had blown up his father's career when Senator Davidson had attempted a run at the presidency, while Thomas' father had left at the end of his last term as a senator on good terms. He had even been quoted saying his son was *carrying the torch* forward.

The two fathers couldn't be more different, more diametrically opposed in their beliefs, and the sons seemed to be the same way – except *apparently* both Thomas and Jaxson enjoyed BDSM.

Tapping her pen on the space bar she ticked her cursor forward across the document as she stared at the useless words. No matter how much she read there were no answers as to how the two met, or why they would be close enough to talk.

Why do you even care, Maddie?

Slamming her laptop closed, she stood up and walked to the clothing rack that served as her closet. Flipping through the dresses she couldn't let the question go in her head.

Why the fuck did she care? Easy.

She *cared* because Jaxson knew that she'd tried to get into Black Light using his name – a stupid choice, for sure – but then he'd taken the time to call Thomas and tell him, and knowing he was friends with Thomas made it all more complicated.

Yes, she was leaving Thomas' name out of the article. She'd been so careful to craft it in such a way that it was clear she had been inside, that she had attended with someone, but there were no hints as to who.

Except… the people who had seen her face would know.

Danny the security guy, Luís in the shop, the friends he had in the club, and ultimately Jaxson *fucking* Davidson. The man who would end up at the center of the shit storm no matter what. He had taken the brunt of the attention during the drama around his father, while Chase and Emma had been names, pictures in photographs, and this would be the same way. Him at the center of the storm, and everyone else swept along with it.

Including Thomas?

Shoving the clothes away from her she walked back across her studio apartment, which didn't take nearly enough steps for her to think properly. Every time she passed her desk and saw the job offer, the beautiful heading from The Washington Post, she felt that surge of excitement. Joy, achievement, finally a thing she could bring home to her parents so they could tell everyone back home about how Maddie had achieved her dream. She was a *real* journalist. They could get a subscription to the paper. They could see her articles. Her mom would probably scrapbook them all, while her dad would start sending her possible leads, delving back into those detective novels he used to love.

It was everything – *everything* – she had wanted when she'd moved to Washington, D.C.

Her phone lit up when she passed her desk for the twentieth time. It was a text from Thomas, and Maddie felt her heart rate pick up, felt the butterflies that filled the spaces behind her ribs with a fluttering hum. A different kind of excitement, a tingling buzz that brushed her all over before it centered between her thighs. She wanted to pick it up, to read it right away, but that only confirmed what she already knew – Thomas Hathaway was dangerous. Like a drug that she'd had a taste of and now she wanted more. Wanted to know everything he could show her, everything they could do together, and then do it. All of it.

"Fuck, fuck, fuck!" Maddie walked to her fridge and opened the freezer, pouring more than a reasonable amount of vodka into the bottom of what *had* been her water glass. She started to drink it just as her phone started ringing, and she moved back to the desk. It was him. Of course, it was him. She tilted the alcohol up to finish it before she scooped up her phone and hit the answer button. "Hi!"

"Well, hi to you, Maddie." Thomas was laughing on the other end of the phone, and she hated how much his voice affected her. There was still that aristocratic edge that had caught her attention the first night in Black Light, only now she could hear the edge in it without effort. The purr that turned her name into something sinful when it left his tongue. "I wanted to give you a heads up so you don't get surprised, or pay for one, but I'm sending a car to pick you up."

"Why?" she asked, but her eyes were drifting between the job offer, her rack of dresses for their date, and the bottle of vodka still calling her name on the counter.

"Tonight is about spending time together, and I figured you didn't want to be late again." His tone was playful, he was in a good mood, and she was contemplating getting drunk. Not exactly the same page.

"You don't have to send a car, I can –"

"I know I don't have to, Maddie, I want to. In fact, I want to do *so many* things to you. Are you really going to turn down the ride?"

"No," she acquiesced, and bit down on her lip when she found herself smiling as he shocked her once again with his brazen comments. Was he still in his office on Capitol Hill? Saying things like that to her? Could someone hear him? The blush was inescapable as she imagined it.

"Good, I gave Paul your cell number so he could call you when he arrives." Papers moved on his end of the phone, and then he spoke again, "I have a few more things to take care of, but I'll be there."

"On time?" she asked, smiling even wider.

"Oh, Maddie, you are asking for trouble and I'm trying to plan a nice evening." There was a low, hushed growl to his voice, and it turned all those fluttering feelings into something more devious.

"I thought it *was* a nice evening the last time I got in trouble."

Thomas laughed, warm and loud, and it tapered into a groan.

"Then I did *not* do something right. How are you ever going to learn a lesson if you like everything I do?"

"I guess you'll just have to keep trying."

"That would make me a very happy man." His tone was serious for a second, and then it was back to laughter. "Now, go get ready so you don't make Paul late, he gets very upset."

"Oh, does he not like the cane?"

More laughter. "He never sits still for it, and he's not nearly as beautiful as you are wearing my marks. Alright, I really have to go, Maddie, I'll see you soon."

"See you soon," she replied before he hung up, and then she sat down on the edge of her bed. A ridiculous grin plastered across her face, her cheeks aching from smiling so hard, a warm glow filling her up to the point that she wondered why she couldn't see it on her skin.

Why did he have to be so damn perfect?

Chapter Ten

One Week Later

*S*itting in her bra and underwear on the shining, smooth counter in Thomas Hathaway's breathtaking kitchen, Maddie smiled as he finished chopping up a cantaloupe and walked over to set the too full plate beside her. "That's too much food."

"Open up." He speared a bite of the fruit and held it in front of her sealed lips as he moved in close, nudging her knees wide so he could stand between them. "Madeline O'Neill, are you trying to get spanked again?"

"Is that a sincere offer?" She grinned for a moment, and when he just raised his eyebrows she relented and opened her mouth. The melon was sweet against her tongue, and she bit down with a small moan.

"See? Delicious, and I know you're hungry." Thomas leaned

forward to brush his lips down her neck, nuzzling into her hair. "You burned a lot of calories last night."

A blush singed her cheeks remembering the way they had barely made it inside the gorgeous Victorian home that his family owned in Georgetown. After dinner, their *sixth* date as he had reminded her, they hadn't been able to keep their hands off each other in the car. As soon as the front door closed he'd stripped her and fucked her on the hardwood floor in the entryway, and her knees still ached from when they'd moved to the base of the stairs. His fist in her hair, her arms braced on one of the steps, and she'd come so hard she could have sworn she saw stars. Round two had happened sometime in the night, when she'd woken up and taken him into her mouth, and he'd fucked her throat until he came – and then spanked her for not sleeping. But he had kept them up a while longer giving her orgasm after orgasm with his tongue and fingers until she was begging him to let her go back to sleep. Four dates in the last week, two more trips to Black Light, each day better than the last. Being with Thomas Hathaway was like a dream she never wanted to end, a very sexy, kinky, wonderful dream. She swallowed the next bite of melon he tucked between her lips, and then turned her head. "You have to eat too."

"Is that a sincere offer?" he repeated her words back to her, smiling as his hand trailed up her inner thigh, his thumb brushing against her clit through her underwear.

"I'd rather have you inside me." Maddie wrapped her legs around his waist, pulling him closer and he leaned down to kiss her, the food abandoned for a moment as their tongues clashed. He was growing hard against her, the thin fabric of his boxers doing nothing to suppress the friction as they moved together, but then he squeezed her hips and pulled back with a growl.

"We *both* have to go to work today. I'm not going to be the cause of you missing again." This time he lifted a bite of egg white omelet. "Eat."

Grumbling, she let him feed her, because she'd learned how much he liked to, but he finally started to eat as well. Between the two of them the plate was almost empty by the time she shook her head. "I cannot eat anymore, especially if I want to have room for more coffee, which is *very* important."

"I know. You get feisty without it." He placed her coffee cup back in her hands as he went to drop the plate in the sink, along with the pans and utensils from him making them breakfast. *Again.* The doorbell rang suddenly, making her jump, and he wiped his hands off on a towel. "Be right back!"

"Wait!" Maddie hopped off the counter, panicking. "Why is Paul so early?" She was about to follow him when she heard him open the front door, and she froze mid-step.

Another male voice, and they were talking in hushed tones, but she wasn't going to peek into the hall just in case he'd opened the door wide to show all of Georgetown his boxer-briefs. She strained to hear what they were saying, but only caught their laughter just before the door shut again. "Maddie, you can come out now."

He was smiling at her as she stepped into the hallway, the little table in the foyer had a stack of shopping bags on it and she crossed her arms under her breasts. "What's that?"

"Some clothes for you to wear today, a few outfits to choose from. The rest I'll keep here just in case."

"You bought me clothes? Wait, *who* bought me clothes? And *when?* It's barely six in the morning!" She walked towards him, ignoring the bags as her temper flared.

Before she could really start ranting, he squeezed her upper arms and smiled down at her. Gorgeous, even with bed head, his hazel eyes more tawny in the morning and too damn distracting. "My assistant, Alan, has a sister that runs a boutique clothing store in Arlington, where he *also* lives. After you woke me up so *very* nicely last night, I realized we'd planned for you to go back home and so you didn't have anything with you. I sent him a text, with your sizes, and asked him to bring some options by on his way into the office."

"But —"

"Maddie, you needed clothes for work, and I'm sure Alan is going to overcharge me for the clothes to make up for his sister opening the shop early. So… it helps her out, Alan was more than happy to get to expense his commute into work today, and now we've got some options here if it happens again." Thomas leaned down to be closer to eye-level with her, and she was speechless, unable to find another argument. "I wish you'd just let me take care of you."

"But you don't have to do that! You don't have to spend money on me, or have Paul pick me up, or take me to nice restaurants all the time, I —"

"I know I don't. That's the best part. You don't want or expect any of that stuff, but you make me happy, Maddie, and so I *want* to do it." He kissed her softly, one of his hands moving to cradle the back of her head as his other pulled her closer by her waist.

She wanted to tell him that she didn't deserve any of it, didn't deserve him, but her lips were busy and before she could think twice about it she had melted against him. Lost in the way his tongue brushed hers, all of her thoughts scattering.

The kiss ended gently, neither of them trying to turn it into something more, and then he looked down at her with a slight tilt to his smile. "When are you going to stop fighting me every time I do something small for you?"

"This isn't small."

"It's a few outfits."

"I could have just as easily ran home and changed." She crossed her arms again as he sighed and stepped over to peek inside one of the bags.

"Then I wouldn't have had time to make you breakfast, and I like any excuse to watch your mouth." Thomas glanced over at her, his smile turning wicked. "Because you do such delightful things with it."

"Flirting with me doesn't change the fact that you sent your *assistant* out to buy me clothes at some ungodly hour of the morning."

He chuckled. "Well, I know how you can make it up to him."

"How?" she asked as he pulled a beautiful, emerald green sweater out of a bag.

"Let him meet you before he dies of curiosity." A black, flowy skirt, came out of the same bag and he tossed it over his arm. "How does Monday sound? Lunch?"

"Thomas..." It wasn't the first time he'd brought up her meeting people he knew. Friends, other politicians, and now Alan – but she couldn't bring herself to say yes. Even when he'd cancelled on other dinner plans to meet up with her instead that Tuesday.

You make me happy, Maddie. His words echoed in her, and she wished she had said it back instead of focusing on the clothes.

"I'm not pressing you, but just know that *you* are the one

breaking his heart right now, not me." He winked at her and handed over the clothes, including a package of patterned, black tights, and a hot pink thong. When she raised her eyebrows at him, he grinned. "I'm sure he thinks that's funny."

"So, you're saying neither of you are funny? Was that a prerequisite to work for you?" Maddie couldn't even stifle her grin as she dodged his attempt to spank her, dashing up the stairs to the first landing. Thomas stood at the bottom, all lean muscular lines, ready to chase her — and her heart sped up as adrenaline and arousal bloomed inside her.

"Madeline O'Neill, I know this house better than you. You are *not* going to outrun me." He placed one foot on the bottom step, and she countered by moving onto the next section of stairs.

"Who says I *want* to outrun you?" Two more steps and he was prowling onto the first landing, his expression hungry.

"We do not have time for this game, beautiful."

"Then I guess I should go get dressed." She was facing him, slowly walking backwards up the stairs, but he wasn't stopping.

"Good idea, my belt is upstairs anyway." With that comment, she turned and took off at full speed. She could hear his footsteps chasing her, moving faster than hers up the stairs. Heart pounding, laughing as she slid on the hardwoods in her effort to turn right towards the master suite he used, she knew he was going to catch up — but she didn't care if they were both a little late.

He was an addiction, and she wanted another fix.

"So, who is she?" Alan asked as soon as Thomas walked in.

"Nope."

"Oh, come on, give me a name." He got up and followed as Thomas entered his office, tossing his laptop bag onto the couch, and he couldn't help chuckling at the slight whine in the other man's voice.

"Not happening, Alan."

"I won't contact her or anything, I just want to see a picture. I'll find her on LinkedIn, or Facebook, or something – but I *promise* I won't reach out." Alan was standing just inside the doorway, watching as he pulled out the papers he'd taken home to review.

"Let me see… no." Thomas grinned when Alan let out a groan and leaned against the doorframe.

"You've got to be kidding me. You haven't used that house in months. When you asked me to have it made ready, I figured your parents, or your brother, were coming to visit! Then you send me a text at two o'clock in the morning asking me to grab clothes from Sandra's shop and bring them there?" He threw his hands up, exasperated. "Who is this girl?"

"Any updates to the schedule today?" Trying to change the topic of conversation did *not* work, and the deadpan look Alan gave him was priceless.

"I knew I should have just shown up at the restaurant the last time I made a reservation."

"*That* would not be a smart choice."

"Scary voice doesn't work on me, remember?" Alan sighed. "Why are you hiding her? Do I know her? Is she famous?"

The sudden excitement in his assistant's voice made him roll his eyes. "No, she's not famous, but she is wonderful, and if you upset her by stalking us there's going to be a problem. Understand?"

For a moment it seemed like Alan might refuse to drop it, but then he relented. "Fine, its not like I won't meet her eventually if it's that serious. As far as today, Claire Ibson from New York Humanitarian Aid needed to move her meeting from 1:15 to 10:30 this morning, and so I swapped your brief review on the parks into Trisha's schedule. You wanted to meet Claire in person, right?"

"Yes, just make sure Trisha gives me a summary on the parks brief." The world was already coming back in on all sides, and Thomas wondered for a moment how he'd ever handled the non-stop working without moments like that morning. Maddie's peals of laughter were still clear in his mind from when he'd caught her and dragged her with him to get the belt. Her sweet whines as he'd peppered her skin with quick strokes, and then that *look* she'd given him as she'd wiggled free of his grip. Bright blush across her cheeks, her breasts rising and falling with her rapid breaths, and when she'd tried to run again he'd caught her and tossed her onto the bed. The sex had been quick, hard, but it had been the perfect release before a day like today.

Everyone was trying to get everything done so they could leave for the weekend.

"Thomas!" Alan raised his voice a bit, and then laughed as he shook his head. "I have got to meet this girl. You've never looked like *that*."

"Maybe." Thomas smiled, because he'd never *felt* like this either. She was all he thought about in his brief moments between meetings. Even in meetings he caught himself remembering her smile, or the way she would suck her lower lip between her teeth just before she said something particularly naughty.

"Alright, Congressman Hathaway. You've got maybe ten minutes before your first meeting arrives out here." With a wave, Alan grinned and walked out, pulling the door closed.

It was almost seven at night, and Thomas was fighting a yawn at his desk. Even with every light on in his cramped office, he was still fading, but what did he expect when he'd snagged a handful of hours of sleep?

The day had been a never-ending sprint, and his last meeting hadn't left his office until after six, which just left the hundred or so emails in his inbox to go through. There wasn't a moment spent with Maddie that he regretted, but it was becoming very clear what he'd been filling his time with before he'd met her: *work*.

Being single, and relatively young, in D.C. meant that he was taking on more than he really had time for, but he was still new, still proving himself worthy of his father's legacy. Even though he'd been working around most of the other people on the Hill since he was twenty-two, and working at his father's office back in New York since he could walk, he still had to make a name for himself. To be Thomas Hathaway instead of being referred to as Michael Hathaway's son. It was because of that history that the work hadn't really bothered him – it was *his* normal.

"And now you've got too many commitments," he grumbled at himself, filing his emails according to the various bills, and initiatives, and committee members that he had offered to help. When his mom, and sometimes even his father, commented on his relative solitude he'd never really thought twice about it. Working on Capitol Hill had been his dream since he was a kid – marriage? A family? Those were things he'd always put into the 'later' pile, something he'd eventually get around to. But as he'd sat in one of his fellow representative's office today and stared at all of the happy photos of the man and his wife and their kids, it had been the first time he'd actually seen that as something in his future.

Something that he might actually *want* instead of something that would eventually just become a necessity, which was absolutely, positively insane.

Thomas rubbed a hand over his face, refusing to connect Maddie with his sudden interest in a personal future outside of Congress, and eventually the Senate. Just because she wasn't a one night stand didn't mean wedding bells were in his future. *Hell*, he couldn't even get her to meet Alan, or let him buy her some clothes without a discussion.

As if Maddie could sense him thinking about her, his phone buzzed with a text from her: *Still in a meeting?*

He smiled and leaned back in his chair to reply: *Not anymore, just catching up on work. Crazy day.*

The little dots in the text message told him she was typing, and he waited, unable to look away. Eventually a message came through: *Tell Alan thanks for the clothes.* Followed by a breathtaking picture of her bent over in front of a mirror, that hot pink thong framing her ass like the piece of art it was. A few still lingering bruises and marks showed, and his cock twitched, because those were *his* marks.

He groaned and started laughing as he wrote her back: *I will most definitely not be sharing that with him.*

The reply was quick: *Why not?*

Because you're mine. That's what he wanted to answer, he was even poised to start typing, but he pulled himself back. Instead, he wrote: *Go out with me Sunday night.*

Time stretched after he sent it, not even the trilling dots to tell him she was planning to reply. Muttering under his breath, he took a drink of water and turned back to his laptop, leaving his phone beside him. He'd skimmed a half a dozen emails, sorting them as he needed to, before he felt the buzz through the desk. When he picked up the phone his heart did a hazardous little somersault in his chest before pounding hard enough to draw his attention. She'd only sent three words, *'I'm all yours'*, but they had power. Strong enough to make him sit back in his seat, smiling like a damn fool at his empty office.

Chapter Eleven

Monday

*R*eaching over, Maddie pressed the silence button on the side of her phone as she let yet another of Antoine's calls roll to voicemail. Her stomach was turning, and her face felt hot, and she couldn't tell if she was *actually* getting sick, or if she was just such a miserable human being that her body was revolting against her.

The buzz a minute later signaling that he'd left her another message only made her feel worse.

When she closed her eyes she could still feel that golden warmth that always filled her when she was around Thomas. Their play the night before had been incredibly fun, sleeping in his oversized, plush bed had been wonderful, and waking up to toast and coffee had been perfect – even though he'd had to leave extra early to head to New York for something with his family.

"What are you doing, Maddie?" she whispered, burying her face in her hands for a moment. The sound of her breath against her palms usually helped calm her down, it had been an old trick before tests in high school and college, but it wasn't doing a thing to ease the twisting nausea that seemed to be getting worse by the minute.

"It's five o'clock, come on, Ginger." Jamar was beside her desk, his dark skin a sharp contrast to the crisp, white dress shirt.

"I'll leave in a bit."

"No, you're going to come with me now, and we're going to that place with the fancy, glassed in patio, and we're going to drink and watch the snow and you're going to talk." He snapped his fingers. "Come on, up and at'em."

"Jamar." Maddie groaned and dropped her hands to her desk, looking up at him. "Do I look like I want to go drink?"

"You *look* like someone just made you watch Old Yeller on repeat, and I don't know what's going on, but I have two sisters and a wife and I've become an expert at listening." He walked around her chair to pick up her coat, holding it out for her. When she didn't stand up, he stared her down. "Do not make me dress you like I do my nephews."

"I'm not good company right now."

"I can tell, but we're going to go and drink until you get whatever is going on off your chest. I cannot deal with this place without the Ginger to my Gilligan, alright?" Jamar shook her coat, and angled his head towards the exit.

"Fine." Pushing her chair back, she ripped her coat from his hands and pulled it on, piling on the scarf, hat, and gloves that would help her handle the falling snow outside.

The walk was a slushy mess, but it was why she'd worn her boots, and once they were inside the heated patio with vodka in her hand she had to admit that the alcohol wasn't a bad idea. Jamar sat in silence for a few minutes, nursing his drink as he people watched, but eventually he gave up on waiting for her to start the conversation.

"Alright, talk to me about it. Is it about the guy?" He tilted his head down towards the table to catch her gaze, and then he sat up, nodding. "That's a yes. Did he break up with you?"

Maddie sighed and looked up at him, and he watched her for a moment.

"Nope, that is not the '*I've been dumped*' face. Trust me, I know that face. So, what is it, Ginger? He not making enough time for you or something?"

"Shouldn't you be home with Nina?" she asked, a little snarkier than she meant to.

"Absolutely, but you're my friend and I don't like watching you mope around the office like some zombie." He nudged her cape cod towards her, and then waved at a waiter for another round. "Drink up."

That she could do, and she finished it in a single go.

"Did you break up with him?"

"No," she said, and the pain in her voice was something tangible. That's what she *should* have done before any of this started. Before she saw how good he was, how kind, how wonderful. She should have left it at a kinky encounter, crossed off something on her life goals list, and moved the fuck on – but instead she'd used him again, and again, and *again*.

"Did he hurt you?" Jamar asked, an intense edge to his low voice that she'd never heard in him before, but the question made her laugh. Tears burned the edges of her eyes as she thought about all of their enticing times inside Black Light – but *that* was not a conversation she'd be having with Jamar. "Ha, ha, Maddie. I don't find this funny. Something has you off, and if this guy has hurt you I want to know about it."

"I'm fine," she lied. She most definitely didn't feel fine, but there was no way in hell she wanted to talk about Thomas Hathaway with him.

"Is he married?"

She scoffed. "No."

"Is he terrible in bed?"

Maddie rolled her eyes, fighting the urge to smile at his question. "Definitely no."

"Thank fuck, the alcohol is here. Can you go ahead and just bring us two more of those for her?" Jamar smiled at the waitress that had brought them, and Maddie gawked at him.

"Trying to get me drunk?"

"I'm trying to get you to talk, because you obviously need to, and if I need to pour you into an Uber and help you up the stairs to your apartment to get the normal Maddie back, I'll do it."

"Nina would *not* like that."

Jamar sighed, shaking his head. "Nina likes you, Maddie. You guys have met multiple times. She just wishes you had more than one friend."

"I have other friends," Maddie retorted, defensively crossing an arm over her stomach as she scooped up the next drink.

"Who?" he asked, and she stared at him.

It was true, at one point she'd had some people she used to hang out with, meet for drinks like this, but other than Antoine there weren't many people she saw in D.C. anymore. "Okay, so I haven't made a ton of friends here, but it's hard."

"Is that what's bothering you?"

"No," she waved a hand at him as she worked her way through another cape cod. The steady warmth of the alcohol was bleeding into her veins, and she realized that she'd been avoiding people, avoiding friends, so that she'd have more time to look for a story. For her big break. "You know, I used to go to these happy hour mixer things for people in journalism in the District."

"Why'd you stop?"

She shrugged. "I made some good contacts, but they all made it pretty clear that breaking into a job here was hard. So many of them just kept telling me to go to other cities, other markets, to get a job *somewhere else* and then come back later. After I had a résumé, something to get my foot in the door at one of the big papers here."

"So, why didn't you do that? It makes sense." His expression was neutral when she looked at him again. No judgment, just waiting to hear her answer.

"I don't know." Maddie took another long drink, trying to anesthetize herself against the uncomfortable questions.

"Come on, Ginger. Talk to me about it." When she just stared down at the table, tracing a groove in the wood with her thumbnail, Jamar finished his first drink and reached for his second. "Alright, then I'll talk first. You know that Nina is a lawyer, right?"

Maddie nodded. "You've mentioned it before."

"Well, before we moved here we lived out in LA together, met at UCLA and I knew she was the one the first week we met. I was a Junior, she was a Sophomore, and I saw her and it was just… *boom*." He tapped the table in front of him. "I was done. Gorgeous, smart, funny − could kick my ass at poker − I was in love before I even knew it. So, after I graduated we moved in together. I got a journalism degree, just like you, but the papers in LA were the same way. They all wanted experience, a résumé like you said, and so instead of working at a newspaper I worked one or two random jobs at a time building a life for us. Bought her a ring doing that, married her during her first year at law school. Then she graduated, got a great job at a firm doing corporate contract law, and I started to get involved with some of the papers. A little freelancing, nothing major, but the LA Times was using some of my stuff. Then, they started talking about a job."

"So what happened?"

"Nina got a call from one of the firms out here. Lambert, Urbanski, and Reed. Big time clients, a lot of money, and I knew she wanted it. I could see how excited she was, but she was holding back for me."

"And you moved here," Maddie finished for him.

"Yep." He raised his glass and took a long drink. "Took the job at Daily Saver D.C. and here I am."

"Aren't you angry about that?" She shook her head, shocked that Jamar had never shared that story, even with all their discussions about their journalism degrees. "I mean you worked *so hard* to get to that point, and then just threw it all away."

"I won't lie and say it didn't hurt. It was hard for a while, especially since she works seventy-hour weeks, but I always wanted a family. So does Nina, and because of my job we're okay to do that. If I was some hotshot reporter, traveling all over, we'd never see each other and having a kid would never have happened." A small smile lit up his face all over as he stared down at his drink.

"Wait – are you guys?"

Jamar grinned wide, and her mouth dropped open in shock, but then he was suddenly more serious. "We're not even ten weeks yet, I'm not supposed to talk about it. Bad luck and all that."

"Holy shit, congratulations!" Maddie almost shouted it, and a few other tables looked over to see what was going on, but he just laughed and waved a hand at her to calm down.

"Don't you *dare* mention anything, she'd kill me." He shrugged. "But, yeah. We'll have a little boy or a little girl in time for Christmas next year, and in the grand scheme of things working some exciting, high-profile gig just doesn't compare."

"I'm just so happy for you guys." It was more than the alcohol giving her warm fuzzies when she looked up at him. He already looked like the proud papa, swiping at his phone with a glowing smile before he turned it around.

The grainy image didn't mean much to her, but there *was* a blob in it. Jamar pointed to the blob. "That was the first ultrasound. Strong heartbeat, but Nina is a mess. Trying to figure out how she'll handle maternity leave without ruining her career, etcetera. But I keep telling her that I'll be there, that I can take time off too, that I can pick the kid up from daycare. Feed them, change them, all that stuff."

"You're going to be a great dad, Gilligan." She smiled, and he smiled back, locking his phone to pick up his drink.

"Thanks, Ginger, but I've talked plenty now. Talk to me about why you haven't pursued the fancy reporter job if that's what you want." He snapped his fingers. "You know, you could totally go back to Pennsylvania and build up some experience and then come back, it would –"

Maddie groaned, cutting him off. "No, *no*. That's the issue. I wanted to be a reporter in D.C. doing important work. I wanted to cover politicians, and world leaders, and do something *meaningful*." As the words left her mouth, she realized they were true. She'd become so focused on getting the job at the Post she'd forgotten *why* she wanted to work there at all… and it wasn't to write tabloid fodder.

Shit.

"Who cares if it takes you a few more years to get there? You're what, twenty-five?"

"Twenty-four," she corrected.

"Jesus, Maddie, you have time. Nina didn't even graduate law school until she was almost twenty-five. You can do anything you want right now, you can *go* anywhere you want. If that's really your dream, go for it."

His words settled somewhere inside her, grating against everything she'd defined herself by for more than a year. Meeting Antoine at that event had been life-changing for her. An editor at one of the biggest papers in the world talking to her like she mattered, telling her she could do it, she could achieve her dreams the way she'd always imagined – no matter what other people told her. It had been everything that mattered to her, *all* that mattered for so long that it was difficult to get anything else by the idea – and now she was so close. "But, what if you had been offered the job in LA. If it had been within your grasp, would you have taken it?"

Jamar didn't answer right away, he took a slow drink and let his eyes stare somewhere in the middle-distance between them. "I don't think I can answer that, Ginger. It's like some sci-fi movie, if I were to go back and say yes to a job at the LA Times, where would my life be now? Would Nina resent me? Would we have a baby on the way? Would we still be together? Would you be sitting here with someone else getting even worse help?" He shook his head. "In life, sometimes I think we just have to make the best decisions we can at the time, knowing we don't know where they're going to lead us. It all comes down to what matters most to you, and once you know that – you know what choice you need to make."

"Right..." Maddie took a drink, thinking over his words.

"I feel like we kind of got off topic from your man troubles." Jamar chuckled.

"Not really."

"Well, you definitely look better, but that could be the alcohol talking." When he grinned she wadded up her napkin and threw it at him.

"You're such a dick, Gilligan."

"So, tell me, what's really bothering you? Career stuff or man stuff?" He was relaxed, leaning back from the table as he held his glass and watched her. Jamar was probably her best friend, and definitely the only person who would have taken the time to have *this* conversation with her, but she didn't really have an answer.

"It's both."

"Both?" He let out a low whistle. "No wonder you look all Dawn of the Dead."

"You're doing wonders for my ego right now."

"Ah, just keep drinking, you'll feel better soon." Laughing, he raised his glass over the table and she leaned forward to clink them. "Did any of this help, or am I now just using you as an excuse to enjoy happy hour before I head back into hormone central?"

"You helped. I'm just not sure what is going to happen when I do what I need to do."

"That's part of the fun, isn't it? If we knew how our lives were going to turn out, they'd be pretty fucking boring." Jamar tilted his drink up, and nudged the last cape cod across the table towards her. "The only thing left is to find out where your decisions are going to lead you."

Chapter Twelve

Tuesday

*M*addie woke up the next morning with a violent headache, and her alarm screeching much louder than it normally did just a foot or two from her head, or at least it didn't normally *feel* that loud. Like a marching band of fire alarms setting off small explosives. Groaning, she turned it off and shoved the thing onto the floor as punishment. She'd been toasted by the time she stumbled into her apartment the night before, the quick drinks catching up to her in the car, and as she peeked down she realized she hadn't even undressed.

Nice.

She really had to stop drinking so much. Hopping out of bed, she started the coffee before heading into the shower, hurrying through her routine to make herself a travel cup to nurse the hangover on the way in. Jamar looked even worse than she did when she saw him – but even with the nasty side-effects of their happy hour, Maddie felt okay for the first time in a month.

Work breezed by that morning, she ordered surprise, greasy subs for Jamar and her for lunch, and then Brenda came by in the afternoon, and the brakes screeched inside her brain. "Madeline, do you have a minute?"

Doing her best to keep the wobble out of her voice, she spoke quietly, "Sure. Is something wrong?"

"No, actually I just want to talk real quick. Can you come to my office?" The older woman gave her a small smile, but Maddie still felt nervous as she stood.

"Okay, I mean, are you *sure* nothing is wrong?"

"Let's talk in my office." Brenda started walking towards her door, and Maddie stared down Jamar as she walked by, but he looked just as bewildered as she was. *No help there.*

As soon as the door closed, Maddie started talking. "Listen, I'm really sorry about those mistakes I made, but I'm really –"

"Madeline, please take a seat, and relax." The woman seemed much warmer in the seclusion of her office, and even though her nerves were making her hands shake, she sat down in one of the uncomfortable little chairs in front of the desk. "I wanted to tell you that I know you were having a rough time a couple of weeks ago, but I appreciate you taking my feedback to heart and getting back on board with the team."

"Right, I was just a little distracted, but I'm good now."

"I know you are, you're back on track, and that's why I'm so glad to be able to give you this now." Brenda opened her day planner and pulled out an envelope, handing it across the desk. "Go on, open it."

More confused than ever, Maddie tore open the top of the envelope and took out a piece of paper. It was mostly typed, and Brenda's signature was at the bottom, along with the owner's name. Forcing herself to read more slowly she finally processed what the paper said. "Wait, I'm getting a promotion?"

"We were going to tell you at the beginning of January, but then you started acting so strange. Your performance slipped, and we had concerns." Brenda waved a hand. "None of that matters now, I can see it was just a rough patch, and we're very happy to have you here at the Daily Saver."

"This is my new salary?" It was an almost fifteen thousand dollar increase over her current salary, and she couldn't help popping out of her chair when the woman smiled and nodded.

Holy shit.

"It took a lot of string pulling, they really felt like we only needed one senior level copy editor, but I put my foot down about it. I said we were lucky to have you, and *damn it* you deserved the title." Brenda looked a little uncomfortable with her use of the curse word, but Maddie walked around the desk and pulled her into a hug. She was stiff for a moment, but then the woman relaxed slightly and patted her on the back.

"Thank you, thank you so much! You have no idea what this means, it's just — it's perfectly timed, and I'm so sorry about that stuff a few weeks ago. I had some personal things, but that's done. Over with." She leaned back from Brenda, smiling, and her manager squeezed her free hand.

"I'm glad it's done, you would be some challenging shoes to fill, Madeline."

"You know, you can call me Maddie, Brenda."

Looking even more uncomfortable, the woman nodded. "Okay... Maddie. Well, that was it. Now that I've told you, I'll go ahead and send it through payroll processing, and you can change your email signature as soon as I send out the email announcement."

"Thank you so much, Brenda. Really, this is fantastic."

"You're welcome, but it was your hard work that made it possible." Brenda was standing next to her desk, her fingers toying with the edge of her day planner, and Maddie finally just moved to the door.

"I appreciate you going to bat for me." She offered a smile, and then left her office before things got any more awkward. The smile wouldn't leave her lips though and Jamar gave her a questioning look, but she held up a finger asking him to wait.

Feeling like she was about to burst with the news, Maddie pulled up her phone and sent off a text to Thomas: *I just got a promotion at work!*

Jamar threw a pen at her and she looked up to see him shrugging his shoulders, his hands out. "What's going on?" he whispered.

Rolling her eyes, Maddie clicked on her inbox, waiting for the email to come through. A minute or so later she saw the message from Brenda to all internal staff, and she snapped her fingers and pointed at her computer screen. "Email!" she hissed at Jamar, and he sighed and turned back to his computer.

"What? Congrats, Maddie!" Jamar announced across the floor, standing up at his desk. Heads popped up around the room from various departments.

"Would you sit down?" Maddie laughed, her blush creeping into her cheeks, but then a few of the coworkers around her started to lean over the cube walls and congratulate her. Email responses started to tumble in telling her congratulations, and she waved at Brenda as she peeked out of her office for a moment.

"Totally well-deserved, Ginger."

"Thanks, Gilligan." Smiling at him as he snagged the spot on top of her filing cabinet, she waited for him to crack a joke, but he didn't.

"Does this affect your decision at all?"

Shaking her head she toyed with the case on her phone. "Not a bit, I think I knew what I was going to do before we even left the bar last night. I think this is just the universe telling me I made the right choice."

"This is big time enough for you?" He gestured at the dingy, rather small office, but when she looked around it didn't bother her like it used to.

"I think it's where I need to be right now. I've got plenty of time, right?"

"Plenty of time," Jamar laughed. "You're not even knocking on thirty yet, Ginger. World leaders will be there when you're ready for the leap."

"Right, thanks."

"You're welcome, *Senior Copy Editor*." He said the last words way too loudly and she tried to kick him as he hopped off her cabinet, but she missed. Instead, he laughed as she scrunched up her nose at him, but she knew he was only messing with her because he was proud of her, and because he was her friend.

Her phone buzzed and Maddie snagged it, excited, but that faded when she saw Antoine's name. He was asking about the article again. Swiping her phone open, she tapped out a quick reply: *We need to talk.*

The response was quick: *When?*

Sighing, she wavered, and then sent: *Tomorrow.*

Setting her phone down, she tried to focus on work, but she was too amped up. So, instead, she updated her email signature, and then did some math on what she estimated her new paychecks would be. With that bump she could probably afford an apartment with actual rooms. The last two hours of the workday were spent making sure her queue was empty, and replying to delayed congratulations as people saw the email. It was all a sign, a sign that what she'd felt in her heart was the right choice.

Just before the end of the day her phone buzzed, but this time it was Thomas, and she couldn't hide her smile. His text took her day from amazing to spectacular: *I am so proud of you, beautiful. We're going to celebrate as soon as I'm back. No arguing, I get to spoil you on this one.*

Jamar kicked her desk just as she was about to type out a reply. "Come on, time for your big dinner, Ginger the Senior Copy Editor. Nina is even going to meet us."

"We're not doing a repeat of happy hour, are we?"

"No way, moderate drinking only." He laughed and clapped his hands together. "Party time! Let's go!"

A few of the people around them stood, asking if they could join in, and she was a little surprised that anyone else cared. Jamar looked at her, clearly signaling it was her choice, but she shrugged. It was a work thing, and they probably just wanted to avoid the bustle of people commuting out of the city. Raising her voice, she announced, "Anyone can come to dinner if they want!"

"Italian food for all!" Jamar laughed.

People started to gather their things, and she rushed to finish her text to Thomas, hitting send: *I can't wait to see you.*

"So, where are we going, Gilligan?"

"Just around the corner, we can walk."

Brad stood up then, her ultra-quiet neighbor who did some of the graphics support for their ad clients. When he saw her looking at him, he stopped. "You did say anyone could come, right?"

"Of course." She smiled and waved him over. "Come on, Charlie Chaplin." Maddie laughed when he looked confused, pausing with his coat half on. "It's a joke, you know, because you're so quiet?"

"Oh, like how you pretend Jamar's name is Gilligan?"

"Exactly." Laughing on the way out the door, she was a little overwhelmed by the small crowd of people that left with her. Even Brenda tagged on to the end of the group. By the time they walked into the Italian place, she counted everyone up and realized they needed a table for twelve, which was almost half the freaking office. Jamar held a seat open for Nina, and Brenda snuck into the seat on the other side of Maddie, and as soon as appetizers arrived, and the wine started flowing, everyone was talking. Actually talking to each other, which was a little weird. It was a little stilted and awkward at first, but then people were chatting about TV shows they watched, and Maddie joined in on the ones she'd caught on Netflix.

Talk turned to the nicknames she and Jamar had for each other, and Brad proudly spoke up that he was Charlie Chaplin. Groans of jealousy came from around the table, and she realized that while she'd thought the little joke with Jamar had just been a stupid running gag – it actually mattered to the others. Soon enough, everyone was picking out names of old television and film characters for each other.

One of the ad guys got the nickname Don Draper for his job and his smoking habit, a woman in distribution got the nickname Dana Scully, both for her hair and her affinity for sci-fi. By the end of the meal everyone there had one, and people were picking out ones for others back at the office, texting them the names with more excitement than she'd seen any of them display in almost two years. After a while, Brenda spoke up and asked everyone to give her a nickname, but only Jamar was gutsy enough to speak up, "Definitely Leslie Knope."

"Who?" Don Draper asked.

"She's the lead on Parks & Recreation? Plucky, blonde boss who thinks her tiny department in some no-name town is the best in the world?" Jamar started laughing, and Maddie couldn't hold it in, and then the whole table was laughing – including Brenda. Their manager's single-minded pride of the Daily Saver D.C. made her a perfect Leslie Knope.

"To Leslie!" Maddie raised her wine glass, and everyone else cheered back.

It felt like her life had turned a page in the last twenty-four hours. A really big, really scary page, but when she looked around at all of the people she'd spent a year and a half working with – she realized she'd never even given them the chance to be her friend. Never really taken the time to try and *make* friends. Jamar had bullied his way into her life with his loud, funny personality, but everyone else had been mostly ignored. She'd been so focused on leaving, on getting a *different* job, that she hadn't even paid attention to what was possible right in front of her. Fun coworkers, an office that didn't have to be miserable and quiet… and this was just the beginning.

The beginning of a new kind of life in more ways than one – a job she was discovering she could actually enjoy, an exciting new relationship, and a whole world of kink to explore – and it felt *right*. As if pieces of a puzzle she hadn't been aware of were slowly clicking into place right before her eyes.

It's all about the choices we make.

Maddie was on cloud nine as she hopped out of the car in front of her apartment building. It was frigid, the snow was dirty, and she almost lost her footing in the slush by the curb. Muttering to herself, she clutched her phone in her hand and tried to walk carefully towards the stairs, but a few steps away from the handrail that would have kept her upright – she slipped on some hidden ice, and went down hard. "Fuck!"

Her nice, office jeans were soaking up the grime on the ground as she tried to get herself upright without falling again, and then she heard someone shout her name. "Maddie? Maddie!"

Looking up, she was simultaneously thrilled and mortified by what she saw. "Thomas?" He almost slid too as he got to her, but managed to retain his footing *and* help her off the ground, just like the knight she knew he was. Always rescuing her.

"Are you okay?" His strong arms wrapped around her, hugging her tight, and she smiled against his chest as she breathed in the scent of his cologne, her embarrassment starting a fire in her cheeks.

"I'm fine, I just can't believe I fell. So stupid." Leaning back she felt like she had to make sure it was really him, but those hazel eyes met hers and they were definitely his. Still the mixture of forest green and brown that she loved. "How on earth are you here? I thought you were still in New York."

"I was going to fly back tonight anyway, but I snagged an earlier flight so we could celebrate your promotion." He chuckled. "But I think you might have celebrated a little too hard already?"

Rolling her eyes, she shook her head. "Not at all, I just had one glass of wine. It was a bunch of work people that went to dinner with me. The falling was, unfortunately, *all* my complete lack of coordination."

"I think you're pretty coordinated." Thomas smiled down at her. "So, if you've only had one glass of wine, then having a cocktail with me isn't out of the question?"

"Once I get some dry clothes on, cock sounds fantastic." Maddie grinned at him when he started laughing, and then he squeezed her ass and turned them towards the steps.

"Alright, beautiful, let's get you changed. Then I'll happily give you one of each."

"That sounds like a perfect celebration, but – wait, *shit*, I dropped my phone when I fell. Can you see it? It's got a bright blue case." Trying to turn around carefully, she looked for it, but it was hard to see in the dark, and the lights from her building weren't helping much.

Thomas pulled his phone out and flipped the flashlight function on, and a moment later he let go of her to reach down and pull the little miracle of technology from a pile of slush. "Got it, but we're going to want to dry it off quickly."

"Fantastic," Maddie groaned and he nudged her up the steps.

"Go on, I'll work on it while you change. No need for you to get sick standing out here in wet clothes."

"Right." As soon as they were inside, she turned and kissed him. "Thank you, Thomas."

"I haven't even done anything yet," he grinned, and then kissed her again. Nipping at her lips before leaning her back to deepen it – right in the middle of the lobby.

Grinning like a fool, she pulled away and pressed the elevator button. "You've done more for me than you could possibly know, and you are the perfect end to an already wonderful day."

"Oh, I have a few ideas for how we can make it even better."

"Really?" Her voice was a soft purr as she pulled him with her into the elevator, and after she'd pressed floor six he pushed her against the wall, shamelessly capturing her mouth. It was delicious, but they were both in *way* too many clothes for this to be happening. Not to mention they were on camera, in her building's elevator, and she was starting to shiver from the snow that had soaked into her gloves and her jeans.

Thomas' laugh sent a thrill down her spine when the ding signaled they'd arrived at her floor. "I'm going to need you to get changed quickly, because my *plans* are just getting more elaborate the longer I'm thinking about them."

"Plans," she repeated as they stepped into the hall, and she pulled him in the direction of her apartment.

"I'm thinking one drink to toast your promotion, and then I'm going to tie you down to the bed and make you come over, and over, and over." He leaned close to her ear as he spoke, and she practically panted.

Definitely need to get changed. Fast.

"I'm all yours." She smiled, but just before they got to the door she flinched, remembering he'd never seen her place. "I do have to give you fair warning, my apartment is kind of small, and so it's pretty much always a wreck."

"Now I'm curious." Thomas watched her as she dug in her massive purse for her key, and fiddled with the lock until it finally turned over. In the hall light she finally had the chance to check him out. Dark slacks, with shining shoes, a black peacoat that fit him like it was custom cut – which was completely possible – and his warm, brown hair seemed to have been styled by the wind to look absolutely perfect.

Ridiculously hot.

Maddie shook her head, and shoved the door open. As soon as

the lights came on she groaned, because her apartment looked worse than she thought. Dirty clothes scattered across the floor, a pile of unwashed dishes in the sink, and then Thomas moved in behind her. "Please, just, ignore all of it. I swear I'm not this big of a wreck all the time."

As she hurried over to the corner of the room that held her dresser, her clothing rack, and the laundry basket of stuff she still hadn't put away – Thomas looked like he was struggling not to laugh.

"I know, it's tiny, but it's an expensive area and I don't need much." She stripped out of her soaked gloves, and tossed her coat over the empty end of her clothing rack, before she sat down on the floor to pull off her boots.

"I'm not judging, Maddie. I spend most of my nights in my office, on a very uncomfortable couch because I'm too lazy to use the blow up mattress tucked in my closet."

"Really?" She stared at him as she stood back up to shimmy out of her jeans, which were even more disgusting than she'd guessed when they'd been out on the street. Her hands and legs were grimy, and she really needed to wash off.

"Yep. A lot of the representatives sleep in their offices."

"But you've got that huge, gorgeous house," she hurried over to the bathroom, the only door in the room besides the one to the hall, and watched him shrug.

"It's a big, empty house. No point in sleeping there alone when I just need to be back at the office. Usually less than twelve hours later, you know?" He smiled at her, his eyes trailing down her bare legs. "I think I might have to fuck you in nothing but a sweater, because *that* looks good on you."

"Is that a promise?"

"Well, maybe in the morning. I want you completely naked when I tie you up." The subtle edge to his voice made her shiver for entirely different reasons than the lingering chill on her skin.

"I —" Maddie's voice failed her for a moment, and then Thomas raised his eyebrows at her. "I am going to clean up, and make myself look at least somewhat presentable. Quickly."

"Quickly sounds perfect."

She shut the door before she wasted more time, and turned on the bath to get some warm water going. While it heated up, she scrubbed her hands in the sink, rolling her eyes at her reflection. Only *she* would wipe out in front of her own apartment building, right in front of one of the hottest, most amazing men she'd ever met.

"Where's a towel for your phone? Or do you want it in rice?" Thomas' voice was hard to hear over the bath, but she shouted back.

"I don't have rice, but there should be a towel in the laundry basket by the rack of clothes!" Grumbling to herself, she grabbed her face wash. The make-up she'd put on that morning was raccooning around her eyes, and since she had a few minutes she might as well fix it.

Before he ties you to his bed?

She bit her lip as she visualized it, remembering the way he liked to tease her to the edge as he licked her, holding her against his mouth so she couldn't escape.

You should be getting ready.

Cursing herself for getting distracted, she scrubbed at her face, using make-up remover on her eyes, and then patted dry so she could sit on the edge of the tub to rinse off her legs. Her knees were sensitive to the touch, and she was sure she could see the beginnings of bruises where both had landed on the ice, but at least she hadn't twisted an ankle. Scrubbing as fast as she could, she washed the soap off her legs and then made sure the tap wasn't leaking as she called out, "I'm almost done!"

She didn't catch his answer as she grabbed a towel. Hair brushed, teeth brushed, and then some quick make-up. Mostly focusing on her eyes so she at least looked *alive*, instead of a pale, freckled mess. Practicing a smile in the mirror, she frowned at her hair, but gave up because she'd taken too long already and she knew it.

"Thomas?" Maddie stepped out of the bathroom, still trying to tame the impossible frizz, and then her heart stopped. He was sitting at her desk, her laptop open, and she *knew* what was on the screen before he even turned around. "I can explain."

"*Antoine* was texting you while you were getting ready. He asked if you'd finished the article for him." Thomas tossed her phone onto the bed, raising his eyes to hers. "He called you as well, but I thought it might be awkward if I answered."

"Thomas, wait –"

"I was confused, because I thought you didn't write articles at work. I was even trying to think of some explanation, and then I saw this." He held up the job offer from the Post, and it felt like the floor dropped out from under her. She wanted to speak, but his expression was something she'd never seen. Cold, hard – angry.

"I –"

"You're a fucking reporter?" He almost shouted the question, sounding more like an accusation than anything else, and then he let out a bitter laugh as he stood up. Pacing away from her desk, he clenched his fist around the pages of the offer, crumpling the edges. "I can't *believe* I fell for your bullshit. I can't believe I brought you in there!"

"Please, please listen to me. I wasn't going to –"

"What, Maddie? Or – wait – is that even your fucking name? Who the *fuck* are you? Tell me! Who the hell have I been fucking for the last two weeks?" His voice was a roar when he asked the last question, his footsteps carrying him towards her until she backpedaled, tears springing to her eyes.

No, no, no, this wasn't supposed to happen.

It was over, I'd decided.

I'd made my choice.

She was sniffling, backing up from him as if she were afraid of him, and *fuck* if part of him didn't feel like a bastard for making her cower like that. Growling, he forced himself to walk away from her, throwing the damn offer letter from The Washington Post into a pile of clothes. He shoved his hands into his hair, pulling at it, trying to focus.

Jaxson is going to kill me.

"Thomas…" Maddie's voice was shaky, and she was crying now, but he refused to let her manipulate him again.

"Am I in the fucking article? Was I just some mark to you because I'm in the House? Did you put me –"

"NO!" She shouted, shaking her head. "No, you're not in there. I swear!"

"I saw you wrote about Jaxson, and Chase – and fucking

Emma? You don't even know them! What have they done to you? What has *anyone* at Black Light done to you?"

"I wasn't going to publish it, I wasn't. I swear, Thomas, just *please* let me explain." Maddie walked towards him and he recoiled, backing up towards the front door.

He wanted away from her.

"I don't want to hear it. You *used* me. You used me against my own friends. You used people's personal lives as a fucking sideshow – and for what? So you could get some shit reporting job?" He laughed, grabbing his forehead as he stared at her. "Was that the promotion? Were you going to have me celebrate you destroying one of the only safe places in the fucking city for people to play?"

"NO!" She was starting to hyperventilate, her breaths turning into hiccups as she stood barely six feet away from him, and he had to squash the tiny part of him that wanted to make her sit down and slow her breathing. Maddie wasn't his to watch over, she wasn't his sub, she wasn't *his* at all. "It's not – that's not it. I chose *you*, Thomas. I decided, I decided you were –"

"I was a fool, that's what I was. I thought you'd been hurt, I thought *that* was why you didn't understand some things – but you were just a fucking liar. You lied about everything!"

"I'm sorry, I'm sorry." Maddie had her hands in front of her, her fiery red hair in waves over her shoulders, her breaths cutting short as she sobbed. "Please, don't leave. I never meant…"

"Why don't you call Antoine and tell him how you feel? He seems desperate to talk to you." Turning away, he pulled the door open and slammed it behind him as he stepped into the hall. The wail he heard as he started towards the elevator plucked at him, tempted him to go back and comfort her, to stop her pain – but *she* wasn't who he wanted to hold. She was a lie wrapped in a pretty, distracting package. He wanted the girl he'd thought she was, and he hated himself for feeling anything for the woman in there now.

His head was buzzing and everything was a haze as he left her apartment building. Paul didn't even have the chance to get out to open the door before Thomas was settled in the backseat, his rage completely out of control.

"Is Ms. O'Neill not coming?"

"No, she's not. I need to go to the Georgetown house. Immediately."

"Of course." Paul nodded and immediately pulled away from the building. The drive to the house was a blur, because he spent the whole ride replaying the argument in his head. Maddie's tears, the sobs, her pretty voice shaping even more lies. His chest ached as he remembered her pleading, but then he would remember the way her phone kept buzzing with texts from *Antoine Cano*.

When do you want to meet tomorrow? Had made his possessive streak twitch, but he'd pushed it down. Then came the text that had confused him: *Are you done with the article?*

At first he'd just wanted to sit down, and so he'd pulled out her chair, but her desk was covered in pieces of scrap paper with BDSM terms scrawled on them, quick definitions, and then he'd seen the job offer. His head had spun, trying to process it all, and before he could think about it he'd opened her laptop. The article was waiting on the screen like she'd just been working on it, and then Antoine had called, and she had come out and –

"Fuck!" He shouted, slamming the side of his hand into the door panel. Paul jumped at the sudden break of silence in the car, and Thomas forced himself to breathe slowly. "Sorry, Paul. I just got some bad news."

"Is Ms. O'Neill alright?" The question was a strange break in normal protocol for the man, and Thomas met his eyes in the rear view mirror.

"She's fine."

Paul nodded, and then put his eyes back to the road, staying silent the rest of the drive, which wasn't long at all. When the car pulled up to the curb, Thomas opened the door before it had even fully stopped. "Head home, Paul. Thank you."

"Of course, Mr. Hathaway."

As soon as he got into the house, dark and empty and quiet, he walked into the library and poured a large scotch. It burned, but it dulled the raw feeling inside him as he sat down and tried to clear his head enough to figure out his next steps.

First, he texted Alan that he would need to delay his return to the office another day, and then he took a big drink and called Jaxson. The line rang, and rang, and went to his voicemail. Thomas debated about what to say, but figured the discussion would be better if they were talking – because *then* Jaxson could tear him a new one in real time. He took a deep breath and tried not to sound as insane as he felt, "Jaxson, it's Thomas. I need to talk to you as soon as you get this. It is very fucking urgent. Call me, or come to the Georgetown house. I'm here."

Chapter Thirteen

Wednesday

*T*he extended chime of the doorbell echoing throughout the house made Thomas jerk out of the chair, and then he groaned as his head pounded. Prying his eyes open he could see the unfinished glass of scotch on the table beside him, but whether that had been his fourth or fifth pour – he couldn't remember.

Shit.

Everything from the night before came rushing back in full, horrific Technicolor, just as the damn doorbell went off again. Growling, he stomped to the front door and knew before he'd even opened it who was out front. One tall, broad frame in tailored clothes, another a little shorter, with slightly longer hair.

Jaxson had brought Chase with him. Flipping the deadbolt, Thomas pulled the door open. "I called you, Jaxson. *Just* you."

"Where I go, we all go. You're just lucky Emma had plans."

Jaxson shrugged, and pointed towards the interior. "Are we going inside for whatever emergency you're having, or are you going to tell me while I freeze on your front porch?"

Rolling his eyes, he opened the door wide and let the two men into his house. Chase gave him a grin as he walked in. "This is a beautiful home."

"Thank you." Thomas kicked the door shut, the windows shaking with the force of it, but he didn't even flinch — he just walked back into the library and picked up his unfinished scotch.

"This is a whiskey at nine in the morning kind of problem?" Jaxson asked, crossing his arms as he paused just inside the room, Chase filling the rest of the doorway to his right.

"It's scotch, actually, and I have a feeling you're about to want some."

"Why?" Chase asked.

"Because Maddie is a fucking reporter." Thomas should not have felt the dark surge of self-satisfaction as the shadow passed over Jaxson's face, but he did. Now, the man understood the situation.

"*What?*" His old friend's voice was dangerously quiet, but Thomas had spent half the night torturing himself over every mistake he'd made, every stupid choice, and he'd numbed them all with liquor.

"Madeline O'Neill has written an article exposing Black Light for The Washington Post."

"Are you fucking kidding me?" Jaxson roared, but Chase just stood there silent and wide-eyed. "When does it go out? What kind of lead-time are you giving me on this colossal fuck up? God dammit, Thomas!"

"From what I understand, she hasn't turned it in yet." Thomas flinched as he remembered her voice, unsteady with tears, but then he pushed it away. "She told me last night she wasn't going to, but I honestly don't believe a fucking thing she says."

Jaxson laughed, a bitter sound as he walked over to the scotch and poured himself a glass, and Chase shadowed him to do the same. His friend took a rough drink of the liquid and then looked up at him. "So, you discovered this last night."

"Yes."

"How?"

"I was picking her up at her apartment, and I saw some things while I was waiting for her to get ready. Then I saw the article, and…"

"And?" Chase prompted.

"I lost it." Thomas finished the last of the scotch in his hand, letting it burn all the way down as he remembered how he'd shouted at her, the way she'd backed away from him with genuine fear.

"Jesus Christ, this is a nightmare. Please tell me you didn't hurt her, I cannot deal with that shit right now."

He lifted his eyes to Jaxson, and for a moment he was angry that he'd even suggested it. "You really think I'm capable of that?"

Jaxson ran a hand through his hair, pacing away from him to take a drink before he turned around again. "Look, you said you lost it, which I understand, but I've been dealing with a lot lately when it comes to friends making stupid choices when they're angry."

"I have *never* hit a woman," Thomas growled, taking a few steps towards Jaxson, but his friend didn't even shift a foot.

"Non-consensually." Chase's voice floated over and both he and Jaxson turned to stare at him. "I just think that's an important distinction to make in this conversation, because you *have* used things on women consensually. Hit them with crops and floggers and stuff, but not to really hurt them. I just mean that it's probably a good thing to clarify. You've never *non-consensually* hit a woman."

Thomas turned his eyes back to Jaxson, but instead of the annoyance he felt, he saw humor in the tilt of Jaxson's mouth. "Seriously?" Thomas asked.

"Chase has a point, and for the record, Thomas, I'm glad you didn't do anything to her, but I'll handle it from here."

"Wait, what are you going to do?" Some fractured part of him still felt the urge to protect her, to put himself between Jaxson and Maddie. *Fool.*

"Talk to her. Scare her a little. Remind her that we do have her signed NDA on file, and a lot of lawyers that will make her life hell if she breathes a word about the club, or you." Jaxson shrugged. "If I have to approach the Post, I'll have my lawyers handle that. They won't want to fuck with a legally operating entity, especially when their only source is in violation of a contract. Don't worry, I'll make her regret the day she met you."

"Right." Thomas nodded, knowing he should have been comforted by the words, by Jaxson's commitment to helping clean this mess up – but none of this felt good. Chase approached him, swapping the empty glass of scotch in his hand for a fresh one.

"I know you liked her, Thomas. I'm sorry this happened." The blond dropped a hand on his shoulder and squeezed, staying beside him for a moment before he walked over to Jaxson. Chase whispered something too low to hear, and then took Jaxson's unfinished scotch and left both glasses on the wet bar.

His friend looked up at him, taking control of the situation. "We need her address, Thomas."

"I've got it in my phone." His stomach twisted as he brushed his thumb across Maddie's contact information, remembering the way she'd stood dazed in front of him after their first night at Black Light, still coming back from subspace as she'd told him her number. Clenching his jaw, he pushed away the image of her blush, and sent her info to Jaxson. "There. You should have it."

His friend slid an iPhone from his pocket, stared at it for a moment, and then nodded. "I do. Don't worry about this, we'll handle it."

"Just —" Thomas swallowed the first set of words, and chased them with some scotch. "I'm sorry, Jaxson. This was my fault."

"You're right," he agreed, but then he shrugged. "If it helps at all, I thought she was a different person too. At least, based on what I'd heard."

"What had you heard?"

His old friend waved it off, moving towards the doorway. "It doesn't matter now."

"Tell me," Thomas demanded, and Jaxson turned to face him, pity etched into his expression for a moment.

"I'd heard you two were well-matched. That she was a submissive with a penchant for pain, but whether or not she could handle a crop —"

" — or nipple clamps," Chase added.

"She wasn't who she pretended to be, Thomas. No matter what she did, no matter what you did with her, it doesn't matter." Adjusting the coat on his shoulders, he waited for Chase to come stand beside him. "We'll handle it," Jaxson assured him.

"Thank you." Thomas' throat felt tight as he spoke, and he self-medicated with more alcohol.

"I'll call you later."

He nodded in reply, but the sound of the front door opening and closing seemed to sap the rest of his energy and he sunk into the nearest chair. A behemoth leather thing that was large enough to swallow him, even at his height.

She wasn't who she pretended to be.

Right. It was all a bunch of lies. None of it had been true. Not her submission, not her moans, and not her smiles or the peals of laughter that he'd heard in this very house.

I'm all yours.

No. It was all a mirage, and he just needed to wash it away. *He needed more scotch.* Enough of it to make him stop picturing her biting her lower lip, staring up at him with blue eyes that he'd thought held something good within them.

"You don't need to come with me," Jaxson muttered as the elevator rose towards the sixth floor, but Chase didn't even react. He just stood beside him, *quietly*, which was weird. "I'm just going to talk to her."

"Mmhmm." Chase made a sound of agreement, but even that sounded doubting, and it was making him defensive.

"She deserves to get scared a little. She lied her way into Black Light, she's planning to expose everyone. *Everything.*"

"I know." The elevator dinged, and Chase waited for him to step out of the doors first.

"She lied to Thomas, too." Jaxson continued, checking his phone again for her apartment number.

"Yep."

Muttering under his breath he scanned the doors, looking for the right one. Thomas was one of his oldest friends, one of the few people who had understood the crap he went through growing up, and seeing him that morning had been a shock. The man was normally perfectly put together, pristine like most politicians, but he'd looked completely destroyed. All thanks to Hurricane Maddie. His anger flared to life again. This bitch had used Thomas, just like so many women had done to him, for her own selfish purposes. Without even a second thought about what would happen when she wrote her fucking article.

Six, two, seven. This was her apartment.

Raising his fist he banged on the door, rattling the thing on its hinges. He waited a few seconds, and then banged again even louder.

"She may not be home, we can –" Before Chase could finish speaking the sound of the deadbolt turning silenced him. Then the door creaked open and the redhead peeked through the opening.

"We need to have a fucking conversation, Ms. O'Neill." Placing his foot against the door so she couldn't shut it, he leaned forward. "Now."

"You're Jaxson Davidson." Her voice was quiet, shocked, but he didn't have time for her to play the star-struck female.

"Yes, I am, and for the discussion we're about to have I don't want to be in the hallway."

Maddie just let go of the door and took a few steps back into the apartment, so Jaxson pushed it the rest of the way open, letting

Chase follow him in to shut it. He didn't waste any time before he started talking, "I want to make something very clear – if you have turned in that article, I am about to make your life a living hell. You signed a non-disclosure agreement when you tricked your way into Black Light, and whether or not Thomas paid for you, I can promise you that *you* are the only one my lawyers are going to tear apart."

She nodded, her arms coming up to cross just under her breasts, but she didn't speak. Instead, she was chewing her lip so hard he wouldn't have been surprised if it started bleeding.

"You need to listen to me. There's nothing illegal about Black Light, everything that happens there is consensual, and I don't really care what you fucking think about it, but if you breathe a word about it to anyone, much less the fucking Post, I will destroy you. And I won't be pulling any punches after what you did to my friend."

Maddie's blue eyes went wide, and then he watched as her face collapsed. Tears came, and then she was sobbing, and Jaxson was so taken aback as she bent at the waist, hugging herself, that he couldn't think straight.

"I didn't – I wasn't –" Her words were getting caught by the gasps of air she was pulling in between raw sobs.

Shit, either she was the best actress he'd ever met, or she was actually upset.

"If you think this is going to help you –"

"I don't want your fucking help!" she screamed at him, sniffling hard and wiping at her cheeks as she turned away from them. Maddie started stacking things on her desk, ripping cords out of her laptop, and the wall, piling them up. "You can have it all, it doesn't fucking matter. None of it fucking matters."

"Maddie," Chase spoke up, but she didn't even react as she picked up the messy pile of papers and technology.

Stomping back towards him she shoved the pile at Jaxson's chest, and he raised his arms on instinct. "Just take it, take all of it. None of it matters. I wasn't going to turn it in! I *wasn't going to turn it in…*" her fingers were still touching the pile in his arms for a moment, and then she broke down, folding over again as the sobs returned.

Jaxson turned to look at Chase who had an *I told you so* look on his face, and then they both watched as Maddie stumbled to her bed and sat down on the edge, hiccupping as she tried to breathe through the tears.

Well, fuck.

With his prepared threats delivered, he finally took a moment to look around the tiny space. Everything was in one room, and the place was a wreck. Her kitchen was against one end of the room, her bed in front of it, facing the windows. She must have eaten, and done everything else, at her desk because it was the only real surface in the apartment. The opposite corner had a dresser, a clothes rack, and a laundry basket full of more, and then there were little shelving units on the wall closest to the front door. It was small, *too* small for an experienced reporter at the Post.

Chase approached her slowly, easing to his knees in front of her, and Jaxson knew why his lover had insisted on coming. He'd somehow expected this.

Maddie lifted her eyes to look at him, and for the first time that day he really *saw* her. Her red hair was a tangled, frizzy mess down to her shoulders. Nose raw and red from crying, skin ghostly pale other than the smattering of freckles, which only served to make the contrast sharper. If he had thought Thomas looked bad, this was a whole new level of disaster.

"Just talk to me, I'm here. I'm listening." Chase was whispering to her, using that soft voice that he always did when someone was in pain – a skill Jaxson was still trying to develop for Emma.

The girl shook her head, another round of sobs making her shake, and he found himself standing awkwardly with an armful of stuff, across from the woman he'd planned to ruin just fifteen minutes before. *Time for a new tactic.* He may not be good at the emotional side of things, but he did have one thing he'd always been good at. Jaxson turned on his Dom voice, authoritative and clear, "Explain. Now."

Maddie stilled instantly, a sniffle the only sound she made for a moment as she looked up at him with effervescent blue, blood-shot eyes. "Why? He doesn't care."

Debatable. And that was one of the main reasons he was still standing in the room.

"You said you weren't going to turn it in, so what *were* you going to do?"

"Nothing. I turned down the job at the Post."

"You don't work for them?" he asked, confused.

She shook her head. "My contact there said I had to bring him an article, something that would *wow* them, before they'd hire me." Maddie hugged herself a little tighter, dropping her head for a moment as more tears fell... and then she told them both her story. How she'd shown up at Runway looking for a story, *any* story, and then noticed the D.C. elite arriving – but she wasn't able to find them once inside and it piqued her interest. The rest flowed fast. Her discovery of the secret entrance, her sneaking in, Thomas choosing to pay for her guest pass.

It was a mess. A really big mess that pointed out some weaknesses in his security he needed to tighten up, along with some new directives to members about how to enter Black Light – but when it came to her tears, her breakdown over Thomas, he still wasn't sure what to believe.

"I chose him, I don't care about the rest of it. Any of it. Everything was going to be perfect, I was *his*, but it doesn't matter now. I ruined it, I ruined the best thing I've ever had, and there's no point to anything because he doesn't care about me anymore."

"How about some water instead?" Chase was talking to her again, easing a bottle of vodka out of her hands, and then he was in her kitchen opening cabinets to find a glass.

"Is this everything?" Jaxson asked, jostling his armful of papers, cords, and technology that included her laptop and what looked like an external hard drive.

"You can have this too, it doesn't matter. I'm not going to talk." She grabbed her iPhone off the little folding table that sat at her bedside. "The passcode is four, two, eight, eight."

"Drink this," Chase demanded, employing his Dom voice with her as he gave her the water, and then he took the phone from her hands, looking down at it for a moment as he stood before her.

Maddie sat on the edge of the bed, mostly limp as she took a small sip of water and then held it between her knees. The nice green sweater looked strange with the pink, plaid pajama pants, but Jaxson didn't comment.

"Well?" Chase whispered as he moved close and offered Jaxson the phone, open to her home screen with a backdrop of a starry sky. They shifted the pile of stuff between them so he could look at it.

"I'm not sure," Jaxson answered quietly, trying to decide what to do next. He raised his voice when he spoke to Maddie, "Look,

I'm not taking your only phone, but I need to be sure you've removed everything from it."

"Feel free," she answered, wiping at her face with her sleeve. "I took some pictures of the guest stamp, I've got a note in there, just wipe it all. Smash it. Throw it away, I don't care."

Jaxson sighed, her defeated tone tugging at him as he focused back on the device. He deleted the note first, a collection of names and details that never needed to see the light of day. Then he opened her photos and started swiping through. Chase almost choked next to him as an image of what *had* to be Maddie's ass appeared on the screen. He swiped past, seeing a few more images that he instantly tried to erase from his memory. Then he found photos of the stamp, and others of Runway, and cars in front. He deleted them all before he walked over to her. "Is that everything?"

She sat back, staring up at him as he towered over her and offered her the phone. "Yes."

"No more back-ups? Other things?"

"No." Her sniffle was almost cute, and he could see what Thomas had seen in the girl. She was probably gorgeous when she was crying for different reasons.

"If there's anything you're holding back, you're going to regret it." The threat was probably not necessary, but he felt like he had to leave no doubt in her mind. "And you're not welcome back at Runway or Black Light."

"Right." She nodded and her breath shook as she sighed.

"I'll have my people go through your equipment and return it once we've cleaned it, but the NDA is still in effect. If you suddenly change your mind and —"

"I won't change my mind."

"Okay. Then, we're going to go." Jaxson stepped back from her, but she was already staring at her lap.

Chase was still looking at the girl, concern plastered all over his face, as he passed him to move to the door. Jaxson could tell that his lover wanted to stay, wanted to comfort the girl, but he wasn't sure she deserved that kindness. Without another word they left her apartment, Jaxson making sure the door was pulled tight, and then Chase spoke up, "She seems sincere."

"Yeah, but whether the tears are for getting caught, or for something else, I'm not sure yet."

As they walked towards the elevator, Chase scoffed. "You know as well as I do why she's so upset, and it has nothing to do with the article."

"First things first, we need to go through this shit and see what she was able to write about. I'm going to have someone dig into what the Post knows – because if she gave them too much they might be trying to look at Black Light even if she pulled her story." Jaxson sighed as he pressed the call button. "Then, and only then, am I going to even think about what else might need to happen."

"Good."

"It may not even matter, Chase." He glanced at him as they stepped inside the elevator and headed back downstairs.

"I think it will," the blond smiled at him, full of unbeatable optimism.

Jaxson huffed. "We'll see."

Chapter Fourteen

Thursday

"Whoa, Ginger, you *really* don't look good." Jamar sat the cup of coffee on her desk, pale and milky, just like she liked it, but she wasn't even interested.

"I know."

"What was it? Food poisoning?" He looked around the office, which was buzzing with chatter, a burst of laughter off to one side. "I don't think anyone else got sick, and I'm pretty sure Cruella had the lasagna too."

"Who?" Maddie looked up at him in confusion.

"Tammy in IT, she's got the blonde hair with the black streak underneath? They called her — nevermind. Look, I'm worried about you. You still feel sick?"

She shrugged. It would be so much easier if what she felt was food poisoning, but instead it was worse. So much worse. "I'll be fine."

"Okay, well, if you need anything all you have to do is ask." Jamar started to turn towards his desk, but Maddie stopped him.

"Actually, I think I want to go see my parents next week. They've been on a cruise and I haven't told them about the promotion yet, it would be nice to surprise them." *And get the fuck out of the District for a while.*

"Are you saying I'm going to have to handle the queues by myself for a whole week?" He sighed as he asked the question, but she knew he wasn't upset.

"I'll buy you guys a *really* nice baby shower gift."

"No need. Of course I'll do it. Bribery isn't required," he grinned, "but it is very much appreciated."

"Thanks, Gilligan." She forced a smile, but it felt strange and brittle on her face. Fortunately, he seemed to ignore it.

"Back to work we go! Heigh ho, heigh ho!"

Shaking her head at him, she tried to focus on her work. To block out the bitter taste in her mouth whenever she remembered the last words she'd had with Thomas. He had been so angry, his face empty of any of the charming kindness she'd fallen in love with.

Shit.

There was the pain just behind her ribs again, a twist that made her rub over her sternum in an effort to ease it. Before Thomas Hathaway she'd thought heartbreak was just a phrase, but now she understood the word. It actually felt like her heart was broken, nothing but shrapnel in her chest, but it was too late. Everything had been too late.

Discovering how she felt about him. The call to Antoine where'd he shouted at her for lying to him, for making him wait around for a non-existent story.

She should have come clean when she'd had the chance. That first morning when she'd woken up in his arms, in his bed, and known that he wasn't something she could live without.

Except, now she had to. She'd never get to hear him call her beautiful again. She probably wouldn't hear him say *anything* again unless she watched C-SPAN for the next decade, and that would be exactly what she deserved.

A lonely, empty life.

His cell phone buzzed in his pocket, but Thomas squeezed the button on the side to silence it, keeping his face placid as he tried to pay attention in the meeting.

The rest of the world hadn't stopped just because his had fallen apart.

There was a list of people who wanted time with him, a litany of meetings booking his calendar from eight in the morning to eight at night because of his absence. Alan had even apologized for the back-to-back nature of them, but Thomas didn't even mind. It kept his mind off everything else, off her.

"What do you think, Hathaway? Will we have enough support?" Congressman Bowen was looking at him, and the collection of aides and other representatives turned towards him as well.

"I think we're in a good place, as long as we verify with Richard and get one more of the swing votes."

"Who would you recommend?" Bowen asked, and Thomas wanted to just tell him to do his own damn research. Do his own job. Be as familiar with their peers as he was, but *that* was the only reason Thomas was even in this meeting. His comfort level with the Democrats in Congress. As one of the more junior members, he should have been grateful to even be in the room.

Focus.

He took a slow breath, running through the people in his head until a name appeared. "Charles, from Georgia. I think he was on the edge."

"Not Laura Cohen out of Maine?"

"If you think you can swing both of them, talk to both of them." Thomas sounded as tired as he felt, and the sudden buzz of conversation in the room was more irritating than invigorating. His phone vibrated in his pocket again, and he closed his eyes to try and push back the rush of frustration.

"Thomas – why don't you talk to Charles, and Mary Beth will talk to Laura. Then we can meet again on Monday when we're all back. Does that sound good to everyone?" Bowen looked around the room, and Thomas followed suit with the chorus of agreements. Anything to end the meeting so he could have five minutes to grab some water before the next one.

"Great, see you all then."

It was several hours later when Thomas was finally walking back into his office, and Alan was right there with a notepad in hand. "I ordered you dinner again, it should be here soon. Trisha wanted to talk to you before she left for the day about the brief summary, and Representative Billings' assistant asked me *again* about the golf tournament in the Spring. They need an answer."

"Fine," Thomas agreed as he walked back into his office and Alan followed.

"Perfect, I'll confirm that then. Your mother called, by the way. Asked you to call her back whenever you got a chance." He held out a short stack of post-it notes. "And here are the other messages from today."

"Thank you, Alan." He took the papers from him and settled into his chair, rubbing his hands over his face. "Is there anything else?"

His assistant was standing beside his desk, shifting his weight from foot to foot as he stared. "Did something happen in New York? You haven't been right since −"

"Everything is fine, Alan. When will Trish be in?"

"Probably soon. Friday is a light day with most of the representatives leaving for the weekend, you've got a few meetings in the morning, and nothing in the afternoon."

"Good," Thomas sagged in his seat, not even looking at the stack of work he still had to do. None of which even remotely interested him at the moment.

"Can I do anything for you?" Alan asked, and he knew it was a sincere offer. His assistant, his *friend*, knew him better than most people. He'd joined him just after the successful campaign in New York for his first term, and now they were starting their second.

Summoning a smile for the man, he shook his head. "No, but I appreciate it."

"No dinner reservations?" Alan prompted, a tinge of hope in his voice.

"No. No dinner reservations." Thomas instantly shut down, turning to his laptop like he actually wanted to do work, and Alan took the cue.

"Alright. I'll be leaving after the food gets here."

"Thanks," he answered, and waited for Alan to pull his door closed before he propped his elbows on his desk and pressed the heels of his hands against his eyes. Just as he was trying to empty his head of visions of Maddie, his phone buzzed again and he growled and ripped it from his pocket.

Three texts from Jaxson, and a missed call.

The phone barely rang once before Jaxson answered, "Thomas?"

"Hey, let me guess. More bad news?"

"No, actually. I did confirm she was speaking with an Antoine Cano at The Washington Post, but I made some calls to some friends, and there's no story. Not about Runway, or a sex club in D.C., or anything." Jaxson blew out a breath on the other end of the line. "It seems like she was telling the truth."

"Except for all the lying before that," he retorted, feeling that uncomfortable twist inside whenever he thought about the things they'd done.

"Right." The line was silent for a moment, nothing but dead air, and then Jaxson huffed. "Look, I know she fucked up, but —"

"There's no buts to this, Jaxson. She used me to get into Black Light —"

"For a story she didn't actually do anything with."

"It doesn't matter!" Thomas raised his voice, leaning back in his chair to stare at the ceiling. "I played with her, I had sex with her, and it was all a game. Just a research session to her."

"Have you called her?" Jaxson asked.

"Why would I call her? I have nothing to say." He shook his head, wishing that everyone on his staff had left so he could dig out that bottle of liquor someone had gifted him a month before for Christmas.

"Because you told me last week she was the most interesting girl you'd ever met. That you couldn't stop thinking about —"

"Well, I'm not thinking about her anymore," Thomas lied, and he knew Jaxson didn't believe him. She still popped into his head whenever he had a moment to breathe, only now the memories were tinged with an acidic discomfort.

"My IT guys finished wiping the information off her laptop, and her hard drive. I've got a courier service delivering it tonight. It's all over if you want it to be."

"Good. There's nothing more to be done."

Jaxson sighed heavily, letting out a round of quiet curses on his end of the phone before he spoke again, "You're really going to give up on this?"

"Give up on what? A girl who lied to me about everything she was? Who let me play with her when she was uneducated and had no fucking idea what we were doing?" Thomas laughed bitterly, struggling to keep his voice down so no one outside his door would hear. "I mean, how could she even have consented to what we did? To me tying her up? Using a goddamn cane on her when she didn't have a clue what it even was?"

"You didn't do anything wrong, Thomas."

"It sure as fuck feels like I did, and she broke so many rules I can't even think of them all. She lied to me, *to my face*, so many times…" His voice trailed off as flashes of her flickered through his mind. The sight of her against the cross, on her knees with nipple clamps making her beautiful face contort with pain and panting pleasure. *All lies.* "There's no fixing this, Jaxson. I appreciate you handling this, making sure the article didn't go out, because that would have been the worst outcome – but there's nothing more you can do."

"Okay, listen to me. So, she wasn't into the lifestyle before she found Black Light, before she met you. Did you give her a safe word? Tell her to use it?"

"Of course," Thomas growled.

"And did she ever, even once, accuse you of crossing the line with her?"

"Why would she? I was her fucking meal ticket into Black Light. To *you*. To Chase, and Emma, and every one of the members."

"She didn't send the article, Thomas. I read it. It was done, and she didn't send it in. She's got a journalism degree from Penn State, she's working as a copy editor at a local coupon paper, and she just declined a very lucrative job offer from The Washington Post to join their staff."

For you.

The words hung, unspoken, in the silence on the call, but Thomas couldn't bring himself to feel anything beyond the bitter betrayal that had tainted every moment between them. "There's no fixing what she's done."

"It took a stroke of luck and a leap of faith for me to find my happiness, Thomas, and it wasn't easy. It was messy, and hard, but sometimes that's what it takes."

"I'm happy for you, Jaxson. I've told you that before, and I'm glad you moved to D.C. so we could reconnect, but I don't see a way past this."

"Just tell me one thing, and be honest or I'll come over and call you an asshole to your face in front of all your politician friends." Jaxson's voice had a hint of laughter in it, but it felt serious.

"What?"

"Did you care about her?"

Thomas sighed, remembering soft skin and sweet lips and her perfect voice against his ear. "I did, but it doesn't matter now."

"Alright." His old friend sighed against the phone, and he heard the clink of ice that signaled he was already drinking. "I'm around if you want to talk, or just – I don't know – stare at each other so you're not by yourself."

"Thanks," he answered, but he didn't want to be around Jaxson and all his happiness. He didn't want to be around anyone. After a moment they said their goodbyes and hung up. With the heavy conversation still weighing on him, he tried to bury his mind back in work. Fill in all the cracks with meetings, and briefs to read, and the small part he played in helping the country run.

The first sticky note he picked up was the note asking him to call his mom back, but he knew she would just want to talk about the girl he'd mentioned at his father's birthday lunch – and there was nothing more to say about that. So, instead, he reached for his phone to call Trisha's desk and ask her to come by for their meeting.

Chapter Fifteen

Sunday

*M*addie propped the laundry basket against her hip, and used her free hand to open her door. The phone buzzing in her back pocket at a rhythm that told her it was a phone call, and she pulled it out as soon as she was able to kick the door closed. It was a number she didn't recognize, and so she let it roll to voicemail.

Placing the basket beside the suitcase on her bed, she started to fold clothes, either packing them or putting them on the floor behind her. It was a mindless activity, which felt like all she was good for these days. Cleaning her apartment like she'd suddenly developed OCD, biking endless miles in the building's gym, *anything* to keep her from sitting in silence because that was when she started to think.

Her phone rang again, but this time it said a name: *Chase Cartwright.*

"What the hell?" she dropped the pair of yoga pants in her hand and stared at the screen for a moment. Her stomach twisted, nervous, but she knew he'd just call back if she ignored it. If they wanted to yell at her some more, she might as well take it. Pressing the answer button she spoke softly, "Hello?"

"Hey, Maddie."

"Chase? Why are you in my –"

"I added my number when you gave us your phone, and I was hoping you'd call, but I guess you didn't notice."

"No, I didn't." She'd been avoiding her phone, avoiding everything that brought up memories of Thomas.

"How are you doing?" his voice was warm, sweet, and she knew exactly what he was asking about, but she knew if she even thought about it she'd burst into tears again.

"Fine."

"I thought you were done with lying." It sounded like a playful prod, but it made her angry. Why the fuck was he even calling her?

"I'm hanging up now."

"Wait!" Chase sounded panicked, and so she brought the phone back to her ear.

"What? I'm really busy."

"Jaxson wants to talk to you, but you didn't answer when he called."

"*He* didn't put his number in my phone, and I only answered you because it surprised me. I clearly should have ignored both." The biting anger was in her voice now, but he seemed unfazed.

"Well, will you talk to him for a minute?" Before she could respond, she heard soft words on his end of the line, and the shuffle of the phone changing hands.

"Maddie?" It was Jaxson Davidson, that low voice something she would have recognized anywhere.

"I got the laptop and stuff, if that's what you're calling about, and if you want to yell at me some more just get it over with."

"It's not, but I'm glad you got it back. Actually, there's one more thing we need from you before we can put this all behind us," Jaxson's voice was almost gentle.

"What else could you possibly need?" Maddie asked, defeat taking over the anger in her voice as she sat down on the edge of her bed, shoving the laundry basket further back.

"I need you to come to the club tomorrow night and sign some things. Simple confirmations that you're not going to take any further action with the information you have."

"You have the NDA on file. You reminded me of that."

"Yes, but since that didn't seem to faze you before, the lawyers want a little more assurance from you. How does seven o'clock sound?"

"I'm not going to do anything with what I know. The Post won't even talk to me anymore. What more do you want?" She felt exhausted, and all she wanted was to be back in her parent's house, eating her mom's food, drinking with her dad while they watched some old, film noir detective movie.

"I want you to show up at Black Light tomorrow, at seven PM." Jaxson's tone had shifted, not welcoming any argument.

"Fine. I'll be there. Do you want me to go to the psychic shop, or Runway?" Maddie felt a slim flourish of satisfaction reminding him that she knew about both entrances.

"Runway will be fine I'll be there to open the door for you. Both clubs are closed on Mondays so there won't be a line or anything."

"Guess I'll see you then."

"Good." He hung up before she got the chance to do it first, and she growled at the phone before switching to text her parents, telling them she'd be home on Tuesday instead.

At least then this would all be done, and she could figure out what was next without the purple glow of Black Light haunting her.

∼

Monday Night

Paul was silent in the car as he pulled up in front of Runway just before nine, the neon and lights all turned off, but there was a single security light above the front doors. Thomas sighed as Paul jumped out and walked around to open his car door. "I'll have Jaxson's people give me a ride home when we're done meeting, no need to wait around."

"If you're sure, Mr. Hathaway."

"I am. Have a good night, Paul." Thomas shut the car himself, and then walked towards the doors. He pulled out his phone, ready to call Jaxson, but his friend was standing there when he raised his head again. "Hey."

"Hey," Jaxson answered. "Ready to talk?"

"I told you it wasn't necessary, I'm fine." Following him into the interior of the club, it looked strangely naked when it wasn't packed with people and covered in colorful lights and lasers.

"Look, you're my friend, right?" Jaxson asked as they mean-

210

dered towards the back hall and through the curtain into backstage.

What the fuck was he doing?

"Yes," Thomas nodded and waited in the club's supply closet for him to open the door. "We're going to Black Light to talk? Why don't we just go to your office?"

"It's the best place for this conversation." Jaxson headed down the steps to the security room as he followed. "Anyway, I'm done doing this dance, so I'm just going to lay it out for you. I know you care for Maddie —"

He tried to interrupt, but Jaxson didn't even give him the chance.

"And I know this situation was a nightmare. For you, for me... and for her. But you're my friend, and I'm not just going to ignore something when I think you have a chance to be happy." Jaxson stood in the strange pale, purple light of the locker room, facing off with him. "You're miserable, and so is she."

"She doesn't have any right to feel miserable! This is all her fault!" Thomas snapped, irritated at having to follow Jaxson around like a puppy as he threaded his way downstairs.

"But she does. Do you know what happened when Chase and I went to talk to her?" He barely paused. "She handed over everything. Her notes, her laptop, even her *phone*, and she started crying. Fucking sobbing so hard she couldn't breathe. She kept telling us that none of it mattered, because *you* didn't care — but here's the thing, Thomas, I think you do care. I think you care a lot."

"No, she's right. It doesn't matter, because she lied to me. She's not a submissive, she's not honest, and she used me to try and take down *your* club. Why are you even defending her?" Thomas pushed a hand through his hair, contemplating walking back out the way he'd come. "Is this what you brought me here for? To rehash this bullshit?"

"You're wrong."

"What?" he growled.

"Maddie *is* a submissive."

"You don't know what you're talking about." Thomas felt his anger pulsing again, his temper ready to snap, because the worst part of everything he'd been stuck remembering for the last week had been the memories of how she'd responded to him. It had felt *so real*, but it had all been fiction. A clever ruse by a very smart, very beautiful girl.

Jaxson reached over the desk Danny usually sat at, and then the door to Black Light opened. "I need you to listen to me, Thomas. You got into the lifestyle before me, and we didn't talk for a while, but since we've reconnected there's always been one thing you've told me: it's our job as Dominants to take care of our submissives. To take care of them, to teach them, to guide them – and to forgive them when they mess up."

"This isn't some little mistake, Jaxson." His voice was a whisper, but the younger man stepped close, and they were almost eye to eye, his friend just a little taller.

"Shit happens, Thomas. Life is messy. The question here is whether you're going to let a mistake, big or small, affect the rest of your life…" Jaxson took a slow breath, and tilted his head towards the door. "*Or* if you're going to really look at what's in front of you."

Thomas' heart was pounding behind his ribs, a nervous tension making his shoulders tight. "What did you do, Jaxson?"

"I haven't done anything, I've just laid out the options. For you… and for her." He turned away and pushed open the door into the club, which was eerily silent. Empty.

For her?

Thomas walked forward in a daze, pulling the door shut behind him as he watched Jaxson head onto the main floor, stopping in front of one of the raised, circular stages. There was a wooden whipping post erected in the center of it. "What is this?" Thomas whispered, and Jaxson pulled him towards a pair of leather chairs that had been moved to face the stage.

"Sit down, watch, and *listen*." The authoritative tone in Jaxson's voice made him want to argue, but then he saw Spencer, the club's Dungeon Master, walk out from one of the locker rooms. The man's normal suit jacket was got, the sleeves of his button down rolled up. *What was going on?* He blamed his shock for how he let Jaxson push him down into the seat.

Spencer paused beside a couch, leaning down to rip a girl in a gray shirt and black yoga pants upright, fiery red strands in his fingers as she gasped. *Maddie?* "Come on, girl."

It was her.

He saw her face the second Spencer turned her around to push her towards the raised platform, and Thomas immediately tried to stand up – but Jaxson's hand on his shoulder forced him back into his seat. "Listen," his friend whispered.

"Up," Spencer ordered, and she walked barefoot up the steps to the stage. Part of him wanted to call out to her, but he pushed it down, reminding himself that whoever this was – she wasn't his.

So why the fuck was Jaxson making him watch?

"Before we begin, tell me why you're here." Spencer walked the floor around the stage. "Speak, girl."

"To be punished," she whispered, and it was only the relative silence of the room that made her audible.

"Excuse me?"

"To be punished, sir," Maddie spoke louder, but her eyes stayed down at her hands, fingers twisting together.

"Good. Strip down to underwear." The command was given as Spencer walked away to the wall of toys and implements, but Thomas' eyes couldn't leave her, his muscles bunching as he almost got up again.

"Stay down, and listen, Thomas," Jaxson urged him, and he tried, but as she started to pull the shirt over her head he wanted to cover her up. Stand between her and everyone else.

She's not yours. She's not yours.

Her eyes found his for just a moment as she finished taking off her pants, but she pulled her gaze away before he could react. Then Spencer was returning with several things in his hands. "Face the post," the man snapped and Maddie turned away from Thomas to obey.

"Yes, sir," she spoke softly, and he hated hearing her say that to anyone else. Even someone like Spencer, who was clearly only acting in his role at the club at Jaxson's request.

The cuffs were on her wrists too quickly, and the other man hooked her to the post, her heels lifted off the floor, leaving her stretched out and taut against the wood. A beautiful expanse of pale skin, where the last lingering marks of their play showed as mere shadows on one cheek of her round backside beneath the edges of her thong.

"Your safe word is red." The Dungeon Master spoke, but she didn't answer, and he spanked her hard. "Acknowledge."

"Yes, sir," Maddie droned, lifelessly. "My safe word is red."

She's not going to use it.

Thomas knew it instantly, but Jaxson's grip on his shoulder tightened to the point of pain, forcing him to stay seated. Spencer leaned down and picked up a long flogger made of a thick, oiled leather. "You told me you're here to be punished. Why?"

The man stepped back, shaking out the flogger, and Thomas tensed. "Because I lied," Maddie spoke the words evenly, but she gasped as Spencer brought the leather across her shoulders in a hard swing, the lines appearing fast.

"What did you lie about?" he asked, and struck her with the flogger again, mid-back.

"I said I was invited to Black Light!" she cried out, whimpering as the leather landed the other direction across her shoulders again. Bright, pink skin already.

"Why did you sneak into my club?" Spencer asked, and Jaxson made a noise behind him just as the leather struck again, turning her upper back into a network of lines from the many falls. Maddie was barely letting out a noise with each strike, but in his experience that kind of oiled leather could sting and thud enough to send other subs into tears.

"I was going to write an article about it." The strike that followed was harder, the crack of the leather loud, and Maddie whined, her fists balling up on the other side of the cuffs. "I did – I *did* write an article."

"That's right, you did," Spencer replied, and delivered a series of hard strikes of the vicious flogger across her ass and thighs. Maddie jerked with each of them, bouncing on her toes at times as she pressed forward against the post, but there was no begging, no pleading, no screaming. Just a stifled whine, or a shortened gasp.

"She's not going to stop him," Thomas hissed, twisting to look up at Jaxson, but his friend's face was expressionless. Neutral. As if he were the one delivering the punishment to the girl.

Looking down at him Jaxson nodded, "I know."

"She's not a sub, Jaxson. You can't make her do this." He felt defensive, angry, but his friend simply lifted an eyebrow.

"*I* didn't make her do anything. I talked to her, I asked her what she wanted, and I gave her an option for how she *might* get it." The man sighed. "And, despite what you think, Thomas, she *is* a sub."

The loud pop of leather striking skin was echoed by a quiet cry, and Thomas glanced back at Maddie's red, striped skin before he turned to Jaxson again. "What do you mean? What does she want?"

"Forgiveness," Jaxson answered quietly. "And I told her a way that submissives can *try* to earn forgiveness, but she chose this. So, will you stay seated? Listen to her confession?"

"Why did you do this?" he asked as his friend released him and moved to the chair right next to his.

"Because you both need it." Jaxson tilted his head back towards the platform, where another strike had just landed on her thighs, leaving glowing marks behind. "Watch. Listen to her – and think about what *you* want."

"Why else are you here to be punished, girl?" Spencer dropped the heavy flogger to the platform, picking up a quirt. The split ends were angled to a point, and he could tell just by the look of it how much it would hurt her.

Maddie lifted her head, shaking her hair out over her shoulders as she looked up at the ceiling. "Because I deserve it."

The first lash across her ass made her jerk, a quiet cry leaving her lips, but then Spencer shook his head as he paced behind her. "I know you deserve it. Confess."

Another strike, harder, and she screamed, "Thomas!"

He almost answered her call, but Jaxson reached over and grabbed onto his arm as she continued with tears in her voice.

"He tried to help me, he brought me in here because he believed me. He was... he was good to me, *too* good. He was perfect, and I – I used him. I did this." Maddie didn't even try and hold back her sobs this time as Spencer delivered the lashes in even, measured strokes. Adjusting to even out each side as he moved from her ass to her thighs, leaving dark red spots that promised bruises. She was pulling at the cuffs, squirming up on her toes, but she didn't even beg. Didn't ask him to stop.

"What else?" Spencer asked, the quirt dangling from his hand like a hungry thing.

"I ruined everything. I was selfish. I lied, and I lied..." she sobbed, her body shaking and he was up out of the chair before Jaxson could stop him. The next lash landed, and he wanted to rip the quirt from Spencer's hand.

"Spencer!" Thomas shouted, and the man turned to look at him. Calm, and cold. "Stop. I'll take over."

"We don't allow punishing while angry in this club. If you have something to add to her list, speak up, but you stay seated."

"I will handle the rest," he growled.

"Not in my club, boy."

Maddie was sniffling, her forehead pressed against the wood of the post as she caught her breath, and he found himself speaking before he could question it, "She's *my* sub. I have it."

"Absolutely not." The Dungeon Master was staring him down,

but he'd already made the decision and he wasn't going to back off.

"Let him, Spencer. You can watch with me. If he goes too far, we'll stop him." Jaxson's words should have felt helpful, but instead he wanted to punch him for questioning his self-control – which wasn't the most level-headed response.

Maybe it was a good idea they were here.

Thomas walked to the wall and pulled out a thin, whippy cane from a rack. Something that would hurt far more than it would mark, since Spencer had left her with so many already. As he stalked up the steps, he found himself face-to-face with Maddie for a moment. Cheeks flushed, blue eyes bright with tears, but she stilled her breathing as she met his gaze.

"You lied to me about being a sub." He accused as he walked around her on the platform, swishing the thing through the air.

"I never said I was, I just let you believe it." Maddie's voice was harder, and it spiked his temper. The swat with the cane across her ass made her yelp through clenched teeth.

"Lying by omission is still lying, *that* is clearly still a lesson you need to learn." Adjusting the cane in his hands he prowled to her other side. "Did you know about me?"

She shook her head, fiery hair flaring. "No. You just showed up after I found my way downstairs, and security stopped me, but then you –" Maddie's breath was shaky, a groan filling in the pause. "But then *I* flirted with you, I wanted inside. I wanted to see."

"So, it was an accident, I was just convenient." He heard the angry hiss of his voice, but he purposefully kept the cane still at his side.

"I didn't even know what was downstairs. I didn't know you

would be there, I had no idea about any of it, about how much I'd like it —"

He landed the cane across her ass and she screamed, twisting in the cuffs. "Don't lie to me!"

"I'm not lying!" Maddie bounced on her toes, her legs shivering, the high cut black underwear framing the marks on her ass.

"You liked this?" Thomas asked and delivered another strike, and another, and another, and then he saw Jaxson and Spencer stand up in his peripheral vision and he stopped. Breathing hard, finally able to hear the desperate whines coming from her as she pressed her hips forward to the post trying to avoid the next blow.

"Yes," she choked out. "I don't know why, I don't understand it, but *yes*. You called it subspace!"

"She's a masochist, Thomas," Jaxson interjected, moving to the edge of the stage.

"I know!" Thomas roared, and he threw the cane down to the floor, off the platform so he couldn't reach it. His mind was spinning too fast, a flurry of emotions making it impossible to think straight. "God dammit, I know!"

"Why don't you let us take her down now?" Jaxson offered, but Thomas ignored him.

"I want to hear the truth!" He moved until he could see her face, tear-streaked and red. "Was any of it real?"

"*Everything* was real with you. All of it," she spoke softly, just for him, but the pain was back in his chest. Doubting, questioning.

"I don't believe you." Thomas turned towards the steps, unwilling to let her hurt him again, and then she shouted after him.

"Then punish me until you do! Do whatever you want! Just please, *please* forgive me!" Maddie's voice broke at the end, torn by her sobs, and it stopped him halfway down the steps.

He turned to face her, but her eyes were closed, tears tracing paths down her cheeks, strands of her red hair stuck to them. "That is a very stupid request, Madeline."

She opened her eyes as he came back, stepping close to her. "I don't care."

"You're not scared?" Thomas asked.

"I trust you." Her words were surprisingly steady, and the flash-back to their time in this very club, in front of the cross inside the dungeon room, overwhelmed him.

The fire inside his hazel eyes was something she couldn't look away from, because it was so perfect, and because part of her was worried it would be the last time she'd see it. For a moment she'd wondered if he'd really leave her there, if all of the discussions with Jaxson, and Chase, and Spencer had been for nothing – but then she heard the jingle of his belt as he undid it, followed by the whisper of him pulling it free.

"You had so many chances to tell me the truth," he growled as he stepped behind her, but she settled against the post, ignoring the ache in her legs, her ass, her back.

"I know, sir," Maddie nodded, and he landed the belt hard, overlaying the other marks peppered across her backside, and then he did it again, but she bit down on the cries of pain.

"You pretended to be someone you weren't, whether you said it aloud or not."

"Yes, sir, I know," she agreed, and the confession made the bite of the belt easier to take, even though she couldn't hold back the cry as he landed swat after swat after swat down her ass and thighs.

"Thomas!" Jaxson yelled, a note of panic in his voice, but she needed this. Everything was getting out in the open, every dark thing she'd hidden exposed to the light, and he'd told her this was her only chance. There would be no second meeting with Thomas Hathaway. Heavy footsteps came around the platform, muttered curses accompanying them, before Jaxson growled, "That's it. Back off. Now."

"NO!" she shouted at him as he got to the bottom of the steps, and he paused, his face questioning as she forced her breathing to even out, trying to stop the tears. "Don't. I want this. *Please...* I'm okay, I swear."

"Ask me for another, Maddie," Thomas growled behind her, and she nodded.

"May I have another, sir?" Just as she asked, he delivered. Stroke after stroke until the pain blurred, and she found herself leaning hard against the wood, bracing her forehead to it so she could alternate which foot held her aloft. So much guilt, so much pain and loneliness in the last few days, and she'd already seen her future stretched out before her without Thomas in it – and she didn't want that. She wanted him more than she'd ever wanted anything. A particularly sharp strike made her scream, and then she shouted the words she'd never said, but always should have, "I love you! I'm yours. I'll always be yours..." She sobbed, her mind humming in some glorious place between pain and pleasure.

"What?" He moved to her side to pull her head back by her hair so he could meet her eyes, the hard grip sending a sparkling rush down her spine.

"I love you," she repeated.

Thomas' eyes flickered over her face, a pained look pinching his brows together, and then he kissed her hard. It was forceful, leaving her lips feeling bruised before he parted them to delve his tongue inside and claim her mouth completely. She arched against the post, wishing her hands were free to touch him, but the low hum of his moan was perfect just before he pulled back and leaned his forehead against hers. "Dammit, beautiful…"

"I'm so sorry," she whispered. So grateful to feel his skin on hers that the tears started again, but in a moment he was unclasping her arms from the post, catching her around the waist when her legs decided they were no longer interested in keeping her upright.

"I need you," he groaned as he pushed her back to the post, pain flashing somewhere underneath the haze in her mind.

"Yes, sir. Please." Maddie's world spun as he picked her up and tossed her over his shoulder, stomping down the steps to move towards a wall of curtains. She caught sight of Jaxson and Spencer, both standing with their arms crossed, as he walked them away.

Thomas didn't put her down until they were inside the curtain, tossing her onto a narrow bed, waking up the vicious network of welts, but it didn't matter when he immediately covered her body with his. Their lips clashed again and she moaned against him as they shifted backwards on the bed. "Maddie…" he whispered, sliding his hand between her thighs, beneath her underwear, to stroke at her wetness.

"Fuck," she hissed, lifting her hips into his touch as he slid two fingers inside her, and then a third, making her whimper as he dragged her back to that fine line between pain and pleasure that was so blurry it may as well have not existed. "I've missed you so much."

"Swear to me you'll never lie to me again." Thomas nipped her lips after he said it, kissing her, and she had to turn away from him to answer.

"I swear. I will never lie to you, sir." Another thrust of his fingers, stroking at that spot inside her that was pushing her towards delirium. "Please fuck me, *please...*"

Sitting up he pulled his touch from her and ripped her underwear down her legs, the welts across her backside a second thought as he shoved her back to the bed, pinning her down so he could spread her legs with his knees. Thomas traced her collar bone with his mouth as he worked at his pants, and then he growled and sat up suddenly. "Dammit!"

"What?"

"Nothing," he snapped. Climbing off the bed he ripped his shirt off before he grabbed a condom from a bowl on the small table near the curtain. Thomas kicked off his pants and shoes and climbed back onto the bed with her. He looked as desperate as she felt as he tore the package open, and she sat up to wrap her hand around the steel of his cock, nudging his boxers out of the way. The low, barely contained groan he released was music to her ears, and she quickly shifted until she could lean forward and take him into her mouth. The taste of him was everything she'd craved, and as his fingers threaded into her hair, sliding his cock deeper, she moaned. He brushed her throat, and then pulled free of her lips. "No, I need you under me."

"Yes, sir." Maddie nodded as he moved them, forcing her back to the sheet, the condom rolling on just before he pushed her knees wide.

"For the record, I've missed you too, beautiful," he spoke right by her ear, just before he plunged deep. Her body arched against his, and she felt complete as he bottomed out, making her ache in the best of ways.

"I'm yours," she whispered, and then he bit down at the place where her neck met her shoulder, holding her still so his hips could swing to deliver each hard thrust. Nails dragging down his back, she tried to fight back the orgasm, wanting to ride the delirious wave as long as she could, but soon the edge was too close, each shift of him inside her too perfect – and she came. Sparks exploded behind her eyes as she gasped out his name and held on to him, while he thrust again and again.

"Maddie," he groaned, and then he came, his cock kicking deep inside her, and she wrapped her legs around his hips holding him to her. His breaths pistoned against her ear, their hearts racing. "Maddie, Maddie, Maddie…"

His voice brought tears back to her eyes, and she buried her face against his shoulder, trying to stifle it, but she was too grateful, too happy. "I'm so sorry, sir. I'm so sorry."

"Forgiven, beautiful. I promise, I forgive you." Thomas lifted up to kiss her, and the sweetness of it mended something inside her as their tongues brushed, a soft moan rising up to meet them as they held onto one another.

"Really?" she whispered when he slid from her, moving to her side so he could look down at her.

Thomas brushed her hair from her forehead, cupping her cheek. "Yes, but not just because you took the punishment."

"Then why?" she asked, looking between his eyes, a shade of forest tinted gold.

"Because I love you, too." He smiled when she felt her face light up, all of that warmth and post-orgasmic joy overflowing until she hugged him, rolling until she was on top of him.

"Are you sure?"

"I am." His thumb plucked her bottom lip from between her

teeth. "This past week has been the worst week of my life, and it was all because you weren't there. I couldn't text you, call you, or see you when I got home. It was empty, and dark, and I hated every minute of it."

"I am so sorry, Thomas." Maddie felt the tears coming on again, but as she sat up on his hips he reached up to cup her face.

"I love you, Madeline O'Neill, and what hurt the most was thinking you'd never felt anything for me. That I was just so blinded by how I felt for you that I'd ignored every signal." He shook his head, sighing as he stared into her eyes. "Seeing you tonight, I realized what an idiot I actually was, because I didn't see what Jaxson knew the first time meeting you."

"What?" she asked, her heart racing so hard she thought she might faint.

"That you have always been submissive, that our moments together were real, and that you're mine." His thumb brushed across her cheek. "I'm sorry I didn't listen to you when you tried to tell me."

"No, *no*, this was my fault. I was horrible, I was —"

"Forgiven, beautiful. I just hope you can forgive me for putting us through the past week. I promise I'll listen in the future, okay?" That election-winning smile crossed his lips as he sat up, face to face with her since she was propped on his lap.

"I will *never* do anything like this again."

Thomas chuckled a little. "I would hope not. If you didn't learn a lesson after *that* punishment, I think you might be beyond all help."

At the mention of it, she realized just how sore she was, the pounding ache in her back, and ass, and thighs. Even her shoulders were throbbing. "I got the message, sir."

"Good," he spoke softly and then kissed her. It was gentle, and she knew she was lucky to even be near him again. "I love you, Maddie."

Tears threatened, but she was able to hold them back. "I love you too, and I'm yours, Thomas, always."

"And I'm so glad that you are." He was about to kiss her again when someone cleared their throat outside the curtain.

"Are you two safe to leave alone? Because I have Chase and Emma to get home to, and Spencer probably wants to go sharpen his knives, or oil something." Jaxson's voice made her blush furiously, and she dropped to the far side of Thomas, covering her face.

"Give us five minutes and we'll be dressed. I want her back home."

"Fine, but be quick. Listening to you two fuck has me very ready to be home too."

"We're going to your house?" she asked, fighting the furious blush as she realized they had heard them loud and clear. Thomas turned back towards her, warm brown hair falling over his forehead as he leaned down to kiss her.

"If you'll let me bring you there, yes, but I have to warn you, I might never want you to leave."

"That sounds great." Grinning, she laughed when he picked her up and planted her on the floor beside the bed, lifting her underwear from the floor.

"Then get dressed, Madeline O'Neill, because I have plans for when we get home."

Epilogue

One Week Later

"No one will miss us if we just skip work," Maddie whispered just before her lips collided with his again, and Thomas couldn't help but groan.

So. Damn. Tempting.

Sometimes it really, really sucked being a responsible adult with a job and people waiting on you. Sliding his hand into her hair, he tightened his fist and bent her neck back, watching as she panted, her pupils dilating, perfectly pink lips swollen from their kisses. Her eyes were on his, and he made sure she was focused before he shook his head slowly. "Tsk tsk, beautiful. We played hookie for almost an entire week, and *you* just got a promotion at a job that expects you to actually be there. Plus…" He squeezed her thigh, pushing her knees apart just enough to have her whining quietly. "I have to go sit in meetings all day, thinking of what I'm going to do to you when I get home tonight."

"What are you planning?" Her voice had that dreamy quality that she always seemed to develop whenever she was sliding into full submissive mode – and unfortunately, now was not the time for that.

"You don't want me to spoil the surprise, do you?" Thomas grinned and leaned in to place one last chaste kiss to her mouth before she could start chewing on her bottom lip. Then, as difficult as it was, he released her and pulled back to his side of the car.

"Thomas." She groaned, pushing both of her hands into her hair to drop back against her seat. "You torture me."

"You like it."

"That is *not* the point." There was steel in her voice, but she was smiling at him, the flush in her cheeks making her hair look even more fiery in the morning sun streaming through the window.

To think I almost lost her.

He had to swallow before his thoughts turned dark, but she reached out and took his hand like she could sense it in him anyway. "We're almost to your office, beautiful. Better straighten out your clothes or everyone will know what you were up to this morning."

Rolling her eyes she adjusted her top, running her hands through her hair before wiping at her lips. "Well, how do I look?"

"Positively fuckable." He laughed when she gawked at him, enjoying that even after spending almost every day together since her punishment at Black Light – he could still shock her.

"I am never going to be able to concentrate today."

"Yes, you are, because you are smart, and dedicated, and the hottest Senior Copy Editor on the East Coast."

"Only the East Coast?" She grinned at him, that flirty tone becoming a challenge his cock twitched in his trousers to answer.

"I haven't been to the West Coast in a while." Thomas caught her hand when she went to smack his arm, smiling slowly as he tightened his grip until he heard the tempo of her breathing pick up.

So fucking irresistible.

"You're terrible," she whined.

"But you love me."

"I do." The bright smile transformed her face into something beyond beautiful. Angelic. Pure perfection that hid underneath the surface the naughty little submissive he'd had the chance to belt until she'd screamed his name the night before.

Interlacing their fingers again he knew they were getting close to her office, and her eyes wandered out the window as she recognized the buildings as well. Thomas could actually see the moment her mind switched into work mode, her thoughts whirring to life, back into gear for the day ahead. "I'm going to miss you today, too, but we'll be back home soon."

"I know."

"You're thinking about this weekend again, aren't you?" he asked, but he didn't actually *need* to ask, it was written all over her face as she crinkled her nose and sucked her bottom lip between her teeth.

"No," she lied.

"I'm going to spank you for that tonight." He grinned when she turned to stare at him, irritated. "Listen, it's going to be fine. Everyone will adore you, and then we'll be back and we can plan what we'll do for Valentine's Day."

That made Maddie smile again. "Maybe we could go to Black Light?"

"Jaxson *is* planning a special club event that night, but I wanted to do something just for us." He brought her hand to his lips, kissing her fingers. "Doesn't that sound better?"

"As long as I'm with you it sounds perfect." Leaning towards him, their lips met again, and he couldn't resist tasting her one more time. The softest sigh left her as she turned her head so that he could take over, and he took the invitation like he always did.

"We're here, Ms. O'Neill," Paul spoke up with the most perfectly calm tone, one of the reasons he valued the man so much. Discretion, professionalism, and – most importantly – he trusted him with Maddie.

"When will you be home?" she asked as she sat back, bright blue eyes looking up at him.

"As soon as I can, but you need to hop out of the car or we're both going to be late." Thomas nudged her, and she grabbed her coat as Paul opened her door.

She stepped outside, pushing her arms through the sleeves so she could wrap the coat around her to block out the cold, and then she dipped her head back into the car, "I love you."

He probably looked like a lovesick fool when he smiled back at her, but he didn't care a bit – because he absolutely was. "I love you too, beautiful. Now, go!"

"Yeah, yeah," she called over her shoulder as she hurried to the entrance. Paul shut the door and was back in the driver's seat in a matter of moments. The car immediately started forward again, and as Thomas checked his watch he was *sure* he was about to get the third degree from Alan for cutting it close to his first meeting of the day.

"Any chance we can speed a little?" Thomas asked, half-joking, but when he caught Paul's eyes in the rear-view mirror he saw that the man was smiling. "What?"

"Nothing, Mr. Hathaway."

"Oh, come on. Out with it." He waited until the man caught his eyes in the mirror again.

"I'm just glad you have Ms. O'Neill. You're different with her, in a good way." Paul shrugged as he turned down the street that would take them to the congressional offices, weaving between other cars as he ignored the speed limit. "I don't mean anything by it, just an observation."

Thomas was amused, smiling to himself in the back seat. "Is that all?"

"Well, to be honest, as high-strung as you were before her, I would have bet money on you having a heart attack before you hit forty – and then I'd be out of a job." Paul gave a real smile in the mirror, and chuckled.

"I think that's the first time I've ever heard you laugh, Paul."

"There's another thing Maddie has been right about, Mr. Hathaway."

"What's that?" Thomas asked, raising an eyebrow.

"You really aren't very funny." The man had a stoic expression for just a moment, and then they both started laughing. Loud, and freeing, and warm.

"Cutting it close, Ginger?" Jamar asked, as she slid into her desk barely two minutes before her official start time.

"Fuck off, Gilligan." She flipped him off, but he just laughed and turned back to his computer, with the grainy, blobby ultrasound taped to the side of his screen.

Maddie logged into her computer, and waited for the thing to slowly wake up and start loading her emails. Just as the first ones started to appear, filling her inbox with her editing queue for the day, Brad popped up over the cube wall to her left. "Hey!"

She jumped, and then laughed as she looked up at him. "Hey, Charlie."

"Did you get the chance to watch Black Mirror?"

"Oh, yeah, I watched a couple of episodes. It's weird, but kind of in a good way?"

"I know!" He had so much energy to his voice, and she was still astounded that the guy was even speaking to her at all, because in the year and a half before the infamous day of her promotion he'd been so damn silent. "There's this awesome episode in season three, I won't spoil it for you, but my friends and I talked about it for a week straight. It just – *boom* – blew our minds."

Maddie grinned at him. "You know, I think we're going to have to give you a new nickname."

"Why?" His face fell, and she rolled her eyes.

"Because Charlie Chaplin was a silent film star, and *you* aren't silent anymore."

"Oh." Brad shrugged. "I just didn't think anyone wanted to talk to me, and I kind of zone out when I'm working on the graphics. I kind of like the Charlie Chaplin thing though, I made him my background. See?"

Standing up, she peeked over the wall to see the infamous actor emblazoned on the screen with his trademark mustache and bowler hat – and next to him was a quote: *A day without laughter is a day wasted.*

How true.

"Alright, Charlie. We'll stick with that in memory of the days when you used to be quiet. It'll confuse the hell out of any new hires." She couldn't help but grin when he bounced back to his feet.

"Sweet, that's what I was hoping. Everyone knows me by that nickname now anyway!" He shrugged, suddenly a little reserved again. "And, you know, people actually *talk* to me now."

The comment made Maddie sad for a moment. She'd really been a bitch at work. "Gilligan and I were going to order subs from the shop down the street, would you want one for lunch today?"

"Uh, yeah, definitely."

"Great, I'll email you the link to their menu. We usually eat around twelve, or twelve-thirty, does that work for you?" she asked, but based on the barely contained joy in his expression, he was excited.

"That works great! And I'll buy this time, my treat."

"You don't have to −"

"No! I've got it, really." He smiled and sat down in his chair. "Anyway, I know you need to work, I just wanted to ask you about the show."

"Remind me at lunch to ask you about the episode with the grain recording device people implant in them."

"I love that episode!"

"It was pretty cool. Alright, talk to you later, Charlie?" She waved over the cube wall, moving to sit back down.

"Later, Ginger!" Brad called back, and she shook her head. *The things you learned about people when you took the time to talk to them.*

Maddie blew out a breath and started to sort the emails, flagging her to-do list items so she'd have a snapshot of her day before she went to get coffee. It took a few minutes, but she was pleasantly surprised to see that the workload wasn't as insane as it had been the day before. Everyone had been in crisis mode on Monday, but it seemed like Tuesday was going to be smooth sailing – and full of cheesy, greasy goodness at lunch.

Grabbing her Penn State mug she wandered back to the break room to rinse her cup, before pouring the powdered creamer and sugar into the bottom. The Keurig had just started to make coffee when Jamar walked in with his mug. "Hogging the machine already?"

"Jerk." She threw a Splenda packet at him, and he scooped down to pick it up.

"Thanks, I needed one of those." Jamar palmed it and then smiled at her. "So, you ready to meet the parents this weekend?"

Just the mention of it sent Maddie's stomach into knots. "Ugh, please don't remind me, I want to enjoy my coffee."

"Come on, it wasn't so bad when he met your parents."

"Correction – it was a nightmare. Having them show up here in D.C. because I didn't come home when I told them I was going to, was *not* the best introduction." She groaned under her breath as she pulled her coffee cup from the machine and started to stir the mixture together.

"You said they loved him."

"Of course they loved him! He's fucking charming, it's what got him elected!"

Jamar made a face as he stepped up and propped his mug under the spout to start his own cup. "I still can't believe you're with a politician. There's a reason people think they're slimy."

"This coming from the guy married to a bloodsucking lawyer?" Maddie asked, dropping an ice cube into her coffee so she could bring it back from the brink of boiling.

"Hey now, that bloodsucking lawyer is carrying my beautiful child inside her." He grinned at her as he put the single packet of Splenda into his coffee, stirred it for half a second, and then took a long sip just to torment her.

"You're going to have no sensation left to your tongue if you keep drinking coffee that hot."

"Nina never complains," he replied calmly and she almost choked before she was able to swallow enough to laugh out loud.

"Gilligan, that is *so* wrong."

"You don't get to play the blushing game with me anymore. Not when you come in here with sex hair pretty much every damn day."

Maddie lowered her voice to a hiss, "I do *not* have sex hair every day."

"Yes, you do."

"No, I do not!" She huffed, taking another drink of her coffee, because she needed way more caffeine before she was able to deal with Jamar.

"Listen, slimy politician or not, I'm glad you've got him. You're happy, that's obvious, and his parents *are* going to love you."

"We'll see." Maddie shrugged, still so nervous anytime she thought about meeting former Senator Hathaway and his still stunning wife, along with Thomas' older brother and his wife and two girls. An entire family, from an entirely different walk of life than hers, who lived on a veritable estate in upstate New

York. "I'm about ninety-percent sure I'm going to say fuck within the first fifteen minutes of meeting them."

This time it was Jamar who almost choked on his coffee. "Yeah, you might want to avoid that."

"I always do something stupid when I'm nervous like that. Did Brenda ever tell you about how I knocked over my cup of water in my interview with her?"

"Leslie Knope would never speak ill of anyone on her staff," he answered, but then he grinned. "I did have to bring her paper towels though."

Maddie groaned. "See? I'm going to do something ridiculous like that, and they're going to question why on earth he's slumming it with someone like me."

"Ginger?" Jamar said her nickname in a quiet way, and she forced herself to look at him. "They would be lucky to have you in their lives, if that's where this thing ends up, but I can tell you one thing for sure… A man like Thomas Hathaway wouldn't be bringing you within fifty miles of his parents if he didn't have plans on keeping you around, and I mean keeping you around in the *gonna-put-a-ring-on-it* kind of way."

Oh.

She swallowed slowly, suddenly feeling a little dizzy, and weirdly excited at the same time. "We've known each other a month."

With a big grin, he simply shrugged. "When you know someone's the one, time doesn't really matter so much. I knew I loved Nina on our first date, and the look you've had on your face lately tells me that *you* already know."

"This isn't a fairy tale, Jamar. We didn't exactly have the most perfect start to everything." The memories of the dark week when she'd been without him haunted her. That horrible series of days when her lies had been uncovered and nothing seemed to matter anymore because Thomas wasn't there.

"All the greatest love stories start off messy. It's the fact that real love can overcome anything, can carry you through anything, can forgive anything that makes it great."

Maddie couldn't help but smile at him. "Since when did you become a romantic?"

"I've always been a romantic, you've just been cynical." He winked at her, and snagged her left hand from where it hung at her side. "I wouldn't be surprised if he's already got a ring."

"Don't be stupid," she said as she snatched her hand back, but as Jamar laughed and walked back towards his desk she stared at the empty ring finger on her left, and she realized Thomas had kissed that very place in the car that morning. "No way..."

Lifting her eyes, she saw Jamar laughing with someone as he sat down at his desk. He pointed at the little grainy photo with pride, and for an instant she imagined a little boy with Thomas' brown hair running through the halls of the Georgetown house. A red-headed little girl propped on the counter in the kitchen as Thomas tried, and failed, to flip pancakes.

Shaking her head, she tried to brush the visions from her mind, but as she walked back into the office she knew one thing for sure. If Thomas Hathaway asked her to be his, she'd answer like she always did:

I'm yours. Always.

THE END

End Notes

I hope you loved this new story in the world of Black Light. Before you go, it would mean the world to me that if you liked this book that you take a few minutes to write a review and capture how you're feeling right now so other readers can find my work! Reviews are truly one of the most effective ways to help authors out, and I would be very grateful.

Again, thank you for reading and if you enjoyed this one I hope you'll check out one of my other books. They're all listed on the last pages, but *first* I have a delicious sneak peek of the upcoming 'Black Light: Valentine Roulette' anthology which will come out in early February 2017! Eight of your favorite authors, eight very kinky stories, and you're about to see the opening chapter that describes how it all comes about. Not to mention, a special scene with Jaxson, Chase, and Emma from Livia Grant!

Enjoy, lovelies!

SNEAK PEEK

The incredibly hot anthology 'Black Light: Valentine Roulette' will be here soon! Don't skip this sneak peek!

Three hours. Four hard limits. Eight sexy stories.

Early January, Runway Club Offices

"All right. We've been at this for two hours and need to wrap things up." Jaxson Davidson tried his hardest to wrangle the vocal group of managers gathered around the conference table into some semblance of order. He'd purposefully hired strong leaders when he'd opened Runway a month ago, because after spending most of his adult life in front of cameras, he knew he didn't know enough about the dance club and bar industry, even with Chase and Emma at his side.

The good news was that his new business was off to an overwhelming success.

The bad news was that having all of these strong personalities in the same space was not working as the well-oiled machine he'd hoped for, *yet*, which meant he was staying more involved in the day to day decisions than he'd planned.

"I'm sorry, but we still haven't nailed down the Valentine's Day ideas and since we're only five weeks out, we need to finish those plans, even if it takes another two hours." Maxine Torres, Runway's general manager, was the antithesis of Jaxson's style, but although he wanted to strangle her most of the time, he was grateful he'd hired her. He and Chase might pony up the bankroll and name recognition for the club, but he knew Maxine was the reason it was a runaway success. She was a damn fine bar manager.

"Fine. What's still outstanding?" He impatiently tried to push her along.

Maxine clicked away on the tablet she carried with her everywhere.

"We still need to decide on door prizes and gifts to be passed out to all attendees." Carrie Fung, their publicist and media specialist, rarely got a word in edgewise, but she sat at attention, ready to be heard. "It needs to be something we can put the Runway logo on and that people will want to keep and see often."

"How about packets of condoms with our logo? We could add a comment wishing them a 'Happy and Safe Valentine's Day'."

Their DJ, Marvin Washington, better known as DJ Elixxir, had made the same suggestion at their last staff meeting.

As expected, Blake Howard, the head of security, shot the idea down. "I keep telling you that we have to break up enough couples having sex on the premises already without encouraging it by passing out rubbers."

DJ Elixxir grinned. "I know, but it's so fun to look down from my balcony and watch people going at it like rabbits to the beat of my music."

Blake shot back, "There's a place for that shit in this building, and the dance floor isn't it."

Jaxson shot his head of security a warning glare. Most of the people crowded in around the table were not privy to the fact that a top-secret BDSM club was one floor below the dance floor and Jaxson wanted to keep it that way. Knowledge of the secret club was on a need-to-know basis, and blabbermouth Elixxir certainly did *not* need to know.

Carrie interjected with a thankfully better idea. "I was thinking we could buy small tins of breath mints with our Runway logo on it and pass those out. And maybe for the women… long-stemmed roses with a Runway ribbon. And as always, we'll have the step and repeat with the red carpet where the photographer will take commemorative photos – at a hefty profit for us of course."

Jaxson jumped in, "I love those ideas. Let's make it happen."

Maxine glared at him for his continued rush job, but didn't interrupt.

Blake gave a warning, "We've been turning people away at the door every night since we opened so I know it will be a madhouse on the weekend before Valentine's Day. Just a reminder that I'm gonna be riding my boys at the door hard to avoid getting dinged by the fire marshal again. We've already had one warning that we were over our approved capacity, the next one's going to come with a big ass fine."

"Well that's your department so you'd better watch that closely. I'm gonna kick your ass if you get us shutdown." Jaxson meant the warning.

Sensing the meeting was wrapping, Maxine took charge as she always did to recap action items and decisions. She ran a tight ship and as annoying as it was, he knew they needed her.

"So to recap, we'll have the Crushing Stones back again for a concert on that Saturday night. The show will start at 8pm. Doors will open at 6pm and we'll be selling limited VIP tickets in advance at six times the door ticket price."

"Holy shit, that would be $120 bucks," the stage manager, Arianna Esposito, squeaked.

"Yes, and a bargain. Their big arena shows have tickets going for twice that and they'll get an up close and personal view of Cash and the boys here at Runway," Maxine countered before continuing. "We'll pass out the roses to the women and the breath mints to the men as they arrive. Noah, remind us again what you've got planned."

Their head bartender, Noah Garner, piped up, "I've got two thousand glasses ordered for that night with the Runway logo on it. We'll be serving a new drink I've created called a Runway Love Potion and they'll keep the glass as a souvenir."

Jaxson had almost forgot Chase was in the room, sitting on the couches behind him with Emma, until he piped in, "They are fucking awesome. I think we should keep them on the menu year round."

Jaxson hadn't tasted the drink yet, but he'd been the beneficiary of a pretty tipsy Chase and Emma the week before, when they'd come home frisky as hell after acting as guinea pigs for Noah's experiments for just the right recipe. He could attest that the cocktails had worked as a *very* effective love potion that night.

"Alright, that's it for now. We'll have one more staff meeting in two weeks to nail down any last minute items. Everyone have a great day and get back to work." Jaxson dismissed them, anxious to get on to the second and more important meeting of the day.

Most of the occupants of the room stood and headed for the door, chatting amicably. As expected, the head of his security – and the only man who had sat completely silent in the first meeting – Spencer Cook, remained behind. Unfortunately, so did Maxine.

As soon as the door closed on the office, Maxine spoke up, "Okay, it's time I find out what the hell is going on around here."

Jaxson had known this day was coming. He'd been dodging her prying questions for weeks. "Maxine, it's best if you just get back to work. It's getting late and I know you have to pick up your kids after school soon."

She grinned triumphantly. "Not today. I told Eric he had to pick them up because I had to stay late for a meeting."

Blake piped in, "Your meeting wrapped on time."

"Not that meeting. *THIS* meeting. The one you guys always have without me," she glowered.

The serious looking man in the sharp suit, who'd sat silently for two hours, finally spoke. "You're not invited. Out." Jaxson's friend, Spencer, had always been a man of few words. He was used to dealing with women who were the antithesis of Maxine Torres. As a result, Jaxson's top two employees were like two sheets of sand paper when they got close enough to rub each other.

Maxine didn't back down, instead she put her high-heeled shoes up on the now vacant chair next to her as if to convey she was settling in for the long haul. She stared Spencer down with her best glare before responding, "I'm the manager of this club. That means I need to know everything that goes on here."

"You know everything you need to know."

"Apparently not, since I don't have a clue what the hell you guys are up to."

Spencer broke into a threatening smile that Jaxson had seen many times before. "You couldn't handle it."

"I'm a married mother of three kids; one a teenager. We have three dogs, two cats, and one rabbit. My seventy-three year old mother lives next door and I'm the president of the PTA. Not to mention, I put in fifty hours a week making Runway the premier club east of the Mississippi. I can handle anything," Maxine countered with confidence.

"Well, this meeting has nothing to do with Runway, pets, or families, so you are excused," Spencer answered in his condescending way.

Maxine crossed her arms with a humph showing no sign of backing down and Jaxson wasn't surprised.

"Maxine, Spencer is right. It is best if you head to your own office now."

She changed tactics, turning to look back at Chase and Emma still sitting on the couch to the side. "Why do they get to stay and I don't? I'm the manager."

"Of Runway, yes. The following meeting is about another venture we have invested in that is not under your control," Jaxson argued more sternly.

He saw her eyes widen a sliver, excited she had him talking. "But it *is* under the same roof, which means I need to know about it. Don't think I don't notice you all disappearing down the back hallway every night around ten when you think I've gone home for the night."

She'd hit a sore spot with Jaxson. He hated to admit it, but he'd been trying to sneak down to Black Light without Maxine noticing and it was quite frankly pissing him off. He resented having to curtail his movements in his own club because he didn't want to make waves with an employee.

I'm the boss, dammit.

"Maxine, don't forget that you work here. We own the place. Chase, Emma, and I can come and go as we please."

"That's not what I'm talking about and you know it. There is something fishy going on around here and I don't like it. If you guys are selling drugs or running some other secretive underground illegal business, I better damn well know about it. I didn't sign up to be involved with anything like that."

Spencer barked an annoyed laugh. "Oh for Christ's sake, there is nothing illegal going on here."

"Prove it," Maxine shouted back.

"I don't need to prove shit to you. You have your job. I have mine and God willing, never the two shall meet," Spencer's voice was rising. Jaxson knew his friend would blow soon if he didn't get Maxine under control.

She barged ahead with her next argument. "Then why is he even here during the Runway meetings? If I don't get to come to his meetings, he shouldn't be at mine," the manager reasoned.

Jaxson had wondered himself why Spencer chose to come. His friend's answer only increased the tension in the room.

"I need to know everything that goes on in this building."

"And I don't?" Maxine countered. "And what's with that anyway. Blake here is head of security. If anyone needs to know what is going on everywhere in the building, it's him, not you."

"Which is why he is allowed to stay." Spencer's normally unreadable face was turning a bit red as Maxine continued to challenge him.

"Just tell me what is downstairs and I'll leave."

"You couldn't handle five minutes down there."

"What, you have a built-in torture chamber?" Maxine chuckled.

"Something like that." His reply startled her into silence.

Jaxson had had enough. "All right you two. You are both important to our success here. I think Spencer is right, though, Maxine. I can assure you there is nothing illegal going on. I think you'll be happier staying in the dark."

"And I know I won't rest until I know." She changed tactics. "He sat silently for my meeting. All I'm asking for is the same courtesy. I want to sit silently during his meeting."

Tit-for-tat. That was the game she was playing. Spencer's eyes lit up with a dangerous twinkle at the thought of shocking his counterpart.

Jaxson relented. They were barely a month in and Maxine was already acting like a sleuth. They might as well cut her in on their little secret. "Not one word out of you, got it?"

Maxine made a show out of pretend zipping her mouth and then turning an imaginary key before tossing it over her left shoulder and then returning her arms into their defensive crossed position.

Spencer glared at her for a few long seconds before turning his attention to Jaxson at the other end of the long table. He didn't bother getting up to move closer to the other occupants in the room, instead electing to remain removed as he often did.

"You're really gonna put up with her shit?" he challenged Jaxson.

For some reason, Spencer's aggression bothered him more than Maxine's. "She's no more of a prima donna than you are. You both can be a pain in my ass, but I hired each of you because you are experienced and the best. So the answer to your question is, yes. Yes, I'm putting up with her shit because she's right. While Black Light is a secret, as the manager of Runway, Maxine has the right to know what is going on below her club." He paused, turning to pin Maxine with a threatening glare. "But she better keep in mind that what she is about to hear is one-hundred percent confidential. It is not to be discussed with anyone outside of this room. Not her hairdresser, the other employees... not even her husband. She's a smart lady. I don't need to remind her of the NDA she signed when she took the job."

Keeping her mouth closed tightly, she nodded her agreement to Jaxson's warning.

Spencer didn't like it, but he proceeded. "Fine. We've wasted enough time. If she loses her shit over this, it's not on me."

"Duly noted," Jaxson reassured him. "Continue. What have you and the guys cooked up for Valentine's Day?"

"Hold on." Spencer pulled his cell phone out of his pocket and punched in what looked like a short text message. Within ten seconds, the door to the office opened and four men in leather pants and black T-shirts shuffled in. They halted briefly at the sight of Maxine in the room, but recovered quickly, taking the seats around the table recently vacated by the managers of the Runway teams.

Jaxson saw Maxine's eyes fill with surprise, but to her credit, she held her tongue.

Spencer opened the plain manila folder in front of him, taking the top sheet out, and began to fill them in. "We've come up with an excellent idea that's going to get the place packed on Valentine's night. We're going to setup a mixer game of Valentine Roulette."

The dungeon master paused dramatically giving the occupants of the room time to assimilate what he'd said.

Chase stood and pulled out the chair next to Jaxson at the table, taking a seat as he questioned Spencer. "Roulette. As in Russian Roulette?"

Blake looked at him, annoyance in his eyes. "Yeah, we're gonna off the participants until the last man is standing. Nothing like killing participants to drive up membership."

The newest men in the room broke into snickers at Chase's expense, which annoyed Jaxson.

"Explain. Now." He knew how to talk to Spencer. The snickers ended abruptly.

"We'll have a private sign-up period starting next week. Dominant and submissive club members will be able to read the rules and decide if they want to sign up and consent on-line in advance. The night of the party they will be randomly paired up to scene with one person. They won't know who they will play with in advance and they can't refuse their play partner without using their safeword which will disqualify them."

Jaxson was intrigued, but he had a lot of questions. "So, how do they get paired up?"

"We'll have two large roulette wheels, just like in a casino only the first one will have the names of the submissives on it. The

Doms will draw numbers to see who goes first and one by one, they will go up and take their chances spinning the wheel. They play with whomever the wheel names and then we take her name off the wheel and the next guy spins. Rinse and repeat until they are all paired up."

Chase interrupted. "So, is it just a singles night?"

"Not at all. If couples want to play, they can, but they are committing to most likely playing with other partners. Couples not wanting to play will be spectators... voyeurs... We'll have small cocktail tables setup throughout the club and we'll serve top-end champagne and appetizers. We'll sell tickets over and above membership fees as a special event since the club is normally closed on Tuesdays."

Jaxson suspected he knew what the other roulette wheel was for. "And the second wheel? They spin for their scene?"

Owen, the dungeon's Master Shibarist answered him. "Exactly. Each participant will be allowed to put three things from the wheel on their hard limit list when they sign up. If they roll something on either of their hard limit list, they can spin again. If not, they have to play the scene they roll for a minimum of thirty minutes before they can take their chances by spinning again."

Chase asked, "How many activities are on the wheel?"

"We brainstormed over twenty activities so far. I think we could come up with a few more ideas, too," Owen replied.

"What kind of stuff are we talking about here?" Jaxson pressed, curious.

Spencer picked up the top piece of paper from the open manila folder and started reading the list. "Bondage, Anal Play, Pet Play, Water Sports, Electrical Play, Suspension, Whipping Post, Medical Play, High Protocol, Pain Play, Humiliation,

Water/Tub, Sybian-Orgasm Torture, Latex Encasement, Fire Play, Age Play, Oral Sex, Breath Play, Blood Play, and Needle Play. We also decided we could put several role-play options on for things like principal/naughty student, royalty, law enforcement. We've accumulated a pretty extensive wardrobe for scenes already and will continue to add to the costume options over time. We could even throw a Dom's choice role-play in there for fun; like a wild card."

Maxine fidgeted in the chair next to him. He suspected she might be regretting promising to remain silent.

Jaxson's cock was expanding in his jeans at the mental image of the sexy scenes that could play out on Valentine's night. He had to admit, the plan was appealing for several reasons.

"I like it. We've wanted to introduce more of a variety of activities and try to get the current members to come out of their shell a bit. This could help with that, but some of those activities are heavy duty. What if we get a novice Dom who has to do a complex fetish like Blood Play or Suspension? If they fuck it up, it could go south quickly."

Spencer reassured him, "That's the greatest part of the plan. Between my four dungeon monitors, and me, we have all of those activities covered. We'll each be assigned stations that we will monitor, but also act as a trainer for Doms who are learning new activities. Safety first."

Jaxson nodded, relieved they had a plan to keep the submissives safe.

Chase challenged Spencer next. "This seems pretty risky for both the Doms and the subs who participate. What incentive is there to get people to sign up?"

"The prize at the end of the night will be one month's dues free for anyone who finishes the night and who played by the rules.

Then the monitors and I can give out extra comp days or weeks for extra good scenes, and we'll choose one couple to award the grand prize of two months free membership."

Jaxson wasn't too crazy about that. "That's a lot of free membership cash to be giving away."

"We plan on maxing out at fifteen couples, and don't forget, I'm sure some of them will drop out when it gets too intense for them. And we'll more than make up for it by selling the VIP tickets for the observers that night. I think what's most important is that we continue to distinguish ourselves as the premium BDSM club on the east coast. Black Light is not only secure and confidential, but also focused on providing safe, sane, and consensual play. We'll be offering training for Doms and subs both."

Garrett, one of the most hardcore Doms of the group spoke up next. "Don't forget, I'm also an EMT. I'll come prepared in case anything gets out of hand with the needle or fire play."

"Well, you'd better make damn sure nothing gets out of control. It's great we are prepared for an emergency, but we can't put subs in danger intentionally."

Spencer spoke up, out of patience. "I'm counting on the sign up process to weed out anyone who isn't going to be able to handle it."

Chase challenged him, "And why is that?"

"Because, it will be a legal document that will scare away anyone not fully committed."

Up until now, Emma had been sitting quietly through both meetings, but Jaxson heard the quaver in her voice when she spoke up softly to question the plan. "So if I were to sign up, I could only say no to three of those things? What if I wanted to say no to more than three?"

Jaxson turned and could see the fear in her eyes. He rushed to help her relax. "You don't have anything to worry about, sweetheart. We'll be observers that night. I have zero desire to play with anyone other than you and Chase, angel."

Visible relief passed across her face before she pressed forward with another question. "And what about sex? Are they expected to have sex with their partner who will most likely be a stranger to them?"

Garrett answered her and Jaxson was relieved to hear the respect in his voice as he recognized he was talking to the boss's submissive. "Intercourse will be one of the things on the list that they can put on their hard list, but if they refuse to have sex then that will leave only two other picks for their limit list."

Emma glanced his way and Jax could see concern in her beautiful violet eyes. "What is it, sweetheart?"

"I don't think that's enough options for hard limits. There are a lot of scary things on that list."

Jaxson gave her a reassuring nod. He trusted her instincts. "You heard the lady, gentlemen. We bump the hard list choices from three to four."

"Now, wait a minute. We're gonna be spinning all night long because there are so many free passes," Spencer grumbled, careful not to direct his anger directly at Emma.

Jaxson closed the discussion. "There will be four options for submissives to put on their hard limits. Next topic."

Chase thought of the next controversial question. "What happens if a male Dom gets paired with a male submissive and they don't bend that way?" As the only switch in the room, Chase had a unique view into the D/s dynamics at play with an event like this.

Jaxson wasn't thrilled to see the surprise on Spencer's face. It told him the others in the room hadn't considered this obstacle, which annoyed him. Just because his employees were strictly male dominants who topped female submissives didn't mean there weren't many other D/s combinations. Jaxson, Chase and Emma were proof of that.

Spencer reluctantly answered, "I don't think we have a large enough membership pool yet to offer anything other than male on female options this year. Maybe by next year, assuming this is a success, we can be more inclusive during the sign up process and try to accommodate our gay and bisexual members, as well as our female Dommes and male submissives."

"I agree with you for this year, but let's make it more inclusive going forward."

Spencer nodded his agreement.

Jaxson glanced at Maxine who was still sitting silently at the table. He had to stifle his grin as he realized she was turning beet red in her attempt at holding her silence. She looked as if a rant was literally bubbling up, ready to spew from her mouth at any moment.

Moving to a more tactical discussion, Jaxson spoke, "So talk to me about the legalities. This obviously goes over and above our normal contract for membership. What are we doing to protect ourselves from lawsuits when one of the participants isn't happy with the way things turn out for them on the wheel?"

Owen answered, "We had the same law firm you used to buy the building and do all of the contracting for Runway and Black Light write up the contract for participants. As they also wrote up the membership agreement for Black Light, we figured they were setup for this as well."

"Yeah, good thinking. How much is that gonna cost us?" Jaxson hadn't been thrilled with the bill they'd got from Lambert, Urbanski and Reed's law firm their last go-round. They'd luckily been able to work out a discount membership, and a set of free months, for the partners of the firm to reduce the billable hours.

Spencer grinned. "They did it pro-bono. I just had to offer Alexander a free pass to participate."

"Excellent."

Maxine shifted in her seat, sitting bolt upright as she took her feet from the chair next to her. She looked as if she were about to spring out of her chair. Jaxson couldn't hide his grin any longer.

"Would you like to be excused now, Maxine?" he prodded.

She hesitated, unsure if she was allowed to speak to respond. He was being an ass since he knew Maxine didn't have a single ounce of submissiveness in her body, but he just couldn't resist. "You may speak."

Her eyes flashed angry at his condescending approval. "Let me get this straight. You barbarians are running a sex club beneath my Runway?"

Spencer looked like he wanted to throttle her, but Jaxson waved him off before responding. "We are running an exclusive BDSM club beneath *my* Runway." He stopped and looked at Chase and rephrased. "Correction. My, Chase, and Emma's Runway. Yes, there is sex involved, but it is way more complicated than that."

"Listen, I'm no prude, but I'm not entirely sure I'm comfortable with this," she objected.

"Which part? The sex or the BDSM part?"

"All of it. Particularly the fact that young women are going to be used and possibly abused for men's satisfaction."

Jaxson leaned forward, placing his hands on the table and leaning closer to her to make sure he was getting his point across as he answered her as best he could. "Emma," he didn't take his eyes off Maxine as he waited for his lover to answer from behind him.

"Yes, sir."

"Have you been to Black Light?"

"Of course. Many times."

"Have you ever seen anyone, man or woman, being abused against their will?"

"No, sir."

"As my submissive, have you ever felt abused by our lifestyle?"

He could hear the humor in her voice as she answered. "Abused? Goodness, no. More like pampered and loved."

"Even when you've been punished?"

She hesitated before answering this question. He suspected she didn't care admitting it, but he knew her answer was the truth. "Especially when I've been punished."

"Good girl," Jaxson praised.

"Good girl? Seriously? She's not a fucking puppy!" Maxine's anger was bubbling up.

"That's enough. We asked you to leave. You insisted on staying. You said you could handle it."

"That was before I knew what was going on," she countered. "I'm not sure I can deal with this."

Jaxson pressed her hard. "Then I'm sorry to see you go. Accept it, or I'll be expecting your resignation before you leave today."

Her eyes widened at his threat. He prayed she'd back down. He really didn't want to lose her. She was a damn fine manager for Runway, but he also knew he wouldn't put up with her giving them shit for their lifestyle or running Black Light.

An awkward silence hung in the air as he and the bossy woman in the room squared off. He could see indecision flitting through her eyes as she weighed her options. He was a bit surprised when Emma came into his peripheral view, coming to sit in the chair next to Maxine, recently vacated by her propped up feet.

"It really is okay, Maxine. I remember not understanding the whole lifestyle at all when I met Jaxson and Chase. It confused me too. After all, I'd been raised to be a Type-A career woman. I never would have dreamed I'd enjoy being a sexual submissive, but honestly, I've never been happier. I've met so many submissives in the club and I can assure you, everything that I've seen has been consensual. It may not be for you, but please don't quit over this. We need you and you're great at your job."

Jaxson could have kissed Emma. She was saying exactly what needed to be said, and with a credibility that only a woman could pull off in this situation.

Maxine glanced back up at Jaxson and hesitated only a few seconds before giving her answer. "Fine. As long as you all keep it private, I'll back off. I'm not sure I understand it all, but it's none of my business."

Spencer couldn't contain his response. "That's what I said in the beginning."

She glared at him and then went to work. "So, who do you have designing the website sign-up for the event?"

Spencer glanced at his four employees for support, but all five men got a deer in the headlights look on their face.

Maxine continued on. "That's what I thought. I assume you

have a food and beverage operation down there? Where are you getting your liquor? Are you doing any product ordering that we could combine with Runway to get volume discounts? How about your scheduling, memberships, accounting?"

The more tactical things Maxine rattled off, the more sheepish the Master of the Dungeon looked. Jaxson had to hide a new grin – this time at his friend's expense. He was enjoying Spencer being schooled by the real outlet manager in the room.

"Maxine, you bring up excellent points. I'm sure there are some scales of economy we could gain by combining some of the resources between the two clubs." He paused to pin Spencer with a glare. "You are an excellent Master Dom, Spencer, but you don't know shit about running a club. Effective immediately, I'd like you two to work together on the non-BDSM components of Black Light."

"You have to be shitting me. You want me to work with *her*? You told me Black Light was all mine to run."

"And it is. You have complete creative control over the BDSM components, but Maxine can help with the F&B and purchasing. Let her help you with the website setup for the event. Keep in mind, it has to be 100% confidential and have a login/password setup to protect identities."

Maxine did her best to ignore the grumbling at the other end of the table as she turned back to Jaxson. "I understand the need for confidentiality, but I'd like to let Noah in on the secret. He does all of our ordering of supplies and liquor. Trying to add anything to orders without him knowing will be impossible, and I've put him in charge of inventory control."

Jaxson and Spencer answered, "Agreed", and, "No fucking way", simultaneously.

Spencer grumbled. "I already hired my own bartenders for Black Light. We don't need his help."

Maxine rounded on him. "Let me guess. Old friends of yours?" When Spencer sat silently she had her affirmation. "I'm not suggesting Noah work downstairs. I'm only saying he helps with inventory control and purchasing. Don't worry. He won't interfere with your boy's club."

"All right, I think we've had enough for today. Getting the website setup is a top priority and then sending out a confidential email to all of our membership with the invitation to participate or attend as observers comes next. Let's get back together in two weeks at our next staff meeting. I'll expect to hear how we are doing with participation. And Spencer?" He pinned his friend with a glare. He knew the Dom wasn't going to like his next request any more than he'd liked the rest of the meeting. "Emma is our accountant. I'd like her to run the numbers with the planned participation and ticket sales to understand where our breakeven number is. We need to set target sales thresholds to make sure we aren't losing money."

"For Christ's sake. You act like you're running a huge corporation or something. I thought you wanted to have a private place for the BDSM elite to play safely here in D.C. without fear of being outed with the media or public."

"Yes, but I never once said I wanted to open Black Light to lose money. It's a business. Just like Runway. I'm willing to give it a few months to get things rolling, particularly since we can't do any wide advertising and keep our anonymity. We'll only get business through private referrals, which will take time to happen, but let me be clear. We either figure out a way to start making a profit within the next few months or we'll shut it down. I'm not running a charity here, particularly since almost every Dominant member we've signed up so far is a millionaire."

"That's the problem. We are heavy on Doms and since many of them already have regular subs, they pay the couple rate. It is single submissives we are short on. Many of them don't have the money for the hefty membership fees."

"Well then, this is a great opportunity for many of them to come and play with the possibility of winning a month's free membership. Just be careful who you invite. Even if they are a guest, they have to still agree to all of the confidentiality clauses."

Terry, the burliest of the four dungeon monitors, had sat quietly in the meeting up until that moment. Jaxson always thought he'd earned his nickname, Muscles, honestly.

"I'm still doing part-time security over at the Overtime BDSM club next to the Capitol Building. Been there a couple of years now. I can get together a short list of submissives I think would be a good fit if you'd like. Most couldn't afford the monthly fee for Black Light, but I think they'd love to participate in the Valentine Roulette event, especially if they had a chance to win a month or two of regular membership to come and play."

Spencer cautioned, "That's a good idea, but just be careful. Confidentiality is a top priority."

Jaxson had worried about this. "We are in a bit of a bind, though. We can let the subs in for free for the event to get the interest up. We'll never have enough members to make the business work if we don't widen our invitations a little bit." As his dungeon master started to argue back, he closed the meeting with, "I'm not suggesting we take out a full page ad in The Post, but we need to get a buzz going among the known BDSM community if we plan on getting enough members."

In the brief silence that hung in the air, he heard Emma's tummy growling. The blush across the bridge of her nose was adorable. As their eyes met, he knew they needed to wrap up so he could take care of filling her tummy. His growing cock wanted to feed her an appetizer of cum before taking her out for a proper dinner.

"So we have a plan. Let's close this meeting. We'll get back together in two weeks for our next meeting. Don't wait until then if you need to run anything past me. Have a good evening, everyone." The tone in his voice didn't leave room for uncertainty. Everyone around the table knew they'd just been dismissed.

Maxine grabbed up her tablet and cell phone and almost sprinted from the room to avoid further interaction with the men of Black Light. Spencer hesitated as if he wanted to stay to debate something with Jaxson, but eventually left, trailing behind the four dungeon monitors, and Blake.

Once the three lovers were alone, the atmosphere switched in a flash from business to pleasure. Chase almost attacked him, sliding to his knees and crawling under the table to start grasping at Jaxson's pants zipper.

"I fucking love watching you dominate the meeting like that. Watching you keep Spencer and his boys in check is the hottest thing ever. I've been like steel for the last thirty minutes."

Jaxson chuckled until he felt his lover's warm hand pulling his own hardening cock free from the confines of his underwear. His touch was the perfect aphrodisiac to add to the growing sexual need hanging in the air. Jaxson reached his hand out as an invitation to Emma who sat nearby watching her lovers starting without her.

"Come here, sweetheart. I want to give you a big kiss. You were perfect in the meeting."

"Are we really going to have front row seats that night for the Valentine Roulette?" He saw excitement in her eyes.

"That was the plan."

Emma rushed to stand next to his chair where he could pull her down into an urgent kiss. Jaxson let the pleasure of the two mouths connecting with him intimately wash over him. Within seconds, his cock was rock hard and ready for the next phase of their tryst. As tempted as he was to let his lovers finish him off, he knew they deserved to come too, and he really did want to feed Emma his growing load.

He broke out of the kiss and pushed his rolling executive chair away from the table, leaving a panting Chase on his knees under the table.

"Get on up here, Chase. You're gonna pound our Emma while she kneels on the chair. Come here, sweetheart."

He pushed to his feet so she could place her knees on the seat his ass had just vacated. She faced the back of the chair. "That's it. Lean over the back of the chair and I'll feed you while Chase services your hot little pussy. Don't forget. We all come together."

Chase was already on his feet, freeing his own manhood from his pants and stepping up to bare Emma's core. Jaxson waited until Chase's eyes met his own, telling him all was ready. The only indication to Chase that it was time was a small nod. The men both entered Emma, one in her mouth and the other in her pussy, in one strong push. Jaxson felt her gagging as the tip of his engorged penis hit the back of her throat. Her gurgling cry as Chase went equally deep at the other end of her enhanced Jaxson's pleasure. She was holding on to the back of the chair for stability, which meant he had complete control over the speed and depth he fucked her mouth. The sound of bodies slapping together was joined by the slurping of wet channels being plundered front and back on their submissive.

The soundtrack of the room was too fucking sexy to let any of them last for long. He could feel Emma trying to pull off his cock as she attempted to ask permission to come. He was too close to allow her to stop, even for a second. Instead, he wrapped his fingers through her long dark hair and used her wet orifice to chase his own pleasure.

Jaxson was so focused on plunging into Emma's throat he missed Chase leaning in, seeking his own intimate connection to his Dom. The men's mouths connected in an open mouth kiss, completing their favorite triangle of connection for the trio.

Within seconds, they all tipped into a loud orgasm with the men depositing their loads into Emma's warm body.

Chase grinned his lopsided smile as they began to peel apart from each other. "That should tide us over for a few hours. I'm starving. I vote we go to dinner before we head down to Black Light for round two."

Jaxson pulled one of the cloth hankies he always carried with him out of his pocket to start cleaning up Emma's spunk filled mouth where she'd dribbled drops of sticky cum she couldn't quite swallow.

"That's one idea. I kinda thought we could order up a pizza and start round two while we waited."

Emma giggled as Chase got to work stripping her. "Perfect plan. You order the pizza."

Excited to see what comes next? We can't wait to show you!

Watch for the release of 'Black Light: Valentine Roulette' to dive back into the world of Black Light!

Books by Jennifer Bene

Dark / BDSM Erotic Romance:

Security Binds Her (Thalia Book 1)

Striking a Balance (Thalia Book 2)

Salvaged by Love (Thalia Book 3)

Of Fog and Fire (Parts I & II)

Taken by the Enemy

Lethal Sin (Dangerous Games Book 1)

Early Sins (Dangerous Games Book 0)

Black Light: Exposed (Black Light Series Book 2)

Tying the Knot (Thalia Book 4)

Dark / Paranormal Romance:

Fae (Daughters of Eltera Book 1)

Tara (Daughters of Eltera Book 2)

BDSM Erotic Romance Novellas:

The Invitation

The Rite

Christmas at Purgatory (Thalia Extra #1)

Reunited

Anthology Appearances:

The Dark Forest: A Collection of Erotic Fairytales

Black Light: Valentine Roulette (Black Light Series Book 3)

Hero Undercover

Royally Mine

About the Author

Jennifer Bene is an international bestselling author of erotic romance. She's had #1 top-selling books in BDSM, Suspense, Thrillers, Action & Adventure, Fantasy, Science Fiction, and Horror. While she's been writing for years, it's always been the dark stuff that makes her tingly, so her books are full of aggressive alpha males, feisty women who may or may not have a submissive streak, and intense, psychological storylines. Don't worry though, she also insists on having a nice little happily-ever-after! Because without the dark, we'd never appreciate the light.

Want to get a FREE book, news about upcoming releases, giveaways, appearances, and more? Sign up for her mailing list!

Keep in touch with Jennifer Bene:
jenniferbene.com
jbeneauthor@gmail.com